Also by Miss Read

VILLAGE SCHOOL

VILLAGE DIARY

STORM IN THE VILLAGE

THRUSH GREEN

FRESH FROM THE COUNTRY

WINTER IN THRUSH GREEN

MISS CLARE REMEMBERS

COUNTRY BUNCH

CHRONICLES OF FAIRACRE

OVER THE GATE

MARKET SQUARE

THE HOWARDS OF CAXLEY

VILLAGE CHRISTMAS

FAIRACRE FESTIVAL

MISS READ'S COUNTRY COOKING

NEWS FROM THRUSH GREEN

TIGGY

EMILY DAVIS

TYLER'S ROW

THE CHRISTMAS MOUSE

FARTHER AFIELD

BATTLES AT THRUSH GREEN

NO HOLLY FOR MISS QUINN

VILLAGE AFFAIRS

RETURN TO THRUSH GREEN

THE WHITE ROBIN

VILLAGE CENTENARY

GOSSIP FROM THRUSH GREEN

A FORTUNATE GRANDCHILD

AFFAIRS AT THRUSH GREEN

SUMMER AT FAIRACRE

SUMMER AT FAIRACRE

MISS READ

ILLUSTRATED BY J. S. GOODALL

Houghton Mifflin Company
Boston
1985

First American edition 1985

Copyright © 1984 by Miss Read

All rights reserved. No part of this work may be reproduced
or transmitted in any form or by any means, electronic or
mechanical, including photocopying and recording, or by
any information storage or retrieval system, except as
may be expressly permitted by the 1976 Copyright Act or in
writing from the publisher. Requests for permission should be
addressed in writing to Houghton Mifflin Company,
2 Park Street, Boston, Massachusetts 02108.

Library of Congress Cataloging in Publication Data

Read, Miss.

Summer at Fairacre.

I. Goodall, John S. II. Title.
PR6069.A42S9   1985   823'.914   85-2432
ISBN 0-395-38016-2

Printed in the United States of America

P 10 9 8 7 6 5 4 3 2 1

To Dotti
With love

Contents

1   The First Day of Spring

'**W**HAT the Hanover d'you make of this, Miss Read?'

Mr Willet took the cap from his head and shook the snow from it, spattering the schoolroom floor with dark spots.

'Twenty-first of March,' he went on. 'First day of spring, and I reckon there's a good inch of snow all over.'

'Well, it can't last,' I replied. 'It's melting already in the playground.'

A clashing of pails from the lobby told of the presence of Mrs Pringle, our school cleaner. Both she and Bob Willet, the caretaker, come soon after eight each morning to see that Fairacre School is in good trim to start the day.

'And how's Madam Sunshine today?' asked Mr Willet, nodding towards the source of noise. He was prudent enough, I noticed, to lower his voice.

As village schoolmistress, Mrs Pringle is one of the crosses I have to bear. Mrs Pringle enjoys the gloomier side of life, and is never so happy as when she is discussing distressing ailments, other people's peccadilloes, impending disasters or a really slap-up funeral, preferably with inner knowledge of how much money was left by the deceased and to whom it is going.

Square, sturdy and sixtyish, Mrs Pringle is as tough as an old boot, but she has 'a Bad Leg' which dominates our lives at Fairacre. If Mrs Pringle decides that she is over-worked, and this happens quite often, the afflicted limb is liable to rapid deterioration, and gives its owner a pronounced limp. One can always tell, from the severity of Mrs Pringle's hobbling, what sort of mood the lady is in. There is no love lost between Mr Willet and our cleaner, and I have to be very circumspect in dealing with both.

This is not always an easy task, as both parties can be over-sensitive to the reaction of the other. I have to tread as warily as Agag, and then, more often than not, I find that one of them has taken umbrage.

Usually, of course, it is Mrs Pringle, who is always on the look-out for the odd insult. One need only comment, in a perfunctory way, about the amount of grime children can collect on their hands, and Mrs Pringle begins to bridle and to point out, with unnecessary acrimony, that there is always a plentiful supply of soap put out in the lobby. Moreover, that very soap has been put there with her own two over-worked hands, and the basins have been cleaned so thoroughly – again by those same hands – that it would be possible to eat your dinner in them, should you feel so disposed.

When I first came to Fairacre as the village schoolmistress I used to try to stem this flow of umbrage-taking by making ineffectual apologies and explanations. I know better now. It is far more satisfactory to let Mrs Pringle have her head, and to allow the torrent to flow over one. She thoroughly enjoys it, and I have now become so hardened that it makes very little impression. Over the years we have shaken down together pretty well, and the occasional clash of wills does neither of us serious harm.

On this particular morning we all three had cause for dismay. A particularly cold winter was being followed by an equally unpleasant early spring. The tortoise stoves were still needed to warm the school, and the children continued to wear their winter clothing. My own tweed skirts and thick cardigans had been in use for months now, and we all longed for sunshine, flowers and lighter clothing.

'When I was a boy,' said Mr Willet, 'I reckoned to go birds' nesting this time of year, and there was primroses and violets in the hedge bottoms. And my old dad's rhubarb was sprouting real steady. Look at it these days! We don't get no spring worth spitting on, and nothing don't start stirring till May. There was some chap on the telly t'other night as said the seasons are just the same as ever was. He don't know the half.'

'I agree,' I assured him.

'And this other bloke he said as the earth's axle – or some such word – has tilted off true a bit, so the weather's changed. I reckon that's more like it.'

He pulled an old-fashioned red and white spotted handkerchief from his corduroys' pocket, and blew his nose with impressive trumpeting.

'Never got rid of me Christmas cold neither,' he informed me, stuffing the handkerchief away. 'Ah! I near forgot! Could you do with a morsel of winter savoy? Good thing to have a bit of fresh greens this weather. That frozen stuff's all very well for second best, but you can't beat the real thing.'

'I'd love some,' I said.

At that moment, the door burst open, and Joseph Coggs and four more boys rushed in bearing a furious cat.

'It's a stray, miss,' they chorused. 'It was under Mr Roberts' hedge, miss. It's *starving*, miss.'

The cat was struggling frenziedly in Joseph's tight clasp. It was certainly cross, but did not appear emaciated to my eye.

Mr Willet scrutinised it closely.

'That's one of Mr Roberts' farm cats,' he pronounced. 'I know it very well. It's like its ma, with one white leg. You take it back, boy, or you'll be in trouble.'

Five pairs of eyes turned anxiously in my direction.

'You'd better do as Mr Willet says,' I told them. 'At playtime you can go back to the place where you found him, and if he's still there you can take down some bread and milk.'

3

Mollified by this compromise, the deputation and its victim departed.

Mr Willet looked at me and shook his head.

'You're too soft with 'em by half,' he told me. 'In my day, Mr Hope would have given 'em all a clip round the ear for trying on a trick like that.'

'Teachers are not allowed to strike children these days,' I said.

'More's the pity,' replied Mr Willet, making for the door.

His way was barred by the formidable bulk of Mrs Pringle who was advancing with an outstretched hand.

Upon it were balanced a few fragments of a small paint brush.

'What's all this 'ere, may I ask?' she boomed.

Mr Willet and I surveyed her wet palm and the debris.

'Don't need much eyesight to see it's been a paint brush in its time,' replied Mr Willet with withering sarcasm.

'Then what's it doing down the plug hole of the wash basin?' demanded Mrs Pringle, fixing me with a stern glance.

'Someone's been trying to hide evidence,' I said. 'Put it on my desk and I'll sort it out.'

Mrs Pringle deposited her burden, and a number of soapy drops, dangerously near the register, and turned to face me, arms akimbo.

'What them children need,' she announced, 'is a bit of old-fashioned discipline.'

'I've been telling her that,' said Mr Willet.

And the two departed, in rare unity, as I went to ring the bell.

By playtime, almost all the snow had vanished. There was still some whiteness under the school hedge, and the tiles on the north-facing roof were edged with shallow snow.

The children were disappointed.

It only needs a flurry of snowflakes to set them agog with anticipation. Making snowmen, complete with pipe, hat and pebbles for eyes, tobogganing down the hill near Beech Green, scoring off old enemies with well-thrown snowballs – all these delights seem within reach, but usually melt away as swiftly as the snow itself.

Joseph Coggs and his rescue party prompted my memory, and were allowed to dash down the lane to see if the cat was still languishing under the hedge. As expected, they returned somewhat crestfallen.

'Mr Roberts was up the yard,' Patrick said, 'and we told him about that poor old stray, and he said it wasn't no stray, but one of his'n –'

'His,' I corrected automatically.

'That's right, miss. His'n. So we just come back.'

'Came back.'

'Like I said,' agreed Patrick. I let the matter rest.

Village schoolmistresses, and no doubt those who teach in town schools too, recognise the utter futility of trying to correct certain phrases. Fairacre's intractable examples include:

'Miss, the nib of my pencil's bin and broke.'

'Miss, could you threadle my needle?'

And, of course, 'I never done it.'

As for the correct usage of the verbs 'to lend' and 'to borrow', I despair of ever getting this particular piece of grammar across.

'Can I have a lend of your duster, miss?' This is the usual phrase. Sometimes it is 'a borrow of'. If I had as many five-pound notes as the number of times I have carefully rephrased these requests I should have retired from teaching long ago with a comfortable income.

Now that the affair of the cat was settled, a lesson on fractions was undertaken until the dinner van arrived. Sliced cold lamb, beetroot and coleslaw, followed by bottled plums and pink blancmange is not my idea of a cheering lunch on a bleak March day, but the children tackled it with their usual gusto, and rushed out to play afterwards with their spirits as boisterous as the wind which buffeted them from the downs above.

That evening, sitting by a log fire as though it were December instead of the first day of spring, I had a surprise visit from my old friend Amy.

We were at college together many years ago. She is now married to a businessman who seems to earn a great deal of money. This busy life involves much travelling, and Amy is often left alone while he is away either here or abroad.

James is a charmer, and devoted to the opposite sex. Personally, I am sure that he adores Amy, but whether he is wholly faithful to her, I have my doubts. Although Amy is far too loyal to voice her suspicions, she is pretty shrewd, and I think she knows quite well that some of these so-called business trips include other interests.

'A fire! How marvellous!' she said, holding out her beautifully manicured hands to the blaze. 'Nothing like the first day of spring for making one appreciate a log fire.'

'Coffee or sherry?'

'What sort of sherry? You aren't still offering that stuff you won at the last raffle?'

When you have known Amy as long as I have you do not take umbrage at this sort of remark.

'That was jolly nice sherry. Good and fruity. The vicar and I finished it off last week.'

'Coffee, I think after all.'

'Instant,' I said, 'and you're lucky to get that!'

Amy chuckled, and fished in her elegant Italian handbag for a cigarette. She followed me into the kitchen.

'I often wonder why you don't get matching kitchen units,' she said, surveying my equipment.

'No money to pay for them,' I told her, spooning out the coffee. 'Top of the milk, or hot milk?'

'Top, please.'

'Good. It saves messing up a saucepan. No point in making work.'

'If you organised this kitchen you could cut down the work. For one thing, all your working tops would be the same height.'

'But I don't want them all the same height,' I protested. 'If I'm mincing I use the table. If I'm washing lettuce, I need the sink which is deeper. The draining board's just the right height for chopping cabbage –'

'Very well, very well! You needn't go on! Obviously, you've become quite accustomed to these primitive surroundings and don't intend to change now.'

7

'That's right,' I said amicably. 'Would you like a ginger nut?'

'I should love one. I haven't had a ginger nut for years, but I warn you, I'll have to dunk it. I've got a filling that's cracked across.'

'I think we've both got to the stage where it's permissible to dunk ginger nuts. Won't be long before we're mumbling our gruel with our gums.'

'Speak for yourself,' said Amy.

We settled ourselves by the fire.

'I've brought the Caxley Festival programme with me. I thought we might go to a few of the events.'

'What's on offer?'

'A concert in the Parish Church. Modern music mainly. Lots of Bartok.'

'Count me out, Amy dear. Those pews nearly crippled me at the carol service, and at least we stood up now and again. Besides, I can't take Bartok.'

'The trouble with you,' said Amy severely, 'is that you close your mind to progress. Well, what about this exhibition of modern sculpture?'

'Where's that?'

'It's all hefty outdoor stuff, I gather. They've roped off part of the common.'

'It sounds nice and peaceful. But what happens if it rains?'

'As the Duke of Norfolk said, with admirable brevity, when asked the same question about the Coronation: "*We get wet!*" '

'Carry on.'

'Your Henry Mawne appears to be giving a couple of lectures on British birds.'

'He's not my Henry Mawne, I'm thankful to say, but I expect I've heard those lectures several times in our village hall.'

'Eighteenth-century silver in the museum? Demonstration

of hand-weaving? Three mid-European plays about the rise of the peasant classes?'

'The silver sounds agreeable,' I said cautiously.

'You do live dangerously, don't you?' said Amy. 'Tell you what, I'll leave the programme here and you can look it through and let me know. Frankly, I'm game for anything. James will be away for most of that time.'

'Where is he going?'

'Holland first, I believe. Something to do with diamond merchants. Not that James will see much of the diamonds, but the money gets put into other things.'

'The Dutch are very clever at trading, I believe.'

'So I gather. Didn't they own the East Indies at one time? All those spices and jewels?'

'My knowledge is pretty hazy. I only know they were jolly good sailors and had the cheek to sail up the Thames, or perhaps it was the Medway, and had to be chased off by someone who had a broom on the mast.'

'I don't believe it! Why on the *mast* anyway?'

'Amy, I really know nothing about the Dutch except that Holland gets flooded very easily, and the housewives are exceptionally clean. I should ask James about them when he gets back. After all, he will have first-hand knowledge.'

'Not of the housewives, I hope,' said Amy, with unusual tartness. She stubbed out her cigarette viciously. 'If that's the time, I'd better be off. James makes an early start for Edinburgh tomorrow.'

'He certainly keeps busy,' I said accompanying her to the door.

'Too busy at times,' replied Amy, getting into her glossy car. 'I've told him not to be surprised if I take a leaf out of his book and have a break myself one day.'

It was said lightly, but there was an underlying grimness which disconcerted me.

She blew me a kiss and drove off, and I returned to the fireside with food for thought.

The chilly weather continued for the rest of March. A few hardy primroses had braved the elements in the garden, and knotted bluebell flowers crouched in their glossy leaves, obviously unwilling to do more until the weather grew warmer.

The leaves were still tightly furled on the trees. The winter silhouettes of the beeches and limes still showed up starkly black against the grey sky.

At night, I was glad of my comforting fire, and still put a hot water bottle in my bed halfway through the evening. The frosts were severe, and it would be many weary weeks before the geranium cuttings on my window sill could be put out in the garden.

I remembered Mr Willet's words about the Marchs of old, and I knew that he was right. Somehow, nowadays we seemed to get no real spring, none of those balmy tender days when one could walk in the woods admiring the rosettes of primroses, noting the glutinous stalk of a trampled bluebell, with the whole vista lit by a spangle of young leaves.

The children coughed and sniffed as they had done all the winter, yet would still attempt to go out into the bleak playground without their coats until bullied into them by their elders. Winter ills were rife in the village at large, and the March meeting of the Women's Institute, a hardy collection of souls, was cancelled as the village hall stove had gone on strike, and no one could brave the arctic conditions there with the windows glazed, both inside and out, with thin ice.

One frosty evening when I was settled by the fire marking essays, and getting rather tired of correcting 'brids' and 'grils', someone rang the front door bell.

As I crossed the little hall I remembered all the warnings

about opening doors to strangers, particularly if one was alone in the house. I am always advising people to go upstairs and find out who the caller is from an upstairs window, but naturally I never do this myself, as I don't remember such things until the door is wide open.

Luckily, tonight's visitor was only Henry Mawne with some draw tickets to sell, and he seemed glad to come in.

'I shouldn't really,' he said, wiping his perfectly clean shoes vigorously on the mat, 'but to tell the truth, it's a good deal colder than I bargained for when I set out, and I shan't call anywhere else.'

I nobly stumped up fifty pence for a book of tickets to support some wild bird project dear to Henry's ornithological heart, and offered him a drink which he refused.

He stretched his legs out to the blaze, and looked settled for the evening.

I stacked the exercise books away and fetched a block of mint sweet.

'Well, indulge yourself with this,' I said, breaking it with some difficulty. 'It says it is as supplied to *successful* polar expeditions. I suppose the *unsuccessful* ones were foolish enough to forget to pack the stuff.'

'Ah! My favourite sweet,' said he, taking the largest fragment. 'Where do you get it?'

'Mr Lamb at the Post Office keeps it.'

'I never knew that!' He crunched happily, and I wondered if he proposed to stay for some time. I had two telephone calls to make, and had planned to wash my hair, but obviously a host's duties came before these things.

Why is it, I wondered, surveying my guest's relaxed attitude, that people generally imagine that a single woman is dying for company? After all, a woman living alone has just as many chores to do as her married counterpart. In fact, she is probably busier, as she has to do them all herself.

When I return from the school I still face my household tasks, correspondence – far too much of it – and the ever-present washing, ironing and mending. Gardening, shopping and modest entertaining have also to be fitted in, and I do what I can to help in various village activities, even if it only involves minding the Hat and Shoe stall at the W.I. jumble sale while the chief stall-holder slips off for a tea break. I am also fair game for anyone collecting contributions to various bazaars, and keep a supply of home-made jam and marmalade for instant largesse to these worthy causes.

It is not that I am an unsocial person, but having spent the best part of the day with a host of demanding children, my fellow-teacher, not to mention Mrs Pringle, Mr Willet and various callers of educational complexion, I am really very content to gain the blissful solitude of the school house, and a few hours of peace.

'How's Elizabeth?' I asked politely. Mrs Mawne is an energetic member of the Fairacre community, and keeps her husband up to his duties as the vicar's right hand, as well as his numerous commitments as an authority on birds.

'Oh, she's in Ireland,' said Henry. 'Gone to see an old aunt of hers. The poor thing has always been difficult, and has gone through companion after companion since her husband Roderick died.'

'You make her sound somewhat cannibalistic,' I replied.

'She is, my dear, she is!' Henry sat up, scattering a few fragments of mint sweet on the hearth rug. I was amused to watch him collecting them carefully on a licked finger and transferring them to his mouth.

'Elizabeth's gone over to see if she can persuade her into a nursing home. Fat chance of that, as far as I can see. Nothing short of dynamite will get her out of that barn of a place she lives in.'

'Has she always lived there?'

'Ever since she married some sixty years ago. It's one of those mouldering old Victorian castles, all pepper-pot turrets and cross-draughts, and the most peculiar fungi growing in the attic bedrooms. Still, it does give shelter to some rare owls and bats, and for that reason I should be sorry to see the place pulled down.'

'Is that likely to happen?'

'Very likely, I should think, if she can be persuaded to sell. My chief concern is that Elizabeth doesn't bring her back to stay with us. The position would be quite impossible. We really have enough to do looking after ourselves these days, and I can't think how we'd manage with dear old aunt Thora in our midst.'

'How old is she?'

'Ninety-three, and good for another ten years.'

He sighed heavily, and put two logs thoughtfully on my fire. I watched him in amused silence.

'And when do you expect Elizabeth to come back?'

'Lord knows,' he said morosely. 'The house is deathly quiet without her. It's one of the reasons I came out tonight, to see a bit of company.'

He rose suddenly from the chair.

'Nice of you to have me in like this,' he said, struggling into his coat. 'I'll pop in again, if I may. You always cheer me up and I'm sure you are as lonely as I am.'

I smiled politely as I took him to the door.

'Bang goes my hair wash,' I said to Tibby on my return.

2 Minor Irritations

MUCH to my annoyance, I found that I could not sleep after Mr Mawne's visit.

I had forgotten to put my hot water bottle in the bed, disturbed from my comfortable routine by my guest, and this may have been the reason for my unusual wakefulness.

After tossing and turning for two or three hours, I realised that I was ravenously hungry, and decided to go downstairs for sustenance. While some milk was heating on the stove, I collected an assortment of goodies on a tray. What, I thought, would a dietician make of a banana, a digestive biscuit and a spoonful of stewed plums? It should keep me going until breakfast-time anyway.

It was unusually quiet in the kitchen at one o'clock in the morning. Moonlight had been flooding in when I entered it, silvering the plates in the rack over the sink, and throwing squares of light over the brick floor. In the distance I could hear the wavering cry of an owl, and I stood relishing this rare night-time beauty before switching on the electric light and turning all to prosaic normality.

For years, Fairacre had been without the boon of electricity. When finally it was brought into the school house I welcomed it rapturously, and never cease to marvel at the transformation it has made to my everyday living.

Nevertheless, it is good to be reminded now and again, as in those few silent moonlit minutes, of how things were when I first came to live here, and how they had been for generations of Fairacre folk before me.

I carried my bounty back to bed and enjoyed it whilst reading my ever-present bedside book, *The Diary of a Country Parson*. This good man of the eighteenth century never fails to amuse, teach and enchant me. I felt quite abstemious about my modest trayful as I read that for dinner on November 24, 1795, Parson Woodforde enjoyed 'Hashed-Calf's Head, a boiled Chicken and some bacon, a Leg of Mutton rosted, and a Norfolk batter-Pudding and drippings, after that we had a Duck rosted, Maccaroni and Tarts. By way of Desert, we had white Currants, Pears and Apples, and Filberts.'

In February of the next year he gave 'to an old decayed Fisherman O.I.O.' (This was one shilling.) He goes on to remark:

'He was the Man that brought me once some very indifferent Spratts.'

This last entry made me laugh so much that I finished my snack, switched off my ever-blessed bedside lamp, and was asleep in ten minutes.

Before school the next morning, I was alarmed to see that Mrs Pringle's limp was much in evidence. What could have happened? Had I inadvertently spilt something vicious such as red ink on her immaculate floor boards? Had the sink overflowed, the plug stopped up with that cursed ubiquitous bubble gum beloved of Fairacre's children? Had the stove gone out? All these hazards flashed before me like the drowning man's swift summary of his life, or so we are told.

Luckily, for once it was not my fault that Mrs Pringle's leg had seen fit 'to flare-up'. As had happened many times before, the cause of her discomfort was her niece, Minnie Pringle.

Minnie's I.Q. is extremely low. She cannot read, has difficulty in signing her name and is virtually incapable of doing the simplest work, as I know to my cost. In a weak moment once, I let her help in my house, and it would need a stronger pen than mine, and far more time than I could spare, to catalogue the appalling list of damages she managed to inflict. I will give just two instances. She thought that a cushion cover looked grubby, and put it to soak, complete with its contents, into neat bleach in the sink. I must say, in all fairness, that the sink had never looked so pristine, although the smell in the kitchen was enough to choke one.

Her second effort was to dismantle the electric cooker in order to give it 'a good going-over'. Fortunately Mrs Pringle arrived in time to switch off the current at the main, or doubtless I should have found Minnie electrocuted on the kitchen floor amidst the debris. It took Mr Willet and me all the evening to put the thing together again, and I have never heard so many whispered curses, from that upright churchman, on any other occasion.

This time, it appeared, Minnie had been obliged to take one of her children to hospital, and had deposited the rest with Mrs Pringle at a moment's notice.

'Called in as bold as brass with them four little varmints, just as I was getting down to give the kitchen floor a nice wash-over with some suds I had left from rinsing out the tea-clorths.'

'What had happened to the fifth?'

Minnie's children are by a variety of fathers. True, she is married, not all that long ago, but that is to an elderly man, called Ern, with children of his own. The marriage is a stormy one, which is hardly surprising, and Bert, an earlier paramour, always seems to be bobbing up and distracting Minnie's scatter-brained attention from her wifely duties.

'Well, Ern went up to the Potters' to see if the lawn mower was in good nick for the summer, and he took young Basil with him. Why, don't ask me!'

I had no intention of asking, especially as it was almost time to let in the children, and Miss Briggs, my assistant, was hovering around as if waiting for something.

'Anyway, Ern left the thing running while he went for the oil can and that little faggot put his hand in. Took the tops off of three fingers.'

'Oh no!'

'Oh yes! And that stupid Ern and Minnie hadn't got the plain common sense to take the tops with 'em to the hospital to be sewn on again.'

Miss Briggs emitted a small yelp. I sat down quickly in my chair and concentrated my attention on a rather wispy late hyacinth growing over water. I cannot take gory details, and Mrs Pringle spares one absolutely nothing.

'I think it's time for the bell,' I said cravenly to Miss Briggs. She hurried away.

'And don't tell me any more,' I begged Mrs Pringle. 'Not about the injuries, I mean. I'm very sorry for the child. Is he staying in hospital long?'

'No, more's the pity. Minnie gets him this afternoon and I've said they can all have tea with me, and she can take 'em home straight to bed.'

'Well, that's very good of you,' I said. 'You must be a tower of strength to that little family.'

A horrid thought struck me.

'You're not thinking of keeping any of the school-age ones with you?' This has happened in the past, and of course they attend my school temporarily and a sore trial they are.

'Not likely,' said my cleaner succinctly.

She rose from the front desk and made her way to the lobby. I think my tribute to her had pleased her.

Her limp had vanished.

At playtime, while the children swarmed happily outside, Miss Briggs broached the subject which she had been trying to bring to my notice, without success, as Mrs Pringle's horrendous account of young Basil's mishap was then in spate.

She has been engaged to a cheerful young builder called Wayne for some time now. He was working for Reg Thorn, a local builder, when he replaced our leaking skylight – not altogether successfully, as it is becoming apparent – and that is how the two young people first met.

The wedding is planned for the summer, soon after the end of the school year, and Miss Briggs' urgent problem was the fitting of her wedding dress. Could she *possibly*, she implored me, go half an hour earlier tomorrow to go to the dressmaker in Caxley who had just heard that she must go into hospital and wanted to make a start on the dress before she took to her hospital bed?

'That's no problem,' I assured her. 'The whole school can play Fox and Geese and Grandmother's Steps and I Sent a Letter to my Love. We don't get enough games altogether.'

'It might rain,' said she anxiously.

'I can still read,' I told her.

She returned to her class much relieved, and I remembered her early days with me when I had been obliged to point out to her that it was her duty to remain until all the infants were accounted for at the end of the afternoon, and that the fact that the clock said three-thirty was not the signal for instant departure. She had improved considerably, whether mellowed by love or simply by discovering that she could do her job quite well, was a matter for conjecture.

Mr Willet's summing up had been that she was 'a fair old lump of a girl' when she first arrived at Fairacre. It had been difficult to talk to her, and I had found her downright surly at times. However, we now hit it off very well, and I thought that Wayne's influence had been all to the good. She proposed to continue teaching after her marriage, and for this I was grateful. New appointments are always hazardous, and in a two-teacher school such as ours it is absolutely essential that the pair can work happily together.

Of course, I pondered, there might be babies coming along, but she could always have maternity leave and then come back if she wanted to.

It then occurred to me that, as usual, I was allowing my mind to run well ahead. After all, we had not had the wedding dress fitted yet. It was rather early to be counting chicks.

Furthermore, through the lofty windows I could see a row of moving heads. Obviously, a procession of children was running along the coke pile, and it was high time that that little caper was stopped.

Seizing the hand bell, I made my way into the playground.

That afternoon the first mild breeze began to blow. The weathervane on St Patrick's steeple had veered to the south-west, the clouds scudded along at a merry rate, and here and there the sunshine broke through, gilding the bare branches and raising our spirits. Could spring be here at last?

The children sniffed the air as appreciatively as eager dogs out on a walk, and I let them go to play five minutes earlier than usual, although with stern threats about the consequences of going *near*, let alone *on*, the coke pile.

When I went to call them in I saw that Gerald Partridge, our much-loved vicar, was among the crowd, his venerable cape, green with age, billowing from his shoulders in the breeze.

'My dear Miss Read,' he said, clasping my hands in his. The leopard-skin gloves of winter were not in evidence today, a sure sign that the weather was warmer.

'Come into school,' I said.

'No, no! It's so lovely to welcome a mild breeze. Let us enjoy the air out here. I've brought a letter from my wife. No need to answer it immediately. You may want to consider your reply. That's why she decided not to telephone you.'

'What's it about?' I asked, alarm raising its ugly head.

Was another pot of marmalade needed for some good cause?

Was I being invited to one of Mrs Partridge's cheese and wine parties to meet some eminent divine? If so, a simple telephone call had always been considered fitting, so what hidden complications were inside the envelope?

'Look at it in the peace of your own home,' advised the vicar. Perhaps my consternation was writ large upon my face. In any case, Gerald Partridge, though vague in many ways, is remarkably sensitive to other people's feelings. I stuffed it into my jacket pocket.

'I always think,' said the vicar, changing the subject with aplomb, 'that you have one of the finest views in Fairacre.' He gazed across Mr Roberts' young corn to the massive bulk of the downs on the sky-line.

'So do I,' I told him.

' "*I will lift up my eyes unto the hills: from whence cometh my*

help," ' quoted Mr Partridge. 'You know I find them as much
comfort as the psalmist did. They put our own petty affairs
into perspective.'

'Absolutely,' I agreed. 'Like ducks.'

'Ducks?'

' *"From troubles of the world*
I turn to ducks,
Beautiful, comical things, sleeping
or curled . . ." The rest escapes me but I'll look it up for you.'

'I should appreciate that,' said the vicar gravely. 'Ducks or
downs, we all need to gather comfort where we can, and I find
a great deal in remembered fragments of writing.'

A breathless five-year-old rushed up to us.

'Miss, one of them Coggs kids has been to the lavatory on
the lobby floor.'

'That,' I told her, 'is what is known as a contradiction of
terms, but I'll come at once.'

'In that case,' said the vicar, 'I must let you return to your
duties.'

He departed, I thought, with unnecessary haste, and I went
to find the floor cloth.

What with one thing and another, I had forgotten Mrs Partridge's missive until I was rummaging for a handkerchief in
my jacket pocket, whilst waiting for the kettle to boil in my
peaceful kitchen. Out fell the envelope and up surged my
misgivings again.

I read it while I sipped my tea. After suitable greetings the
letter continued:

'My dear friend Hazel Smith is trying to raise some money
for the Save The Children Fund in Caxley, and is organising
an evening meeting which is going to be billed as "Our
Children".

'She is asking several speakers to say a few words and then to answer questions from the floor. I know she has a local magistrate who will talk about the juvenile court, and a most eminent educationalist, as well as a local doctor who specialises in children's ailments – a *paediatrician*, I believe is the correct word unless I am confusing it with something to do with *feet*, or even *worse* – but a very nice man indeed who once was on TV in one of those upsetting medical series.

'I took the liberty of mentioning your name to her and she may get in touch to see if you would be a member of the panel. Perhaps you could talk on young children in school? Or children's literature? Anyway, I do so hope you don't mind my mentioning you to her. You would be *so good*, and I know you would love Hazel.

'There would be a cold buffet and wine after the meeting, and a chance to get to know a great many people who are *really caring* about the young, just as you are.'

She was mine affectionately after three pages.

'Oh lor', Tibby,' I said to the cat. 'Now what do I do?'

But that unfeeling animal continued to wash his face vigorously, callous to the sufferings of his mistress.

With this awful prospect before me I spent the evening in a fine state of dithering. My first instinct was to turn down the proposal with a flat refusal. I had no wish to turn out for an evening in Caxley, and a downright antipathy to my unknown panel members.

They were probably all as charming as Mrs Partridge's old friend Hazel. They certainly appeared to be much more public-spirited, unless of course they had been coerced into it and were feeling quite as reluctant as I was myself. But I see far too much of people 'who care for the young' and on the whole I find them exhaustingly earnest. I know I care for the young – look at the floor cloth interlude only that afternoon, and you can't get much nearer the bone of caring than that! Nevertheless, the thought of answering a lot of solemn questions about possible damage done to the young child's ego by thwarting it of some simple pleasure such as flooding the bathroom or jumping on the cat, filled me with horror.

Besides what should I talk about? Even ten minutes' speaking takes the devil of a lot of writing, and I know my limits. No, I should have to decline.

Having decided this, I then remembered the many kindnesses that Mrs Partridge has shown to me and the school, and began to feel a mean-spirited wretch. Would it hurt me to give up one evening? (*Yes*, squeaked my baser self.) Mrs Partridge must consider me capable of the job or I shouldn't have been asked. (Probably the seventeenth person on her list, all the others having sensibly made plans to go abroad, have visitors, contract shingles, and so on.) It would be letting down dear Mrs Partridge if I fobbed off Hazel Thingummy with some weak excuse.

At that moment, the telephone bell rang, and I jumped as though I had been shot. This must be it! Well, better answer it and be guarded. Ask if I might ring her tomorrow when I've thought it over.

I gave my number in a cracked voice. To my enormous relief it was Amy.

'Have you got a cold?' she asked solicitously.

I babbled out my present problems, and Amy forbore to laugh, at least out loud.

'What a funny old thing you are,' she commented, in such a loving voice that I very nearly burst into tears. 'You give the impression of being in command of every situation –'

'Surely not!'

'And yet you go all to pieces over a simple little matter like this.'

'But it isn't a simple little matter, Amy,' I wailed. 'It scares me stiff, the whole idea, and yet I'm so fond of Mrs Partridge, I really don't want to hurt her by appearing disobliging. And, of course, it's a very good cause. Saving the children, I mean. Why, come to think of it, I spend my whole life saving children!'

I told her that sad tale of the floor cloth.

'I should think that is evading Mrs Pringle's wrath rather than saving children,' commented Amy shrewdly. 'But do you know what I'd do?'

'No, tell me quickly,' I urged.

'Forget it for this evening. Go to bed early with a nice juicy book to read. Ten chances to one you'll know your own mind in the morning.'

'Thank you, Amy,' I said humbly and put down the receiver.

Within a minute the telephone rang again. It was Amy.

'Don't be so swift putting the phone back,' she said. 'I didn't have a chance to tell you why I was ringing.'

I apologised.

'I just wondered if you'd decided on any of the Caxley Festival items. I ought to start booking, I think.'

'Amy,' I began, 'I'm afraid I haven't got round to –'

'Never mind, never mind! Just tuck it away in your subconscious with Mrs Partridge's proposition, and you can deal with both tomorrow.'

It was her turn to replace the receiver. Her tone had been kindly and forgiving, and I returned to my fireside thanking the gods for the good friends whom I hardly seemed to deserve.

3 Henry Mawne Needs Company

AFTER a night of solid sleep I felt robust enough to accede to Mrs Partridge's proposal, and decided to telephone after school that day to say how delighted I should be if her friend Hazel needed my services on the panel. Really, civilisation has a lot to answer for! What would happen if we all spoke the unvarnished truth?

As my egg boiled that morning, I turned March over on the wall calendar and read the new motto. It said:

> *A man's reach should exceed his grasp,*
> *Or what's a Heaven for?*

Could this refer to my brave decision? Should I find myself the most knowledgeable member of the panel on that fateful night? Would *The Caxley Chronicle* have a paragraph about the brilliance of repartee, breadth of knowledge, personal charm and, of course, the innate modesty of the head teacher of Fairacre School? Fame could go no higher.

While I dallied with this day dream, I noticed two things. This was April Fool's Day, so I must be on my guard in school this morning, and my egg had cracked and was fizzing all over the stove.

When I came to eat it, I found, predictably enough, that it was hard-boiled. Not that I minded. To me, an egg is an egg however it turns up, but I am always amused to hear people say scathingly that they know someone 'who couldn't boil an egg', as though this act of cookery is the simplest thing imaginable.

Strangely enough, it is jolly difficult to get an egg with a firm white and a delectably moist yolk. It all depends on size, freshness, thickness of shell, and naturally, on the accuracy of the egg-timer or clock. Being called to the telephone does not help either, as I know to my cost.

Well, now, I wondered as I spooned mine down, what little tricks would my naughty children have been up to? One April Fool's Day I had managed to stop them from tying a rope just above floor level at the lobby door. Their victim then would have been Mrs Pringle, without doubt, and the consequences not in the least humorous, as I pointed out to them. A little clean fun was one thing. Injury to people was another. They were suitably chastened, and since then have found minor ways of celebrating the day.

At first sight, all seemed as usual in the school room. I opened my desk, alert to find a mammoth spider or even a grass snake, but there was nothing of that nature there. My chair had no drawing pin or blob of glue on it. The piano keys were clean, the hymn book unsullied. Their little jokes are usually perpetrated in the first half-hour at school. Could they have forgotten? After twelve o'clock the magic was supposed to have vanished, and any larking about was reckoned invalid by ancient tradition.

We ploughed gently on through arithmetic and reading. Playtime passed without incident, and I had quite forgotten to be on my guard, as no doubt my wily flock had intended.

At twenty to twelve, before the dinner lady arrived, I set them to copy Robert Bridges' adorable poem 'Spring Goeth All In White' from the blackboard. This was to be a combined exercise in learning a poem and engaging their skills in hand-writing.

It was while I was concentrating on my own fair hand, as I wrote the last two lines, that Ernest's voice rang out with horrid urgency.

'Miss! Quick! Patrick's fainted!'

This has happened before, so that I dropped the chalk, and was at Patrick's side in one second flat. The child had his head on the desk, and as I bent to attend to him the roar of delight nearly raised the roof.

'April Fool, miss! You're April Fool!'

Patrick sat up, rosy with health and mirth, and I joined in the general hilarity.

It seemed to me, remembering the rope in the lobby, the odd spider and stickiness, that I had got off lightly this year.

That evening, full of noble thoughts, I rang Mrs Partridge to say that I should be willing, if needed by her friend, to take my place on the panel.

'How lovely!' boomed Mrs Partridge. 'I've no doubt Hazel

will be as delighted as I am, and I'm sure she will be in touch very soon.'

I replied suitably, and rang off, wondering if a well-deserved bolt from the blue would descend upon me for downright untruthfulness. It is to such passes, I thought gloomily, that Doing One's Duty, commits a frail body.

Far too often, it seems to me, I am prevailed upon, as in this instance, to undertake some task which I abhor. Why do I do it? And how best can one minimise these occurrences?

I suppose that one could give up belonging to certain clubs or activities that engender these minor irritations. For instance, if I were not a member of the Women's Institute I suppose I should not be roped in for providing something for teas, or for manning a stall, or for entering some competition for which I have no natural aptitude but give in weakly, to such strong characters as Mrs Partridge, because they have not enough entries.

On the other hand, should one retreat and become a self-imposed hermit, simply to avoid trouble? After all, I like living in Fairacre, and I am a quite important member of its little community, I suppose, although Mrs Pringle would no doubt think otherwise. Consequently, I must take on my share of the burdens.

I remember an aunt of mine saying once: 'Now that I've turned seventy, I'm not going to join anything which has *meetings!*'

It must be a family failing, I think.

Later that evening I was somewhat taken aback to find Henry Mawne on my doorstep again. He was carrying a fine bunch of daffodils, and came indoors with a beaming smile.

'Thought you'd enjoy these. They're always early in that dell of ours, and everyone likes daffodils.'

'They do indeed,' I said. 'The most cheering flowers of the

spring, I always think. Mine are nowhere near ready. I often wonder what variety Shakespeare's were that took "the winds of March with beauty". Pretty early, I suspect.'

'Poetic licence. After all, he couldn't have had "winds of April". It would've put out the rhythm,' said Henry, sitting down heavily. 'Are you busy? Things are a bit quiet at home without Elizabeth, and I felt in the need of company.'

I could hardly say that he was a confounded nuisance, I certainly was busy, and how soon would he be off, when I was holding a bunch of the daffodils he had so kindly given me. Here was civilised behaviour rearing its ugly head again!

'Would you like a drink?'

'No thanks, I don't tipple much these days. Tends to repeat, like radishes.'

'Or cucumber. Excuse me for a moment. I'll go and put these in water.'

I have a nice Coalport vase shaped like a trumpet which is invaluable for a non-arranger of flowers like me. Drop a bunch into it and the flowers obligingly fall comfortably into place. I carried it back to my sitting room with real pride.

'Good lord,' said my guest. 'That was quick! Elizabeth takes half an hour to arrange a vase of flowers.'

'She does the thing properly,' I told him, 'and gives everyone a great deal of pleasure too. My arrangements are of the Fairacre Primitive school.'

'And none the worse for that,' he said kindly. I began to warm to the man.

'I'm giving a couple of lectures during the Caxley Festival,' he went on, 'and I wondered if you would care to come.'

'It sounds lovely,' I said. 'Which dates would they be?' I added, playing for time.

'I haven't brought the programme, but I think it is on a Thursday. One in the first week, and one in the second week of May.'

'Well, thank you very much. May I let you know?'
'Of course. Elizabeth ought to be back before then, but it's not at all sure. Aunt Thora is giving her the deuce of a time. No nearer getting her into a nursing home, I gather, from what Elizabeth said on the phone.'
'Old people like their own way.'
'That's putting it mildly. As long as she doesn't arrive in Fairacre with Elizabeth, that's all I ask.'
He settled in for another half-hour, but stirred himself when the clock struck nine.
'I'd better be going. Nice to have your company.'
'Well, I'm sure Elizabeth will be home again soon.'
'It's rather doubtful. That's why it would be particularly pleasant if you could attend my lectures. I get in rather a bother about them. Lose my spectacles, or muddle up the pages of my talk. Elizabeth looks after me very well on these occasions.'
I accompanied him to the door and waved him goodbye.
In my early days at Fairacre, Henry Mawne had been thought a bachelor on his arrival in the village. Elizabeth had then been on one of her protracted visits to relations in Ireland, and the local inhabitants, including Mrs Partridge, I recalled, had done their level best 'to bring us together', envisaging an elderly bridal couple tottering from St Patrick's between a guard of honour formed by my pupils and, possibly, some of Henry's bird-lovers' club.
It had been a most embarrassing situation, and I was quite determined not to get embroiled with Henry Mawne while his wife was away. As for accepting his invitation to the bird lectures, that was now completely out. I should just have to find a water-tight excuse for both occasions, or I could imagine the tongues wagging all the way from Fairacre to Caxley.
The Mawnes and I have grown quite close over the years. His great-nephew, Simon, attended my school for a short

time, and incurred the wrath of the whole village by slaying an albino robin which we all adored.

He was still seen here in the school holidays, as his father David had remarried after the tragic death of Simon's mother, and he had bought a house in the village. David was away quite a lot, but his wife Irene did a certain amount of entertaining at Holly Lodge, and I was often lucky enough to be invited to family occasions. Nevertheless, I did not want Henry Mawne's attentions in his present circumstances. I did not flatter myself that my *beaux yeux* were the attraction, but knew quite well that he was lonely at the moment, and simply wanted some company.

Unfortunately, one's affairs are under constant scrutiny in a village, and as a headmistress I must appear to be above reproach. I alone know how many and varied are my failings, but I hope that flirting is not among them, particularly with an elderly and happily married man like silly old Henry.

Before school the next morning Mrs Pringle greeted me with an unaccustomed smile.

'A little bird told me you had a visitor last night. And a nice bunch of daffs,' she added archly.

I forbore to reply.

For a blissful few days in early April we had warm and sunny weather, and the children and I took full advantage of it.

We even had one or two lessons outside, sitting in the playground in the shelter of the old school walls. The elder bushes were sprouting young leaves, and a few celandines turned shiny, yellow faces to the sun at the edge of Mr Roberts' field.

Already some of his lambs frisked in the field near his farmhouse, and their bleating carried to us on the warm spring breeze.

A pair of blackbirds was hard at work gathering nesting

material, and as far as I could see the nest was being built low down in an ancient lauristinus bush in my garden. This shrub, much loved by the Victorians, is rather scorned by Fairacre gardeners today, but I treasure it because of its glossy evergreen leaves and its heartening way of producing pink and white blossom all through the darkest days of winter.

'Scatter-brained animals, them blackbirds,' is Mr Willet's dictum, and he does not waste any pity on them, as I do, when Tibby or any other marauder attacks the young ones. Rarely a spring passes without my trying to screen an obvious black-bird's nest from Tibby's view. It is impossible to keep an eye on the cat while I am at school, and what horrors go on in my absence I shudder to think.

'Well, it's only nature,' says Mr Willet. 'Them blackbirds gobble up worms but you don't wipe your eye about that, now do you? So what's wrong with your Tibby helping himself to a snack now and again?'

The copse at the foot of the downs was also busy with birds, as we discovered on one of our numerous nature walks during the fine spell.

A few early primroses were opening, and the wild honey-suckle had put forth small strong leaves. It was all heady stuff after a long and miserable winter. The wood smelt of moss and damp earth. Every aspect of spring assailed our senses, the warmth, the fragrance, the welcome flowers and leaves. Even the first, bright, fringed leaves of the stinging nettles received our blessing.

Easter Day was only a week or so away. Soon Fairacre school would be on holiday. What better way to spend the last few days of term than relishing this forerunner of joys to come?

During the last week of term, two things happened which gave me much food for thought.

In the first place, I had a very kind letter from Mrs Partridge's old friend giving me details of the dreaded evening when I had rashly offered my services on the panel.

After profuse thanks, the letter continued:

'The other members of the panel include Doctor Eric Biddle who specialises in children's complaints and has very advanced ideas on children's diet. I expect you have met him, as his practice is just south of Caxley. He once appeared in a television programme, so of course we are extremely lucky to get such a notable figure for our little evening.

'The other man is Councillor James Ellis who is a magistrate on the Caxley bench and chairman of the Juvenile Court panel. He is a charming man, and has taken a degree in Child Psychology in the Open University. He has a very sympathetic way with young offenders, as you may have noticed from reports in our local paper.

'The lady who will keep you company is an outstanding educationalist who has set up her own school near the teachers' training college where she is a much respected lecturer. We are very fortunate to get her to come on the panel, as she is in great demand as a speaker, and has an international reputation. Her name is Miss Crabbe.'

Good grief! That wicked old hag? I put the letter down, and took a large gulp of my breakfast coffee to get over the shock.

So our paths were destined to cross again! Miss Crabbe had taught one of my assistants, by name Hilary Jackson, some years ago.

Miss Jackson was an opinionated young woman who had imbibed her lecturer's psychology theories hook, line and sinker. She also had, what was termed in my schooldays, 'a crush' on the redoubtable Miss Crabbe, and everything that the older woman did or said was considered absolutely perfect.

One dreadful weekend I had been obliged to put up this

paragon, and to endure the most awful pseudo-psychological jargon whilst Hilary hung on her every word.

At that time, the girl was going through a highly emotional phase. She had become infatuated with a local gamekeeper who was old enough to know better than to encourage the foolish girl. I was at my wits' end to know how to cope with this crisis, and agitated calls to her parents, and from them to me, aged me considerably.

Miss Crabbe's visit proved in fact to be a heavily disguised blessing, for she soon got wind of the affair, and flung off in a fit of jealous pique.

Things had been most uncomfortable at Fairacre School, and I had privately thought, and not for the first time, what a confounded nuisance love could be. How right of E. M. Delafield to put it far below good teeth and a sound bank balance, in order of merit!

After a few months, Miss Crabbe offered the olive branch and, as the gamekeeper had found another love, Hilary Jackson accepted with alacrity, and the last I heard of the pair was that they were both interested in the progressive school mentioned in Hazel Smith's letter.

Well, well! It would be fun to see if Miss Crabbe was still as formidable as when we last met. Then, I recalled, she had told me she was not a flesh-eater, and a hard time I had had of it trying to find enough non-meat sustenance that weekend. I only hoped that there would be plenty of cheese offered after our ordeal.

The second surprise came one balmy evening when I was dawdling through the village on my way to post a letter.

Hurrying in the opposite direction was Miriam Quinn. She seemed to be in some agitation.

'You're in a hurry,' I quipped.

'I'm a fugitive,' she explained, with a smile.

'From what?'

'From whom, is the right question. As a matter of fact, Henry Mawne.'

Miriam lives in the attractive annexe to Holly Lodge where now David and Irene Mawne live. It is some little way from the centre of Fairacre, a charming house tucked away behind a high holly hedge which gives the place its name.

'He's been coming down some evenings to have a meal with David and Irene while Elizabeth is away. That suits everyone, of course, but once he's had it he will gravitate to my end of the establishment, and I'm really getting rather cheesed off.'

'I can sympathise.'

'So tonight I told a white lie and said I was paying a visit to someone in the village, and here I am on the run.'

'Pay a visit to me,' I said, 'I'd love it.'

'Truly?'

'Truly,' I assured her.

We posted the letter, and wandered back to the school house.

'He's paid me two surprise visits,' I told her when we were comfortably settled in our armchairs. 'He seems to need company pretty badly.'

'Between ourselves,' said Miriam, 'I'm inclined to think that Elizabeth is to blame. Irene was telling me that there have been several periods in her married life when she has just pushed off. Sometimes for months.'

I remembered Henry's first year at Fairacre, with no wife in evidence.

'You don't think this is another protracted absence?' I asked, with some alarm. The thought of choking off Henry's attentions with tact, kindness and firmness, was a daunting one.

'Who knows? The snag is that we're all fond of the dear old boy, but this popping in to see us maiden ladies certainly sets the village tongues wagging, and I don't want Elizabeth to be upset when she does return.'

I told her about Mrs Pringle's coy remark about my bouquet of daffodils.

'I'm going to see how things go for a few days,' said Miriam. 'With any luck we'll hear that she is on her way home, and our troubles will be at an end.'

'But if nothing happens?'

'I've decided to tell Irene how I feel –'

'Me too,' I begged. 'Put in a word for a beleaguered schoolmarm.'

'And ask her to speak to him about it. It's just thoughtlessness on his part, I'm sure. He's too nice a fellow to want to embarrass us. Leave it to me.'

'I shall be only too delighted,' I assured her. 'And now, as you are paying me an official visit, what about scrambled eggs on toast? You can always upgrade them to an omelette if you are questioned about the meal you had.'

'An excellent idea,' agreed Miriam, following me into the kitchen.

4 The Coggs Are in Distress

OUR local paper, *The Caxley Chronicle*, is much esteemed in Fairacre. I suppose that the headlines on the front page are the first to be read, closely followed by Births, Marriages and Deaths, and accounts of cases dealt with by the Caxley magistrates coming in third.

Among the latter, during the last week of term, the name Coggs caught my eye. Arthur Coggs, father of Joseph, girl twins and one or two other offspring, is an incorrigible rogue, and Fairacre has no time for him.

He is out of work more often than in, which is hardly surprising. Any money which he does earn goes mainly on drink, and his poor wife sees very little of it.

He is a very weak character, and easily led by his drinking companions, many of whom are habitual offenders and well known to the local magistrates. Arthur is the fellow that they get to keep a look-out while they are engaged in such pastimes as breaking into shops and offices at night, or stripping lead from the roofs of ancient buildings.

It is Arthur who is persuaded to drive a van to a hide-out in the country, or to deliver stolen goods from one malefactor to another in the chain. Left alone, I think that Arthur might be quite content to do a little poaching, or local petty thieving, but he is helpless to withstand the pressure put upon him by his wilier companions who use him without a qualm.

Of course, he gets payment, but a very small share of the total sum, I imagine, and it is a befuddled mixture of feelings which keeps him on the fringe of this collection of petty criminals. He is proud to belong to these desperadoes, and flattered by their attention. If he is called 'chicken', he will bluster, and then do anything required of him. There is a certain amount of fear mixed up in his general reaction. One or two of his companions are not above menacing him, and there have been occasional injuries, such as a suspicious cut at the throat and a broken finger, which were never satisfactorily explained, although Doctor Martin, who has known the family for years, guesses the cause and has no hesitation in giving Arthur some trenchant advice which, of course, is not taken. Poor old Arthur, we all agree, is past redemption.

This week's *Caxley Chronicle* gave a short account of the proceedings of the case in which Arthur was involved. It ended with the chairman's comment that in view of the seriousness of the crime, and his deplorable record, he would be sentenced to six months' imprisonment.

'Seen the Caxley?' asked Mrs Pringle the next morning. 'The Caxley' can refer to the local paper or to the bus which very infrequently used to serve the village. This time I knew Mrs Pringle referred to the paper, and to Arthur Coggs' tribulations in particular.

'What's six months?' she demanded. 'That means four, I suppose. They takes off a bit for good conduct, though why they should, you may well ask.'

'It will keep him out of the way for the summer in any case,' I pointed out.

'He'll start all over again when he does get out,' said Mrs Pringle, with some truth. 'When I think that Arthur Coggs signed the pledge the same year as I did, it fair makes me grieve! He didn't keep that vow long did he? I mind his sister Ethel took the pledge the same day. As nice a girl as you could wish to meet, with long black hair as she could sit on. When it was down, I mean.'

I had a brief mental picture of a brunette attempting to sit

on her hair when it was pinned up. Mrs Pringle continued
unabated.

'All dressed in white she was. It was her old confirmation
dress, I recall, and very nice too with a crochet collar. Ethel and
Arthur's old ma was a great one for crochet. Yards of it she did.
Bedspreads, table clorths, nothing was too much for her, and
Ethel's drawers, if you will pardon the word, was always
edged with crochet work.'

'Mrs Pringle,' I began, glancing at the clock, but one might
just as well try to stop the Niagara Falls as our cleaner in full
spate.

'She went into the Caxley Co-op when she left school. The
bacon counter. She married Charlie Tibble whose uncle used
to sweep the High Street, if you remember, a funny old party
with a waxed moustache like the Kaiser.'

'No, I don't think I ever saw him. And now, Mrs Pringle –'

'I was always fond of Ethel,' she continued. 'Never deserved
to have a rapscallion like that Arthur for a brother. Mind you,
she's not the good looker she was. Got rather fat, but she'd had
two boys and they was both nine-pounders which don't do a
woman much good, especially is she's narrow in the hips.
They've been in trouble too, so I hear.'

'What sort of trouble?'

'Fighting, and that, in pubs.'

'So they didn't take after Ethel?'

'Doesn't look like it. Both on probation, I was told.'

She gave a massive sigh, and picked up the dustpan.

'Ah well! Bad blood will out, I always say, and I can't stand
here gossiping with you all day.'

There was general sympathy in the village for Arthur's wife,
although it was agreed that by this time she must be inured to
any discomfort caused by her husband's absences from home.

Mr Willet was more forthright.

'She's far better off without that good-for-nothing round the house. He's not above giving her a walloping when he's the worse for drink, and I reckon it's a dog's life when he's about.'

'I suppose she'll be worse off financially though,' I suggested.

Mr Willet snorted.

'She gets the same hand-out as anyone else, plus the children's allowances which ain't to be sneezed at in that Coggs family. And she's got a little cleaning at the vicarage, and I know for a fact she brings home some pretty tasty bits of left-overs what the Partridges give her. She had a basin of beef drippin' last Thursday as fair made my mouth water. Lovely that'd be on toast with a sprinkle of salt. I told her so, and she said she'd try it on the kids. Now, wouldn't you have thought she'd 'ave known that anyway? A poor feckless body, she is! My Alice tries to give her a few tips like getting bones and simmering them with a few root veg, but she still goes on buying them great packets of cornflakes for three times the price.'

I sympathised with good kind-hearted Mrs Willet. I too am constantly casting my pearls before swine. How many of the poems I offer my children carry any weight beside the comics they devour? I like to think that an occasional felicitous phrase will stick, and one day give them pleasure to recall. One must live in hope, as a teacher, or go under for ever.

Although Mrs Coggs' plight was a familiar one, I somehow could not put the little family out of my mind after these two conversations.

Joseph and his younger twin sisters seemed unmoved by this latest disaster, and as they were the only children of school age I had little idea of how the younger ones were faring. There were two toddlers, and a weakly-looking baby which seemed to spend its time in a battered pram which smelled overpoweringly of ammonia and disintegrating plastic fabric.

In many ways, poor, apathetic Mrs Coggs had much in

common with Mrs Pringle's crazy niece Minnie. Both had a tribe of neglected children. Both lived in a state of dirt and muddle. Both had trouble with their menfolk, and neither seemed to have any idea of managing money, as Mrs Willet had discovered.

If anything, Minnie was less to be pitied. Despite her turbulent domestic life, she seemed to enjoy the excitement of two men competing for her favours at the same time. Her bevy of noisy wet-nosed children did not seem to ruffle her. The wide mad grin stayed permanently on her freckled face. She could not read, nor tell the time, relying on the chimes of St Patrick's church to give her a rough idea of the passage of the hours or the arrival of the Caxley bus, when the village was fortunate enough to have such a service. But she always seemed to find life utterly absorbing and pleasurable, living as she did in the present. With her limited intelligence, the past was soon forgotten, and what lay in the future was beyond her comprehension. In some ways, one could almost envy Minnie's dotty euphoria. She seemed immune to remorse or apprehension.

Mrs Coggs was only marginally more intelligent, but was much more pathetic. She certainly remembered the past, and lived in fear of her husband's violence, knowing only too well, from experience, what terror and damage he could cause when drunk. Lack of money, and utter hopelessness, contributed to her neglect of the children, and any attempts to help her met with overpowering apathy, as the local probation officer could testify. Mrs Coggs had once been discovered shoplifting, and the time she had spent under supervision from the probation service had certainly given some help and direction to the family. But once that had gone, the same slip-shod ways returned. Perhaps, as Mr Willet had said, the departure of Arthur to the care of Her Majesty's prison might give his pathetic wife some relief. Time alone would tell.

★   ★   ★

Elizabeth Mawne was still away from home, and no one seemed to have any news of her.

Henry spoke of her quite cheerfully, and with no hint of there being anything untoward in the circumstances. Perhaps he was accustomed to his wife's absences, as Miriam had told me.

He had called again, so Mr Willet informed me, but luckily I had gone to see Amy who lives some miles south of Caxley in the village of Bent, so that I missed him.

'He'd got a great roll of books with him,' Mr Willet informed me. 'Books', I took it, meant magazines. It is the common term here for anything printed. I was just congratulating myself on my timely absence from home on that particular evening when my caretaker sent my hopes plummeting.

'I was oiling that dratted lock on the lobby door, and I says should I take the books for you, but Mr Mawne said he'd come again another time.'

'He could have left them in the porch.'

'Well, he never, did 'e? Strikes me 'he wanted an excuse to pay you another visit. Seems he's a bit lost without his missus.'

Confound the fellow, I thought! However, no point in making a fuss about it, and certainly no need to let Mr Willet see how annoyed I was. It would be all over the village in no time.

I gave Mr Willet what I imagined was a carefree smile.

'Nice to see the hedges beginning to show green,' I observed, casually changing the subject.

'I wouldn't encourage him, if I was you,' said Mr Willet.

He was gone before I could reply. Perhaps it was as well.

But the slight irritation caused by Henry Mawne was overwhelmed in the bliss of breaking up.

All teachers are glad to welcome the end of term, and particularly the end of the winter term when the weather is at its most bitter, playtimes have to be spent indoors, pupils and staff are suffering from coughs, colds and worse afflictions, and tempers are short.

To add to our general happiness, the sun shone warmly, the little birds fluttered about their nest-building and egg-hatching, and a few early tulips ventured into flower. What could be more hopeful?

We set about tidying up the classroom in the afternoon. Desks were relieved of mountains of used paper, the flower vases were emptied and washed, pencils and pens collected, text books and exercise books stacked in the cupboards, so that the time soon came when the children had nothing to occupy them, and we were back to simple games such as I Spy and Left and Right. This invaluable aid to teachers consists of hiding a piece of chalk in one or the other hand, then holding out the two fists, naming a child and then displaying one's open palms. If the child chosen has guessed correctly it is his turn to come to the front and continue. That such an unsophisticated game should give so much pleasure does one's heart good these days.

At half past three we heard the scraping of chairs as the babies, beyond the partition between our two rooms, prepared to depart. Excited voices were upraised in grace, Miss Briggs' stentorian tones preceded a general exodus towards their lobby, and silence fell.

The massive wall clock ticked ponderously. Outside, a robin chattered, scolding the infants no doubt. Patrick stood, fists outstretched trying to decide who should have the honour of guessing 'left or right'.

'Eileen,' he said at last, breaking the spell.

'Right,' she said, and it was.

'Last turn,' I said, one eye on the clock.

The usual groans of dismay assailed me.

'But, miss, I ain't 'ad no turn yet!'

'Eileen Burton's bin twice!'

'It's not fair! The girls have had more'n us boys.'

'Does anyone want to stay in after school?' I enquired politely.

Silence fell. Eileen fiddled with the chalk behind her back. After a lengthy pause, she held out her two fists.

'Joseph,' she said.

'Left,' croaked Joseph in his hoarse little voice.

'Well done,' I said. 'Now you remember, Joseph, next time we play that it's your turn to start.'

'It'll be next term, miss,' he pointed out. It was a joyous thought.

'All stand. Hands together, eyes closed.'

We sang grace, somewhat discordantly, and rather faster than usual.

But we were truly thankful, every one of us.

Later that evening I pottered about happily in my house and garden, savouring the joy of the first few hours of the Easter holidays.

Now I need not watch the clock. I could have my breakfast later than usual. I could dally in the bath. Who knows? I might even get round to washing the curtains.

Mrs Pringle, no doubt, would soon be badgering me about spring cleaning on her weekly visit to the schoolhouse. The fever hits her early. I am fast becoming immune to it as the years pass, and have pointed out frequently to my tyrant that if the house is cleaned regularly, and occasionally 'bottomed', as she puts it, which means a ghastly upheaval, then surely spring cleaning is not necessary.

I lose this battle every time, of course, as I know I shall from the outset. The day will come when I return from school to find the shabbily comfortable chairs stripped of their chintz covers, and Mrs Pringle confronting me with handfuls of debris she has collected from the cracks, such as peanuts, pencils, knitting needles, and once a lipstick of Amy's, which thankfully had not shed its lid.

But so far nothing had been said about our annual upheaval, and in my present buoyant mood I was hopeful. Perhaps she had forgotten? Perhaps the renowned bad leg was in one of its combustible moods, and when this afflicted limb 'flares up', as its owner puts it, any activity is severely restricted. It can work to my advantage occasionally, as in this case.

I woke the next morning to blue skies and a wonderful sense of freedom. Lying back on my pillows watching the unfurling pink tiny leaves of the copper beech fluttering in the morning breeze, I made plans for my first day of the holidays. I should cook myself bacon as well as an egg. Usually, a boiled egg is the standard schoolday breakfast. While it boils, I can rush about watering pot plants, emptying the tidy bin, putting tea towels to soak and generally getting ahead with essential daily chores.

Today I should stand at my ease turning bacon in a leisurely fashion and enjoying its aroma. Tibby should have bacon rinds – a particular treat – and we would both celebrate.

Then I should settle down with the crossword puzzle. It is surely the height of luxury to do the crossword puzzle early in the day. It seems so delightfully decadent when normally one is at work.

I should take my time over a little flower arranging. I might clean the upstairs windows. I might ring Amy and invite her to tea. In fact, the day spread before me full of enchanting small ploys which I might or might not do. No timetable threatened me. No inspectors would call. No children would disturb me. Oh, thrice-blessed holidays!

As might be expected, I was not allowed to live on these

dizzy heights for long. Life always manages to pull the rug from under one's feet and bring one to earth with a bump.

I certainly enjoyed my bacon and egg, and I was happily settled with the crossword at nine-fifteen, when the postman delivered an electricity bill of horrifying size, a pamphlet from an animal rescue society with a distressing photograph of an emaciated dog which I knew would haunt me for nights to come, and a postcard from Henry Mawne requesting the pleasure of my company at a sherry party. He had added: 'Do come. Love, Henry' which I thought quite unnecessary and particularly thoughtless, for he must have known, as well as I did, that Mr Lamb at the Post Office, as well as the postman, would have read it with extreme delight. What an irritating fellow he was! I should certainly decline, and without love.

But these were minor pin pricks. Worse was to come. I was enjoying a rest in the garden. There is a sheltered spot at the back of the house where the sun warms one comfortably and there is no wind. My peace was disturbed by the arrival of Mrs Pringle and her niece Minnie, with a retinue of grubby children.

For one awful minute I envisaged the dreaded spring cleaning, but Mrs Pringle soon put me right.

'Minnie's Basil's got to go up to the hospital in May.' She indicated a minute boy with his mother's tousled red hair, freckles, and a much-bandaged hand.

'She was wondering if the school ones could come for the day, as I've offered to look after the lot while she's up there. Never know what time you'll get back from those places, do you? I mean everyone's appointment turns out to be for ten o'clock, so you might be hanging about till midnight.'

I agreed hastily. May seemed a long way off, and in any case if Mrs Pringle was being so noble as to have that little tribe for the day, it was very small beer on my part to accommodate the older children in school.

'Ain't you lucky?' cried Minnie to her offspring, who simply nodded owlishly without speaking.

'And how is Basil's hand?' I was foolish enough to ask.

Minnie grabbed it, and was about to unwrap the grubby bandage.

'Like to see it? Coming on nice it is!'

'No, no!' I squeaked. I have no stomach for such horrors, and people like nurses who have to cope daily with such matters have my sincere respect.

Minnie looked disappointed. Obviously, she considered it was a privilege to be shown Basil's mutilated fingers.

'I'm sure it's best to keep the wounds covered,' I said weakly. 'Germs and things, you know.'

'Quite right,' said Mrs Pringle with approval. 'Well, that's all right then, Minnie. We'll be getting back for our tea, now you've got things fixed up.'

I accompanied them to the gate.

'By the way,' said my cleaner, 'about time we did a bit of spring cleaning.'

5 Easter Holidays

EARLY in the holidays Amy spent an evening with me. She arrived bearing a beautiful monogrammed suitcase containing contributions to our W.I. Jumble Sale.

Only Amy, I thought, would pack jumble with so much tissue paper and in such an elegant container. Most of the stuff in the hall had been thrust into carrier bags, or was wrapped in all-embracing old tablecloths or motheaten blankets tied up by the corners. A few choice specimens were on wire hangers, and dangled from the curtain rods over the windows. Sorting out was to take place the next afternoon and Amy's things would certainly be quickly snapped up, I could foresee, by the helpers, if Mrs Partridge did not keep a sharp eye on things.

I suppose this craving to have first pick is universal, and it certainly is at its strongest during preparations for bazaars, jumble sales and the like. I often think it is a marvel that anything gets left to put out on the stalls, and I frequently see a handbag of mine in the village, that went directly from my house to a helper in the hall by-passing the jumble sale altogether.

Mrs Partridge, as a vicar's wife, is quite aware of human frailty and has made a sensible and practical rule. Helpers are allowed to buy one article – and one only – before the sale. That is their reward for the time and energy they put into the job. After that they must muck in with the rest of us, milling about from stall to stall. I must say, Mrs Partridge's rule works well. Perhaps my handbag was the sole choice of its present owner as a helper's bonus – a charitable thought.

49

'We'd better transfer it all to another case,' I said, 'then you can take yours home with you.'

'Oh, don't bother, my dear. Leave it as it is and I'll collect the case another time.'

'But supposing it gets nicked?' I protested. 'The vicar's coat was sold once, and Mrs Lamb's shopping basket. I couldn't bear to see this beauty rattling off in someone's van.'

'Don't be so pessimistic. Of course, nothing will happen to it. You should have more trust in your fellows.'

'Well, if I have to tell you that it vanished when my back was turned, I hope you won't forget the gipsy's warning.'

'I promise not to blame you. There's quite enough to worry about, I find, without fussing about a suitcase.'

For one moment, I feared that Amy was about to unburden her problems concerning James's absences from home, and my heart sank. I very much dislike being the recipient of secrets, particularly marital ones, but I need not have worried.

'Do you find,' asked Amy, settling back on the sofa, 'that things prey on your mind more heavily as you grow older? I always imagined that it was only the young that suffered agonies, over spots on the face, or unrequited love, but really I seem to do nothing but plan against all sorts of horrors that may never occur.'

'How d'you mean? Illness, or accidents?'

'Partly. I mean that I never take the car out without wondering if it will break down in some lonely spot. Then I rehearse what I should do if a convict on the run came up and threatened me. Should I give him my handbag without a struggle? Should I attempt to take the axe away from him? That sort of thing.'

'If he had an axe, I should give him anything he required,' I answered.

'More likely, of course,' went on Amy, fitting a cigarette into a long elegant holder, 'is the business of finding oneself in a strange town with the car locked, and one's keys and handbag still inside. Not to mention one's mac, and it's pouring cats and dogs. I often think of that one.'

'What a masochist you are! I had no idea you led such a lurid mental life.'

'I don't enjoy it,' confessed Amy, 'but I can't seem to control all this planning for trouble. Take this awful man, for instance.'

'Which awful man?'

'The one *The Caxley Chronicle* is full of these last few weeks. He's a positive nut-case. One of these wretched fellows who rings door bells, and then throws open his raincoat to the person who opens the door. Of course, he has nothing on, and very annoying it must be to be confronted like that when you are expecting the fish man.'

'Well, you would shut the door and ring the police, surely?'

'My dear girl, that's been done dozens of times, but they simply can't catch him. Actually, I've thought of an excellent plan if he comes to Bent. I'd better tell you, as this is just the sort of house he'd visit, and one really should be prepared.'

'Thanks,' I said. 'Very reassuring, I must say.'

'I propose to keep a small jar of dye on the window sill by the front door, and if there's any nonsense like that I shall throw it all over him.'

'How will that help?'

'At least the police will be able to recognise him. I should only use *vegetable* dye – in fact I've a little pot of green which will do beautifully. Nothing to harm the poor fellow, as he's obviously *non compos mentis*, and will probably go straight from the magistrates' court to a looney bin. But I do advise you to do the same. Two lots of dye are better than one, and we should really be doing a public service.'

She took a long pull at her beautiful cigarette holder, and blew two perfect smoke rings. Then she looked at me sharply.

'Are you laughing?'

A great painful gale, which I had been trying to suppress, broke forth, and Amy joined me in a prolonged bout of refreshing giggles.

'Amy,' I said, wiping my eyes, 'you'll be the death of me.'

'More likely the awful man will be. I wonder what sets them off on this sort of caper?'

'Frustrated passion perhaps?'

'But there are far more obvious ways of expressing frustrated passion. Suicide, for instance, or poetry. After all, some of the most telling poems have dealt with unrequited love. Do you remember those two rather nice young men we met at Cambridge years ago?'

'Which ones? And did they suffer from frustrated passion? Over us, I hope.'

'No, no, no! They just discussed poems about it. We all got rather cross, I remember. We were picnicking at Grantchester, and they were both at Trinity. Can't recall their names now, but there were in the Madrigal Society. Spotty, rather, but nice boys.'

'They've completely vanished in the mists of time for me,' I confessed. 'But which poems did they recommend for sheer desperate longing of the beloved?'

'One plumped for that little sixteenth-century verse:

> *Western wind, when wilt thou blow,*
> *The small rain down can rain?*
> *Christ, if my love were in my arms*
> *And I in my bed again!*

It is harrowing, isn't it?'

'Hits the nail on the head,' I agreed. 'But what did the other one suggest?'

'He was all for "Night and Day" by Cole Porter, and after we'd played it on their portable gramophone about ten times that afternoon we were inclined to agree.'

She tapped ash from her cigarette and rose.

'Well, I must be off. Don't forget about the dye, darling, and good luck with the jumble sale. I must say, a few hours with you does me a world of good. I haven't giggled till my ribs ached since before I was married.'

'I expect marriage brought you to your senses,' I said lightly, and then wished that I had not spoken.

'I'm afraid it didn't do that,' said Amy soberly.

At the front door she kissed me, a rare occurrence between us, and I felt overcome with pity for her as I waved her farewell.

Darn James! He must give her even more trouble than the awful man, poor Amy!

Early April was at its best that year, with far more sunshine than showers.

I spent happy hours in the garden. The hawthorn hedge had put forth small leaves, on crimson stalks, and the polyanthus plants glowed red and yellow in the border. Arabis and aubretia added mats of white and purple, and already the air was beginning to grow heady with the scent of flowers and new grass.

What can beat a warm English spring? Perhaps we cherish it more because it is so rare these days, I thought, picking a minute white violet from under the hedge, and inhaling its fragrance. I remembered Mr Willet's theory that the earth had tilted, which resulted in the chilly weather we had been enduring. When the sun shone so tenderly upon us it was hard to remember those bitter days of only a week or two earlier. I lived blissfully in the present, and drove over to visit Miss Clare at Beech Green.

Dolly Clare must be the best loved person for miles around. For years she taught at Fairacre School, and I was fortunate enough to find her in serene charge of the infants' class when I became headmistress of the school. Ill health forced her to retire to the little thatched cottage at Beech Green, some two or three miles away. She had been a young child of six when she first went to live there with her parents and sister Ada. Always the little house seems welcoming. The furniture gleams, in winter a bright fire cheers the room and always, whatever the season, there are flowers. In the darkest days of January Dolly Clare still manages to find some sprigs of yellow winter jasmine or a bowl of indoor bulbs to delight herself and her visitors.

I have always loved the cottage, and not so long ago Dolly staggered me by telling me that she had left it to me in her will. What such generosity means to me, I cannot express adequately. All I know is, that I was moved to tears – a rare occurrence for me – and I am still overwhelmed by my undeserved good fortune.

On this fine spring afternoon, I took with me a posy of polyanthus and a pot of freshly-made lemon curd. There was a scent of spring in the air, and the lane between Fairacre and Beech Green wound between hedges hazy with young leaf. With still over a week of holiday before me, I sang as blithely as the lark above me, if not quite as tunefully.

Miss Clare looked as pretty as ever. Despite her great age, her eyes were bright and her skin clear. To my delight, I found a fine black cat sitting in an armchair.

'And who is this?'

'Well, my dear, he's been living rough around here for some months, and during the winter I put out a little straw bed in a wooden box the greengrocer gave me. I put it in the woodshed and left the window open, and he used it every night, you know.'

'I bet he did. And I suppose he found a good supper there too?'

Dolly Clare laughed.

'Of course he did! And top and bottom of it is, he moved in

here a week or two ago, and he's such a dear, I really must take him on.'

He certainly was a handsome animal, and graciously allowed me to stroke him.

'He's found a good spot,' I observed. 'What will you do if you go away?'

'I'm not likely to go far at my age,' said Dolly. 'And I've some kind neighbours. Luckily, he eats anything.'

'More than I can say for my pernickety Tibby.'

'Now sit down, and tell me all the Fairacre news.'

I embarked on the ever-enthralling village concerns, such as Mrs Partridge's plot to get me on the panel game, Mr Willet's garden, Mrs Mawne's continued absence in Ireland, a jumble sale threatened for next week, Mr Annett, the choirmaster's, tribulations with the Easter anthem, Miss Briggs' approaching marriage and, finally, poor Mrs Coggs' trials with Arthur in prison.

'Best place for him,' said Dolly calmly. 'But I don't know that she'll be any better off without him, except that she should be less afraid. That poor soul will never be able to cope with life.'

'Bob Willet seemed to think she'd be better off financially, anyway, without Arthur taking his earnings, such as they are, to the pub nightly.'

Dolly shook her head.

'I doubt it. She has no idea of management. Years ago, when the family was arriving thick and fast, Alice Willet and I had a talk with her about cheap nourishing food to buy, and how best to manage the little bit of money she had weekly. We even offered to mind some of it for her to keep it out of Arthur's clutches, but it was quite hopeless. We used to give her clothes too – things she could cut down for the children. Dear Alice even taught her to knit and gave her wool and needles to make simple things like mittens for the children and scarves, but it was all beyond her. In the end, we faced the fact that nothing practical could be done to help her. We just gave a hand when a crisis occurred. But those pathetic children! They're the ones I grieve for.'

'Me too,' I said, 'particularly Joseph.'

'Perhaps she simply lacked early training,' continued Dolly. 'I know our family was quite as poor when we were young. As you know, my father never earned much at his job as a thatcher, and when he had his accident, things were pretty desperate. But somehow, my mother managed. We were always clean and tidy, and there was something in the pot for dinner, usually a rabbit given to us by a kind neighbour, or some good soup made from bones with lots of vegetables from the garden. We never went hungry, and we learned to be happy with very little. I honestly never remember being sorry for myself. My sister Ada and I thought we had a lovely home, and so we did.'

She rose and went into the kitchen to put on the kettle. I followed her and looked appreciatively at the sunny room which would one day – far, far ahead, I sincerely hoped – be my own.

From the rafters near the window hung some drying herbs and a string bag with last season's onions.

A row of blue and white striped china pots stood on the shelf near the stove, labelled currants, sugar, tea, coffee and salt. A fat brown tea pot stood beside the kettle waiting to be warmed, and on the brick floor there was a generous helping of milk, in an enamel pie dish, for Dolly's new companion.

'I simply love this house,' I said impulsively.

'That's why I'm so glad you are going to have it,' said Dolly, pouring a silver stream into the tea pot.

That evening I pondered on Mrs Coggs as seen through Dolly Clare's eyes. My old friend and Alice Willet were both warm-

hearted realists. They must have spent many hours and much
energy in trying to train Joseph Coggs' mother into more
methodical ways. I liked the calm way in which Dolly had told
me that they soon realised that their efforts were fruitless.
There was no recrimination against their poor pupil, and no
self-pity about the time wasted on her. There was simply this
sensible acceptance of a hopeless case, but an awareness too of
their own neighbourly duty to the family should any crisis
occur. I could not help thinking that Mrs Coggs must have
been heartened by the kindness and support of those two good
women, even if her home and family still appeared as slovenly
and neglected as ever.

I felt pretty sure too that Dolly Clare and Alice Willet must
have helped Mrs Coggs with an occasional gift of money, as
well as the more usual presents of garden produce which we
are all proud to offer to our neighbours.

Teachers are not rich people, and Dolly would never have

earned much compared with college-trained and certificated colleagues, for she was of the old pupil-teacher category. Nevertheless, she was always neatly dressed, never in debt, and managed to find something to give to those less fortunate like Mrs Coggs.

Her example made me feel a positive spendthrift. It was true that I was never seriously in debt, that my wardrobe was respectable, though nowhere near as extensive and elegant as dear Amy's, and that my home was reasonably furnished. But I should never be the careful manager of money that Dolly Clare was. I suppose, I thought ruefully, I fall somewhere between Dolly and Mrs Coggs for financial efficiency.

There are feckless bodies in all walks of life, of course, and I was reminded of a passage in one of William Howard Russell's letters to his wife. He was writing from the Crimea in 1856, in one of his rare free moments from following the campaign for *The Times*. Obviously, his wife Mary was adding to his anxieties by her imprudent spending, and I like the diplomatic way he expresses his concern.

'Riches,' he writes, 'are not happiness indeed, but there is great difficulty in living happy without them.'

A universal truth indeed, and one which poor Mrs Coggs would undoubtedly endorse.

I was beginning to count the few remaining precious days of the Easter holiday with as much concentration as a miser with his gold.

Half the things I had intended to do remained undone, but I had cleaned all the windows, defrosted the refrigerator, made four pots of lemon curd, and parted with the more disreputable of my garments for the benefit of the approaching jumble sale.

My chief accomplishment was the partial routing of Mrs Pringle intent upon the dreaded spring cleaning. I made the jumble sale a useful excuse.

'Just the sitting room,' I implored her. 'I've so much sorting out to do on the dining room table, and I promised to write the labels this time, so that I shall be in your way if we try to do too much.'

I feared that this feeble defence would fall before Mrs Pringle's implacable front, but to my surprise she agreed.

'Give me a chance to get to grips with it in there anyway,' she conceded. 'I don't suppose you've ever given the woodwork on them chairs a nice rub over with vinegar and water.'

'Well, no,' I admitted.

'Then that's what it'll get now,' she said flatly, making for the sink.

'I'll start the overall bottoming when you're back in school,' she continued. 'The top of them pelmets of yours would grow potatoes, I don't doubt, up there in your bedroom. Good thing you're not aspergic to Dust and Dirt. You'd be a hospital case in no time.'

Reprieved from the complete chaos of spring cleaning, I meekly said nothing in my defence, and tried to turn a deaf ear to the horrific bangings which emanated from the sitting-room.

I escaped into the garden, and revelled in the spring weather. No doubt, as soon as term started, we should get a return to the arctic conditions we had endured in March, but meanwhile it was bliss to hear the lambs bleating in the distance, and to watch the rooks building their ramshackle nests near the church spire. Did they recognise the gilded weathercock near-by as an inanimate kinsman, I wondered?

Mr Willet spent an afternoon with me and we planted a row of new potatoes, with some Celtic name, such as Aran Pilot or Ulster Chieftain, which Mr Willet assured me were the only really tasty ones to be grown in our soil.

We also planted peas and carrots and I had visions of modest dinner parties with the vegetable dishes overflowing with my own produce.

But the greatest thrill of all came three days before term started. As I shook out my tablecloth after breakfast, there was the unmistakable twittering of swallows, and there on the electricity wire were two little beauties.

For the rest of the day they flashed around the house, arrows of blue-black satin plumage, and before nightfall they had re-discovered last year's nest in the front porch, and were busy putting it to rights for this year's brood.

What did it matter if the doorstep would be plastered with droppings, much to Mrs Pringle's wrath? What did it matter if I had to hustle Tibby away during their rearing activities?

The swallows were back, and now summer had really arrived.

6 Public Duties

THE W.I. jumble sale took place in the village hall on Saturday afternoon. Fortunately, I was not required to man one of the stalls this time, as evidently a bevy of new helpers had volunteered for this hazardous job.

One of them I saw was Miriam Quinn who was in charge of the children's clothes' stall. She smiled across the room at me as I struggled with my own offerings for the produce stall. I had managed to find some pots of marmalade, one of my precious lemon curd – a real sacrifice, this – two cabbages, and a batch of flapjacks which I prayed had survived their journey intact, and not ended up in shame-making crumbs.

Mrs Partridge was in charge of the produce and accepted my contributions enthusiastically.

'Oh, how lovely! Marmalade is always a best seller, and what superb cabbages! Just look, Mrs James, aren't they splendid? May I sell you one for Sunday dinner?'

Mrs James looked at my offerings disparagingly.

'Got better'n them up home,' she announced, passing on to the next stall.

Mrs Partridge, accustomed to this sort of thing after many years as a vicar's wife, remained undismayed.

'Well, well, well! Someone else is going to be lucky, I can see.'

It is no wonder that our vicar's wife is unanimously chosen as president of so many village affairs. She has tact, resilience, and can rise with good humour to any emergency. I am one of her devoted admirers.

Mrs Pringle was in sole charge of the Shoe and Hat stall. This has been her prerogative for all the years I can remember, and she presides over it with implacable authority. Woe betide anyone foolish enough to try to bargain with Mrs Pringle! If a pair of size four grey suede evening shoes with Louis heels, dating from the twenties, has a chalked price of fifty pence on the soles, then that is what any would-be purchaser must be prepared to pay. I once saw a stranger offer her half the marked price for a pair of wellingtons. After Mrs Pringle had finished with him he made straight for the door, poor fellow.

'How's it going?' I enquired of her. She rattled her pudding basin with some satisfaction.

'Doing quite nicely, although there don't seem to be much call for hats these days.'

'People just don't wear them,' I commiserated, eyeing the yellowing panamas, a small feather pill-box with a veil, four identical picture hats in mauve silk with pleated brims, presumable once the get-up of four unfortunate bridesmaids, and several floral confections, among which I recognised a rather fetching one of my own, and was hurt to see it priced at five pence. Why, I'd paid guineas for it ten years ago for somebody's wedding!

'There's a nice one here,' said Mrs Pringle, burrowing under the pile, and surfacing with a battered object which she held out for my inspection.

'Crushed velvet,' she said. 'Suit you nicely, I reckon.'

Crushed all right, I thought, and as it was a particularly dreadful beetroot colour, I turned it down flat. Mrs Pringle began to draw in her breath, ready for some verbal assault, and I fled to Miriam's stall to escape.

Poor Miriam was in the clutches of a middle-aged newcomer to the village who had arrived late with her contributions to Miriam's stall, and was busy shaking out children's garments and suggesting prices.

'These two skirts shouldn't go at anything less than a pound apiece,' she informed Miriam. 'And I'd put a reserve of seventy-five pence on these blouses. I made them myself, from best quality Viyella for my grand-daughters, and they're hardly worn, as you can see. These little track suits too are in perfect condition. A pity to part with them, but they are too small now.'

Miriam cast an agonised look at me. The lady was busy rummaging in another of her many carrier bags, and was now producing children's shoes of all shapes and sizes.

Some customers were beginning to get impatient, and were besieging Miriam with upheld garments and money. I decided to come to the rescue.

'Shoes,' I said firmly, 'have to go to Mrs Pringle next door.'

She looked up with some dislike.

'But these are *children's* shoes!'

'Nevertheless, all shoes have to go to Mrs Pringle. Shall I take you to meet her?'

'No indeed. I know Mrs Pringle quite well, and can deal with her myself.'

She bustled off, and Miriam finished dealing with the batch of importunate customers.

'That was kind of you,' she said with relief. 'Really, I'd no idea of the hazards of holding a stall when I took it on. As for people's exaggerated idea of the worth of the jumble they're delivering, you begin to wonder why they're parting with it!'

'T'was ever thus,' I quoted to her, and went to buy a cake.

As usual, I was far too late to find the sort I like. It is common knowledge that the cake stall, on these occasions, is the first to sell out. The number of fine fruit cakes and toothsome sponges, which are secreted in the shade under the table, tell all too clearly of those wise people who have dropped a discreet word to the stall holders beforehand and have 'Reserved' put on these goodies.

By the time I arrived, there were a few rock cakes with burnt currants in evidence, some home-made crumbly biscuits and one large cake which I eyed doubtfully.

'Madeira?' I asked Mrs Lamb.

'No, dear. It's caraway seed cake. I can't think why it hasn't been snapped up. It's one of Alice Willet's too.'

'If I liked seed cake, I'd have it like a shot,' I assured her, and passed on sadly.

Joseph Coggs was standing by the bran tub, watching several of his schoolfellows diving for treasure. He looked wistful.

'Here on your own?' I asked him.

'Mum's gettin' shoes,' he answered, nodding towards Mrs Pringle, and sure enough, there was Mrs Coggs trying to fit the twins' feet into some of the shoes which, I suspected, had just been delivered by Miriam's tormentor. I only hoped Mrs Coggs would be successful, and I knew that Mrs Pringle would be sympathetic beneath her grim exterior.

I fished in my purse and gave a tenpenny piece to Joseph.

'Have a go, Joseph,' I said.

'But they's only threepence a go,' said he.

'Well then, have three goes.'

'But then there's a penny I owes you.'

'Keep it for luck,' I said.

'Thanks, miss,' he replied, and the smile he gave me was reward enough.

'Time I was off,' I told him making for the door.

I was pleased to have given him pleasure. I was even more pleased to think how well his arithmetic was coming on. Once a schoolteacher, always a schoolteacher, I told myself, on the way home.

The first day of term dawned hazily, foretelling a fine day to come.

Although, as usual, half my plans for the holidays had not materialised, I felt a certain sense of accomplishment. At least part of the house had been bottomed by Mrs Pringle. I had written to a number of neglected correspondents. The cupboards were tidy. I had worked hard in the garden, and done my duty at the jumble sale.

Now these activities would have to take second place to my teaching duties, and I prepared to go across the playground to start the day.

With Amy's warning in mind, I carefully closed the downstairs windows of the school house and locked back and front doors. Of course, it was doubtful if the sort of mentally-disturbed fellow whom Amy had described would be interested in entering my house to steal any valuables. Come to think of it, what would he find? A small silver sauce boat and a couple of silver napkin rings comprised my silver collection. Aunt Clara's seed pearl necklace was hidden in a handkerchief sachet in the drawer of my dressing table, and the only other object of value was a nice Chippendale carver chair which I had fallen for at a local auction some years earlier.

Hardly the sort of piece to be secreted by an opportunist sneak-thief, particularly one who evidently wore nothing but a raincoat.

However, the police had begged us to secure our property as best we could, and I felt a most virtuous glow as I walked across to school with the door key in my pocket.

Mrs Pringle, dustpan in hand, greeted me dourly.

'You promised to let me have that pudding basin back as I lent you last week with the bird food in it. I needs it for dinner today.'

'D_____!' I said, loudly enough to give joy to a knot of attentive children who nudged each other, happy at my lapse.

I turned to retrace my footsteps, unlocked the front door, retrieved the pudding basin, and returned to school.

'There you are,' I said to Mrs Pringle, who accepted it graciously. 'And many thanks for the bits and pieces.'

My cleaner leant towards me, her voice unusually low and confidential.

'There wasn't no call to swear in front of the children. They gets quite enough of that from the telly.'

I took the rebuke with good grace. It was deserved.

Halfway through prayers I remembered that I had omitted to lock the front door.

Ah well!

The swallows were hard at work putting the finishing touches to their nest. I watched them tugging at moss on the gravel path, fluttering clumsily at their task. It was strange to see how awkward they were. In the air, their natural element, they were such miracles of aerobatic movement that it made the contrast even more remarkable.

Within a day or two, the nest was as they wanted it, and the female settled to her egg-laying. She took no notice of the comings and goings at the front door below her. The male was attentive, swooping in and out with food for her, and ignoring any human activity. I wondered how many babies we should have this year. Last year there had been five, and a good squash there had been in the nest, not to mention the mess on the tiles of the floor below.

One year Mr Willet, scandalised at the state of my porch, had hung a plywood tray of his own making just below the nest. The swallows were furious, and chattered away on a nearby wire, refusing to have anything to do with the nest. Meekly, I took it down.

'They'd soon find some other daft body as'd let 'em nest in their place,' said Mr Willet flatly, 'if you was to stand your ground and leave that there board in place.'

'But I want the swallows!' I protested.

'Then you has to have the mess as well,' Mr Willet told me.

'I really don't mind. Visitors must just go to the back door. Most of them do anyway.'

'Well, don't let Ma Pringle see this porch,' he warned me, and made off before I could reply.

The dreaded evening in aid of the Save The Children Fund came round all too soon.

Alas! My usual hopes that an infectious illness would incapacitate me, that an unsuspected volcano had erupted in Caxley, or that Judgement Day had happily intervened, were dashed yet again, and I found myself dressing for the occasion in deepest gloom.

Should I wear my new patent leather court shoes that hurt, or my scuffed grey suede ones with the scratched left heel – a legacy from letting in the clutch – which were comfortable?

The choice of dress was simpler, either my patterned navy-blue silk, or a white lace blouse with a black velvet skirt. I had spent several evenings studying the ladies' attire in television panel games but with little satisfaction. For one thing, I did not own an off-the-shoulder creation in satin trimmed with either sequins or marabou feathers. Neither did I have anything with a neckline which plunged to the nether regions. Nor did I favour the other extreme of fashion which made use of a crumpled blouse of grubby cheesecloth and a medallion swinging on a long chain.

I had felt that perhaps I should rush into Caxley and buy an entirely new outfit for the occasion, but natural lethargy, combined with my usual shortage of funds, soon persuaded me that my present wardrobe would supply something suitable.

In the end, I set off in the navy-blue silk, the painful shoes, and Aunt Clara's seed pearls. I could do no more. My best patent leather handbag contained my few pathetic notes on children's books, a subject about which I thought I knew a little, but now felt positive that I knew nothing at all.

The meeting was held in a Caxley hall some distance from the market square. This meant that the car had to be parked at some way away from the building, and I limped through the streets to my doom.

A kind middle-aged lady was fluttering about the entrance lobby, and came towards me.

'Miss Crabbe?' she asked.

'No!' I replied, rather more forcefully than the query needed. 'No, my name is Read. I'm from Fairacre. Are you Mrs Smith?'

'Oh no!' she said, sounding shocked. 'Mrs Smith is terribly busy inside with the platform arrangements. I've just been told to greet the panel people and take them into the side room for sherry.'

I followed her down the side of the hall, which was already alarmingly full of people, and into a little room which seemed even fuller.

Mrs Partridge's friend, Hazel Smith, hurried towards me with outstretched hands.

'Now let me introduce you,' she said, leading me around the room. 'You are the first to arrive. Dr Biddle has just telephoned to say he will be a trifle late, and Mr Ellis has only just left court, but I'm sure he won't be long. Miss Crabbe has some distance to come, of course.'

I met some three dozen people whose names I did not catch, and whose faces I should not remember, and expressed my delight at meeting them, and accepted a sherry dry enough to wither the tongue. I should really have liked a long drink of water, but realised that this would have looked eccentric, so twiddled my glass and listened to the rising crescendo of noise about me.

At long last my three companions arrived. Dr Biddle I knew slightly. He was a heavily-built man, with dark hair and a careworn expression which was hardly surprising, I thought, if he dealt daily with children in poor health. I was careworn enough, in all conscience, dealing daily with children in good health. He had my sympathy.

James Ellis, a Caxley councillor and chairman of the juvenile bench at the local court, was also known to me through his spate of letters to *The Caxley Chronicle*. The subject was usually child behaviour, and as he was a bachelor he naturally had very strong views about the way in which one should deal with the young, particularly those who appeared before him at court.

Most of the readers of that eminent weekly, including myself, thought that Mr Ellis's attitude to young offenders was gentle to the point of being deferential. Whilst not actually congratulating young thugs on their success in robbing old ladies of their possessions, his sympathy with their reasons for doing so – broken homes, lack of love, low intelligence, uncaring parents and all the usual stuff – was so eloquently expressed and quoted at such length in the paper that some susceptible readers' withers were wrung.

The majority, however, with their feet still firmly on the ground, found their spokesman in Mr Willet.

'My old dad,' said he, 'would have dealt with 'em in half the time, and with no expense. I bet he'd have stopped their capers!'

Mr Ellis greeted me kindly, and wore a beautiful dove-grey suit which I much admired.

He was followed by Miss Crabbe who held my hand and said what a pleasure it was to find that I was still at my old post and doing such sterling work, she had no doubt, which made me feel lazy, unambitious and a failure, which I am sure was intended.

She herself, I thought cattily, had not improved with the years. Her scanty hair was drawn back to a bun, and her face was much lined. She wore a tight frock of an unbecoming burgundy colour, and one of the buttons on the front of the bodice was missing. I felt smugly well-dressed after noticing this.

She was passed into Mr Ellis's care, and I could see that their minds were as one from their earnest expressions and wise noddings of heads. I was happily embroiled with a young reporter from *The Caxley Chronicle* who made notes with an indelible pencil, which one rarely sees these days. Between jottings he sucked the pencil, and I was fascinated to watch his tongue turn from lilac to a rich purple. It would have done credit to a prize chow.

All too soon we were summoned to the door by Mrs Smith. Dr Biddle was to speak first, then it was my turn, then Mr Ellis's, and finally Miss Crabbe would conclude the proceedings, rather on the lines of keeping the best wine until last, I supposed.

The sea of faces was decidely disconcerting, but at least I would have time to compose myself, and have a quick glance at my poor notes, as Dr Biddle did his stint.

He was greeted with warm applause. He is popular in the area, and the fact that he once appeared on our television screens has added greatly to the awed esteem in which he is held.

He gave a brisk little talk about children's ailments, the importance of inculcating sensible dietary habits, and spoke reassuringly about infectious diseases, everyday accidents and the inestimable worth of our local casualty department. All in all, it was just what the audience needed, and the questions came thick and fast.

The good doctor coped brilliantly, even fielding some awkward ones from a dedicated herbalist in the front row who asked his opinion of woundwort for open sores, and the advantages of sage leaves in cleaning teeth.

All too soon he sat down, and I rose, trembling, to my feet. My feeble talk came to life when I gave a few suggestions for general reading, when there was a great scuffling in handbags for pencils and paper, and people scribbled busily. It was just like being in school again.

'Do you think children should read anything they like?'

'Aren't they better off watching telly?'

'Is my five-year-old too young for a dictionary?'

'How can I wean my son from horror comics?'

These were a few of the questions hurled at me, which I did my best to answer truthfully, but with nothing like the dexterity of my predecessor.

Luckily, I was saved by the chairman's bell, and settled back thankfully to listen to Mr Ellis. His discourse was, predictably, on the vulnerability and sensitivity of young things, and the absolute necessity of letting them find themselves in their own way and time.

'Think of a tender young plant,' he exhorted us. 'It grows by throwing out delicate tendrils to climb upward to the sky. If we try to bend those tendrils, if we handle them too harshly, the plant is damaged beyond repair. All we can do, as parents, as teachers or as any one with the care of young people, is to provide a warm and loving atmosphere, and to encourage the upward trend towards light and knowledge.'

There was a good deal more in the same vein, and a certain amount of muttering when he sat down.

A few questions, which might well have been formed by Mr Willet, were asked about discipline, learning right from wrong, parental responsibility, and plain old-fashioned respect for authority, and these drew forth some kindly generalisations from Mr Ellis which made nobody any the wiser. The applause was luke-warm.

Miss Crabbe was much as I remembered her on the terrible weekend she had spent under my roof. She ploughed along with her lecture, in a slightly nasal monotonous drone, complimenting Mr Ellis on his acute understanding of the Child Mind, and enlarging on the need to make use of the wonders of modern psychology when any difficulties in child behaviour became apparent.

I had a pretty shrewd idea that this was one of the lectures she gave regularly to her students, watered down a little for the present audience.

Everyone was amazingly polite, and the questions, though few, were to the point. Time had run on, and we were all conscious of the chinking of wine glasses and the welcome clatter of plates at the back of the hall, where the helpers were preparing to revive us.

The applause when at last Miss Crabbe sat down was deafening. The lady flushed with pleasure, as we all clapped heartily. I felt that our enthusiasm was caused probably more by relief than rapture, but at least the evening had been successful, and the ordeal was now over.

We raised our glasses and our cheese straws to each other, four disparate individuals, bound together for one brief hour by common suffering.

7 More Worries for the Coggs Family

MAY arrived in a flurry of blustery showers. In school the windows rattled, the doors thumped, and the replaced skylight let in almost as fierce a draught as the old one.

The weather had turned chilly enough to warrant lighting the stoves, but now that officially it was summer time, and Mrs Pringle would be at her most militant if the idea were mooted, we did our best by donning winter cardigans again, and hoping for the best.

Every now and again, black clouds brought hailstones to dance in the playground, and to dash the tender spring flowers to the ground. It was sad to see the first blooms of the cherry and plum trees scattered like confetti on the ground after these periodic onslaughts. The early bees, which had been active during the halcyon holiday spell, were nowhere to be seen. It seemed as if winter had struck again.

Tibby, who had spent all his days, and nights too, as far as I could judge, curled up in a clump of catmint, was now content to find indoor haunts, preferably on my bed or on the sitting room sofa. One evening of particularly cold showers I lit my fire, and rejoiced. And so did Tibby. Luckily, Mrs Pringle was not about to chide us.

It was on one of these cold mornings that I went across about eight o'clock to unlock the school in readiness for Mrs Pringle's ministrations.

Squatting against the door, his arms wrapped round him for warmth, was Joseph Coggs.

'You're early,' I said lightly.

He nodded.

I looked at him more closely. His bare legs were cold with goose flesh, his shabby sandals were soaking wet, and I suspected that he had been weeping.

'What's happened?' I asked more gently.

He shook his head without replying.

I unlocked the door, and left things ready for the school cleaner.

Bending down, I hauled the little boy to his feet.

'Come and have some breakfast with me,' I offered. He put a cold hand in mine, and we went across to the school house.

After a cup of milky coffee and some scrambled egg on toast, he looked more cheerful. I forbore to question him. It would all come out before long, I guessed. Probably he had broken something and Mrs Coggs had cuffed him. He was devoted to his poor slatternly mother, and could not bear to have her cross with him. Sudden flight from such a situation would be his natural reaction, and the fact that he was so ravenous meant that he had not had the doorstep of bread and margarine, which I knew was his usual first meal of the day.

I went into the sitting room to collect a pile of exercise books and some new wall charts, and when I returned to the kitchen he was putting the breakfast china very carefully into the sink.

'Shall us wash it?' he enquired. They were his first words. Already he looked better.

'No, forget them, Joe. Let them soak.'

He turned on the tap, and watched the crockery being submerged.

'You'd better pop up to the bathroom and wash your hands and face,' I directed. He knew my home very well, as he often came to help in the garden, and had once or twice given me a hand in moving bits and pieces upstairs.

He vanished for five minutes while I put away the food. When he reappeared, I looked at him without speaking.

He took a deep breath.

'My mum's bad,' he said at last.

'In bed?'

'In hospital. The amb'lance come.'

'Were you alone all night?'

'No. Auntie come and took the girls. I went next door with baby.'

'To Mrs George?'

He nodded. The tears looked very near again. I decided not to question him too closely. No doubt Mrs Pringle would give me all the details, with horrific embellishments, when we met in a few minutes. But I had to know one thing.

'Does Mrs George know where you are?'

'I shouted as what I was coming up here when I left. What's more, I ain't goin' back.'

I had never seen him look so stubborn. The silence in the kitchen was suddenly broken by the sound of the school bell.

'Come on, Joe. We're going to be late,' I said, making for the door. 'You carry the charts, then I can lock up.'

We crossed the playground, dodging games of marbles, twirling skipping ropes, and flying children, and entered the lobby.

Mrs Pringle, arms akimbo, was waiting, heavy with news.

'You got 'im then,' were her first words, as she eyed Joseph with strong disapproval.

'Run along, Joe, and give out the hymn books,' I said. It was plain that there was plenty to be said, and I did not intend the boy to hear.

Mrs Pringle shuffled a little closer.

'His ma was took bad sudden. Appendix or something. Fair screeching in pain she was, so Bella George told me, until the doctor give her a shot of something. No one knows what, of course, but it's to be hoped he knows his business.'

'But what about the children? When did this happen?'

'Sometime after midnight. She banged on the bedroom wall and yelled out of the window to Bella and Jack next door. Lucky they sleeps light. It was Jack called the doctor from the phone box. Bit of luck it hadn't been verminised this week.'

'Vandalised,' I said automatically, ever the teacher. 'And has anyone heard when she will be back?'

Mrs Pringle's mouth turned down lugubriously.

'Who's to say? I mean, once you gets into a hospital there's no knowing, is there? Half the time you're thrown out as soon as you're sewn up, and the other half you lays there being observed for weeks.'

'But the children?'

'Well now,' began my cleaner, settling her bulk upon a wash basin much too frail, in my opinion, to carry such weight. She looked as though her story could continue for hours, and I began to feel anxious about my delayed school assembly.

'Ethel Tibble, Arthur's sister as I was telling you about the other day, she and Charlie come out in the van and took the little girls back to Caxley with 'em. And Bella and Jack took in Joe and the baby for the night. But young Joe never slept a wink, so Bella said, and sheered off when her back was turned cutting Jack's sandwiches.'

'I'd better go and see her at playtime,' I said. 'She may know more about Mrs Coggs by then. But now I must get on. We're all behind this morning.'

'I wouldn't mind betting,' replied Mrs Pringle bridling, 'as Bella knows a lot less than I do.'

I would not mind betting on it either, I thought, hastening to my duties.

I left the school in Miss Briggs' charge at playtime, and drove swiftly to the other end of Fairacre where the council houses stand.

I received some interested glances as I went through the village, and guessed that my dereliction of duty would soon be common knowledge in the community. What would be the conjectures, I wondered? A sudden brainstorm? An assignation with Henry Mawne – still, unfortunately, a grass widower? A dash to the station en route for a train to my distant home, where accident or sudden death had occurred? There was no end to the dramas which could be imagined.

Bella George was a comfortable middle-aged body, whose husband was a long-distance lorry-driver.

She ushered me into her sitting room, and came at once to the point.

'You've got our Joe safe, I reckon?'

'That's true. What's the position?'

'Well, I said I'd take him and the baby, and Ethel Tibble's got the little girls. As you know, they've got a corner shop in Caxley, mainly sweets and tobacco, and they don't have much room upstairs, so they could only manage to fit in the girls. But they'll be all right with Ethel. It's Joe's the trouble.'

'Is it any help if I have him? He's used to me.'

Her face lit up.

'Would you, Miss Read? He don't seem to settle here, though dear knows why not. He sees enough of us. The baby's no trouble. Nice to have him in the house.'

'Any news of Mrs Coggs?'

'None yet.'

'I'll ring the hospital during the day and let you know. And I'd better let Mrs Tibble know what's happening too.'

A thought struck me.

'I suppose I'd better take Joseph's nightclothes if he's settling with me.'

Bella's jolly laugh set the ornaments on the mantelpiece ringing.

'Lord bless you, Miss Read, there's not a scrap of night

clothing among the lot of 'em! Those kids sleep in their vests, if they've got 'em, and if not it's their birthday suits!'

'I should have known,' I said. 'Well, I must get back to the school, and I'll call again when I know more.'

I drove soberly back to school. Were we still the two nations that Disraeli spoke of? It looked very much like it.

Later that evening, when Joseph had been bathed and was tucked up in the spare bed wearing an old singlet of mine, I rang the hospital.

Mrs Coggs, I was told, was round from the operation, and doing nicely. It was too early to say when she would be fit to come home.

Well, I thought, at least I had been spared that irritating word 'comfortable'. I recalled W. W. Jacob's account of one Bob Pretty who was 'what the doctor called comfortable', and what the narrator of the incident said: 'He would not soil his lips by repeating.'

My other call to Ethel Tibble, Arthur Coggs' sister, was equally satisfactory. She said she would pass on my message to Bella George as she was just setting off for Fairacre to collect some of the children's clothes, and it would save me a trip. We agreed to keep in touch, and she said if she could find anything of Joe's she would drop it in.

'Not that I expect much,' she said. 'You know that household as well as I do. I can't say I'm very proud of my brother. That place is a disgrace.'

I made non-committal noises, and rang off, but I pondered on her remarks as I ate my modest supper of soup and cheese and biscuits. The place certainly was a disgrace, partly due to Mrs Coggs' inability to cope with its running and her fear of Arthur's violence, but there must surely be this other cause – the driblets of money which came so spasmodically that regular budgeting was impossible.

I was fortunate. A cheque was paid into my bank account at the end of each month. I was no financial wizard, and often hard-pressed in the week before I was paid, but my store cupboard could provide for me in lean times and, thanks to Mr Willet, my garden produced fresh fruit and vegetables. I need never go hungry.

The Caxley Building Society took care of my modest savings, and I had some sixty or seventy pounds in my cherished Post Office savings' account. Friends in the profession managed far better than I did, raising families, buying houses, taking trips abroad, and still contriving to save regularly. Compared with them, I was a poor manager. But then, I comforted myself, compared with Joseph's mother, I was a paragon of efficiency. It was all relative.

I washed up, and set the breakfast for two in the kitchen. Boiled eggs tomorrow. It would be good to have Joseph's company for a few days.

By nine o'clock, I realised how tired I was, and was about to go to bed when the front door bell rang.

It was Ethel with a carrier bag of Joe's garments.

'No, I won't come in,' she said, in answer to my invitation. 'It's a proper job lot in there,' she added, nodding at the bag. 'And none too clean. I'd burn a few of them things, if I was you.'

She departed into the dusk.

I left the bag in the hall for tomorrow's attention, and went wearily to bed.

Joseph fitted into the household with no bother at all. I found him helpful with the daily chores, keen to wash up, to fetch and carry, and he straightened his bed each morning without being told. For a child with his chaotic upbringing, he was remarkably practical and obviously liked order in his surroundings.

He even straightened piles of exercise books in the process of being marked, and set my pens and pencils in order in my pen tray. The only thing he found daunting was the setting of a table, but after a few demonstrations he soon mastered that art as well.

As I had suspected, young Joseph Coggs was a quick learner, and as he grew older his progress was becoming more assured. I had great hopes for my young friend's future.

He was much more alert than I was to the doings of the birds in my garden. He inspected the sitting swallow at a discreet distance, and it was he who pointed out the sparrowhawk who hunted along the hedges bordering the school playground and the fields beyond.

'He watches out for them little birds,' he told me, 'and catches 'em when they flutters away frightened. I bet he had that hen blackbird as brought off a brood in your lilac.'

'What makes you think that?'

'Her ol' man keeps all on singing for another mate. Been at it all the week. He was the only one feeding them young 'uns, didn't you see?'

I had not, but obviously Joseph was keenly aware of the tragedy. Perhaps he had a fellow feeling for motherless young.

Mr Willet confirmed Joe's findings. He also told me that he had a whitethroat nesting in his garden, and promised to take the boy to see it. I was glad that the child was so happy in his new surroundings. It looked as though his mother would be in the hospital rather longer than we had thought. The trouble seemed to be diverticulitis, and it was plain that her general poor health would retard her recovery. We could only hope that enforced rest and proper diet would be of benefit to her eventually. Bella George, Ethel Tibble and I had all visited her and given her news of the children. It seemed to me that she was hardly aware of any domestic problems left behind at Fairacre, and although she thanked all of us in a vague way, I suspect that she was in such a debilitated state that anxiety was beyond her powers. It was better so.

One evening I was helping Joseph with a mammoth jigsaw puzzle, to the neglect of a pile of ironing, when the door bell rang and Henry Mawne appeared beaming on the doorstep.

Now what, I thought, ushering him in.

'Ah! A young visitor!' he cried, espying Joseph perched on his chair at the table.

'Yes, he's staying here for a little while,' I told him.

Henry began to rummage in his pockets, and finally produced two dog-eared tickets.

'For my two lectures,' he explained. 'I'll pick you up in good time, and perhaps you would look after my notes for me?'

I was taken aback.

'But I thought I had explained that I shouldn't be able to come,' I cried. Obviously, this wretched fellow was not going to take 'No' for an answer. Joseph's eyes went from one to the other of us with intense interest.

'Well, I hadn't taken that in, I must say. Surely you can arrange things so that you can look after me? I'm really relying on you.'

'It's quite impossible,' I said firmly. 'Won't Elizabeth be back by then?'

'Very doubtful. Very doubtful indeed.'

He looked at me speculatively.

'What are you doing on those two evenings anyway?'

'My friend Amy has plans for me,' I said. It was half true, anyway. I decided to carry the war into the enemy's camp.

'Why not find someone who is free? There must be several keen bird people at your meetings who would be far more competent than I am to help you.'

'Perhaps Miriam Quinn would enjoy my lectures,' he hazarded.

84

'She's very busy, I know,' I said hastily, supporting my unsuspecting friend.

'I think I'll trot round there while I'm out, and just see if she will be free,' he said, picking up the tickets. 'I'm so disappointed that you can't come. I really feel quite let down.'

I made no reply, but accompanied him to the door.

As soon as he had shut the gate I rushed to the telephone and rang Miriam.

'Well, many thanks for the warning,' she said cheerfully. 'I shall pay a hasty visit to the wood and pick primroses until the coast's clear.'

'Why don't you like that man?' asked Joseph when I returned.

I did not propose to answer this direct question with a direct lie, nor, for that matter, with a direct truth.

'Here,' I said, bending over the table, 'let's fish out all the blue bits and get the sky done before bed-time.'

When we went over to the school the next morning, I found three children, whom I did not at first recognise, sitting in a row in the front desk.

Mrs Pringle, immense in a flowered overall, emerged from the infants' room, dustpan in hand.

'Minnie's lot,' she said. 'Just for the day, like you said. She's up home, giving Basil a good clean-up. Left him hollering something awful, didn't us?'

The three little Pringles nodded silently. I was relieved to see that their noses were not running. It made a pleasant change. No doubt Mrs Pringle had recently attended to this item of personal hygiene.

'Minnie says as she ought to be back about two or three,' went on my cleaner, 'but you knows hospitals. Time stands still, as they say. Anyway, I've left a pound of sausages at the ready, and I only hope she don't burn the pan.'

'Well, we'll look after these three for the day,' I told her. 'Miss Briggs can have the smallest, and these two can stay with me.'

Mrs Pringle advanced upon the trio, holding out her hand to the youngest. Without warning, all three threw back their heads and began to emit ear-splitting yells.

'Leave them! Leave them!' I begged Mrs Pringle. 'I'll see to it later. They can stay as they are for prayers.'

Obviously, the Pringle brigade was going to be a somewhat disruptive element in our normal routine.

Joseph, standing by my desk, broke his silence.

'I reckons they could do with a sweet,' he remarked conversationally. He made for the cupboard which holds the boiled-sweet tin.

'Not a bad idea,' I said, as he undid the lid. Expectancy was in the air. The room was blissfully quiet. Even Mrs Pringle stood transfixed, watching the boy.

'And take one for yourself, Joe,' I said to my ally.

8 Strange Behaviour of Amy

TWO days later, Amy arrived to take me to a piano recital in the Corn Exchange, one of the highlights of the Caxley Festival.

Kind Alice Willet had offered to sit-in with young Joseph, and arrived laden with enough knitting to keep her hands occupied for three weeks, let alone three hours. I went off with an easy conscience.

Amy was unusually subdued, I thought, as we drove to Caxley.

'I've had a slight headache for the last two days,' she admitted. 'Nothing much. I'm only glad we haven't got to sit through Wagner played by a full orchestra. A nice tinkly bit of Mozart on the piano is just about right.'

'Are you sure you are up to it? I'm quite happy to give it a miss, you know.'

'No, indeed. It's a good programme — light and melodious, thank the Lord. I'm looking forward to it.'

We drove in silence until we approached Caxley.

'There is just one thing,' she said at last. 'I don't think I'll be able to go with you to the outdoor sculpture exhibition. If I gave you the tickets, could you find a companion?'

I explained about Joseph. Could she find two other people?

'Of course,' she replied. She sounded rather relieved. 'I believe it's going to be a permanent display eventually, so perhaps we can go later in the summer.'

And so the matter was left. I told her about Henry Mawne's lectures and my own prevarication, and a good thing it was

87

that I had done so, for Henry was sitting only two rows from us, in the company of a young fluffy-haired girl who seemed somewhat in awe of him.

We met in the interval when introductions were made.

'Eileen Bonamy, one of our most devoted bird-watchers,' said Henry, gazing fondly at his companion. 'She is going to help me during my lectures.'

'I'm so glad,' I said, with absolute truth.

'Miss Read was already engaged with you, I believe,' said Henry turning to Amy.

'Yes indeed,' said that stalwart friend. 'As you know, she is always in great demand.'

We were saved by the bell, summoning us back to our places.

'Thank you, Amy,' I said, 'for coming to my rescue.'

'No doubt you'd do the same for me,' replied Amy.

We settled back to enjoy an elegant little piece by Schubert.

Later, when we parted at my gate, Amy gave me a good-night kiss.

'I may not see you for a bit,' she said, 'so look after yourself. By the way, have you looked out that dye for the awful man?'

'I'd forgotten all about him.'

'As far as I can see,' said Amy severely, 'you'll be one of his easiest victims.'

She drove off with a cheerful hooting, and I went indoors feeling that Amy was herself again.

The unseasonable and chilly weather suddenly changed, and May became 'the loveliest month' which the poets praise.

Sunlight flooded the ancient schoolroom, and chalk dust danced in the slanting rays. The massive brass inkstand on my desk gleamed like gold, and little rainbows glanced from the glass over the photograph of our Queen, centrally placed on the rear wall, in the most honoured position.

The nature table was bright with specimens of coltsfoot, primrose, dandelion, an early wild daffodil and a cowslip. Why, I wondered yet again, are so many of our early wild flowers yellow? No one seems to know.

The cherry tree in the Post Office garden dangled white flowers, and everywhere, it seemed, the fruit trees were breaking into a froth of blossom and tender green leaf. The lilac bush in the most sheltered corner of my garden was in full bloom, and the heady scent floated up to my bedroom window in the warm nights. This old-fashioned pale mauve variety was always ahead of its more sophisticated companions, the white and the dark purple. It meant that the school house garden was fragrant for several weeks, for by the time the first blooms had turned rusty the others followed with their own scent. Later still the double white philadelphus, or mock orange blossom, as the Fairacre folk call it, would continue to delight our noses. It grows by my compost heap, and obviously enjoys its nourishment from that less pleasantly odorous source.

I had planted double dwarf tulips in the urn in front of the house. It is hopeless to grow the stately tall variety in this windswept quarter. I have seen a splendid row of scarlet beauties, tall and straight as guardsmen, flattened in ten minutes by a sudden onslaught of mighty wind from the downs. I learnt my lesson early here, and this year the short rosy tulips held their own against the elements and delighted all who saw them. Even Mr Willet admired them, calling my urn 'a brave show'.

We all thrived in the sunshine. Tibby basked in the shelter of a hedge. Even the little birds, now finding enough chalky dust for a bath, were ignored, as they performed their toilet.

One of the most welcome visitors to the school during this halcyon period was my pupil Ernest's pet tortoise. This hardy reptile survives even our cold Fairacre winters and always comes to school for a spring visit after he has emerged from his hibernation in a box of straw under the stairs of Ernest's cottage. He lumbers around the room, thumping his shell against the legs of the desks, accepting a morsel of fruit or a young leaf now and again, and generally adding his tribute to the coming of fair weather.

I was reminded of Gilbert White's tortoise which he observed so lovingly at a village near Lewes. He noted that: 'The tortoise, like other reptiles, has an arbitrary stomach; and can refrain from eating as well as breathing for a great part of the year.'

We do not see Ernest's tortoise regularly enough to test Gilbert White's assertion that it makes 'an excellent weather-glass'. He goes on to say that 'as sure as it walks elate, and as it were on tip-toe, feeding with great earnestness in a morning, so sure will it rain before night.'

Sometimes I think it would be a good idea to have a permanent tortoise on the strength. Certainly Ernest's is much loved at Fairacre school and his visit is a highlight of early summer.

It was during this warm spell that Mrs Coggs was discharged from hospital, and Joseph went back to his own home.

I missed his company in the house, and his cheerful presence at the breakfast table.

The baby went back to its own home too, but Ethel Tibble had volunteered to keep the little girls for another week to give her sister-in-law time to recover.

Bella George was a stalwart neighbour and the district nurse was calling regularly. It looked as though Mrs Coggs would have plenty of support in the first days of her home-coming.

One evening Miriam Quinn called to ask if I could collect for the Red Cross at the school end of the village. She had undertaken the Holly Lodge part, and Alice Willet, ever willing, had nobly taken on the main street of the village.

'In fact,' said Miriam, 'she's doing two-thirds of the job, but she says she can easily fit it in with her other work, and it's handy if she has to go a second time. It's only when you go collecting these days that you realise how many houses are empty during working hours.'

'Nice pickings for the opportunist thief,' I commented.

'It seems to me that they operate even if people are in,' replied Miriam. 'Joan Benson had her week's groceries lifted, basket and all, while she was upstairs taking off her coat.'

Joan Benson had once owned Holly Lodge where Miriam lived in the annexe. She had sold it to David and Irene Mawne, who now lived there, and had gone to live near her daughter in Sussex after her husband's death.

We all missed her in the village, and I was pleased when Miriam told me that she was coming to stay with her for a few days.

'Do bring her round one evening,' I said.

'I'd love to.' She hesitated for a moment and then went on. 'It would be an enormous help to me if she could call after school one day, perhaps?'

'Of course. Any day she likes. I'm here at four.'

'The thing is I'm going to be unexpectedly busy during that week, preparing for a business conference. Joan understands, but I feel I'm being somewhat neglectful.'

I assured her truthfully that Joan Benson would be welcome at any time. Miriam looked relieved.

'Another thing. Elizabeth Mawne is coming home.'

'Now that is good news! I've had three telephone calls from Henry this week, and my excuses are getting thinner every time. Did Irene speak to him? Or to Elizabeth?'

'Luckily there was no need. You know the fluffy little thing who was hanging on his words at the lecture? Eileen Something?'

'Bonamy.'

'That's right. Well, apparently after that she pursued Henry doggedly, and after the first flush of flattery had faded, Henry began to feel that he was being hunted. One or two friends in Caxley and Fairacre had added their mite by saying he was making himself ridiculous by encouraging an innocent girl young enough to be his daughter. You know the kind remarks people make in such a situation!'

'Indeed I do!'

'Well, Henry began to get desperate – so desperate in fact, that he rang Elizabeth and asked when she proposed to return.'

'And what was the answer to that?'

'Immediately! The ancient aunt had completely changed her tune, and instead of vowing to end up in her own bed with nothing altered in that great barn of a place she lives in, she told Elizabeth tearfully that she needed looking after, that nobody cared for her, the house was too big, too cold and too expensive to run, and she had decided that life in a comfortable nursing home was what she wanted.'

'I should think Elizabeth was flabbergasted.'

'Not too flabbergasted to act at once, and to fix up her admission immediately to the nursing home she'd had in mind for months.'

'So that's settled.'

'Well, she's not there yet, but with any luck she will be within a week. Elizabeth has put the house on the market already, striking while the iron was hot, as they say.'

She rose to go, and I went with her to the gate. The air was balmy, and a newly-emerged bat flitted between the trees.

'What a relief all round,' I said.

'Except for poor Eileen Bonamy. I hear she's considering applying for a post overseas.'

'I hope Henry gives her a very nice farewell present. She deserves it, poor girl.'

It was a week later that Joan Benson came to tea with me after school.

Her hair was a little greyer, but her figure was as trim and her eyes as bright as ever. How was she enjoying life in Sussex, I asked her?

'Well, I feel very much the grandmother with the children so much with me, but I like that. People are very friendly, I'm already on the W.I. Committee –'

'That was inevitable,' I broke in.

'I suppose so,' she replied, laughing. 'All village newcomers get roped in, don't they? Yes, there's lots to do, and it's good to have the family at hand, but it was marvellous to come back to Fairacre. Here, you see, I really ran my own life.'

I must have looked surprised, for she went on.

'I mean, I was still a wife. And a daughter too, as my mother was living with us, you remember.'

I did indeed. Mrs Penwood had been a charming old lady though very frail when she first accompanied Ambrose and Joan Benson to Holly Lodge. She had died within a few months of Ambrose, and it was soon after that that Miriam had gone to live in the annexe, as Joan's lodger.

'I was very much my own person,' continued Joan. 'I felt needed, valuable, appreciated, both by my mother and my husband. I always faced the knowledge that my mother would go very soon after we moved here, and I missed her sorely, but Ambrose's death really shattered me.'

'I can well understand that, although I'm not likely to experience such a loss.'

'I don't know which is worse, the awful feeling that a shared life is broken, or the fact that everything seems so pointless when one is alone. It hardly seems worth the bother of cooking, for instance, or buying new clothes. For the first few weeks I lived on tins of soup, cups of coffee and biscuits, until my daughter made me see reason. What really pulled me together was her good sense. "I've just lost a father, and I don't want to lose a mother too," she said one day. It was blunt speaking, but after that I buckled to, and went shopping again, and faced all the financial affairs I had been shelving, and generally took up living again.'

'You're a brave woman,' I told her.

'Not really, but looking back I realise I was lucky in the way things happened to me then. For one thing, I had the house virtually to myself while I was getting over the shock. Miriam was there at night, but by day I was alone, and it helped me. So many of my friends in the same position have found company absolutely essential, but others, like me, want time alone to adjust to the idea of widowhood. I had that, and then just when I was beginning to get to the recluse stage, my daughter pulled me back into the world, and I bless her for it.'

I refilled her tea cup.

'And that's enough of my affairs,' she said briskly, 'Now tell me how things have been going with Fairacre. Any hatches, matches or dispatches?'

I told her several of each, and brought her up to date with Fairacre and Caxley news.

After tea we inspected the garden in warm sunlight, and then I wrote a note to Miriam, accepting her invitation to supper at the end of the week, for Joan to carry back with her.

'Any hope of you ever coming back here to live?' I asked as she said her farewells.

'When I see it like this, all flowers and sunlight, I'm sorely tempted, but I remember the winters here, and believe me, Sussex is a good deal kinder to my old bones when the cold weather comes!'

'You have to be tough to withstand the winds of Fairacre,' I agreed. 'I've already started knitting a hefty cardigan in double-knitting wool ready for next winter.'

Mrs Pringle regaled me with a blow-by-blow account of how Basil Pringle's fingers had to be dressed, and very upsetting I found it first thing the next morning. As usual it was impossible to quell the flow.

'And how are the others getting on?' I enquired hastily, hoping to lead her to pleasanter topics. The little Pringles' one day with me had been distinctly exhausting, and I must confess I was thankful that they were not my responsibility permanently.

'Much as usual,' replied Mrs Pringle shortly. 'Now, I meant to let you know the latest about Mrs Coggs.'

'She's progressing well, I gather.'

'And who told you that, may I ask? She looks as near death's door as a great many as are now in the churchyard, to my knowledge. What's more she showed me her operation scar –'

'Well, don't tell me!' I cried. But one might as well try to stop the Nile in flood.

'All of nine inches long and double punch holes like boot

eyelets. An 'orrible sight!' said Mrs Pringle with relish. 'I
thought my poor old ma's was bad enough, but this was more
inflamed, if you follow me. I told her so.'

Trust Mrs Pringle to be pessimistic! I could bear no more,
and walked swiftly into the infants' room on the pretext of
speaking to Miss Briggs. I might have known that she would
pursue me.

'And if I may say so,' she boomed behind me, 'you look a bit
peaky yourself.'

'That,' I said firmly, 'is hardly surprising in the circumstances.'

And I shut the door smartly in her face.

Later, I was to rue this lapse on my part. Looking back, I see
now, that this was the beginning of a rapid decline in Mrs
Pringle's comparative patience and good temper.

I think if I could have foreseen the consequences, I would
have made a superhuman effort to control my feelings –
heaven alone knows I get plenty of practice in my dealings
with Mrs Pringle! But I had been sorely goaded, and retaliated
with the slammed door, sad to say.

Other matters cropped up about that time which distracted
my attention from Mrs Pringle's pronounced limp, always in
evidence when she has taken umbrage.

An evening or two later, James, Amy's husband, telephoned. He sounded unusually agitated, and dispensed with
his habitual opening compliments which I found surprising.

'I'm ringing about Amy. Is she with you by any chance?'

'No,' I said, somewhat bewildered.

'Well, it's the oddest thing, but she's not here, and some
of her clothes have gone, and her cheque book and so on, and
not a word left for me. No note. Nothing. I can't make it
out.'

'Come to think of it,' I said, 'she mentioned something

about being away for a time. Naturally, I assumed that you
knew.'

'That I don't!' James sounded thoroughly cross.

'Are you sure that her note hasn't slipped down somewhere
and got hidden?' I enquired.

'Of course I'm sure!' snapped James. 'I've searched everywhere. There's not a clue as to where she can be, and it's jolly
upsetting.'

'Have you rung anyone else?'

'No. You were the first. I thought she might have driven
over to you, and stayed the night, I got home yesterday about
seven, expecting her to arrive during the evening. In fact, I
rang you about nine or ten, and there was no answer.'

He sounded aggrieved. I explained that I had spent the
evening with Miriam Quinn and Joan Benson.

'She'll probably ring you any time now,' I said, trying to
comfort him.

'Well, if she doesn't do so before dark, I shall inform the
police. For all I know, she may be lying murdered in a lay-
by.'

Why a *lay-by*, I wondered? But it was no moment to discuss
this interesting side-line. Obviously, the poor chap was becoming more distraught every minute, and I was hard put to it
to know how best to help him.

'If you think she might have been involved in an accident,' I
began carefully, 'perhaps you should ring the local hospitals.'

'Oh, for pity's sake!' shouted the exasperated man, 'don't
make things worse! What a ghoul you are, suggesting she
might be lying injured in hospital!'

It was hardly the time to remind him that he had imagined
his poor wife lying murdered in a lay-by, which was far more
ghoulish than my modest and reasonable suggestion.

'If I hear anything at all to help you, I'll ring immediately,' I
promised him, and put down the receiver.

'Now I wonder,' I said to Tibby, 'is Amy really in trouble, or is she just enjoying her freedom somewhere, with thoughts of what's sauce for the gander holds true for the goose?'

9 Troubles Never Come Singly

THE mystery of Amy's disappearance had to be shelved in the pressure of day to day school problems, but I intended to get in touch with James to find out if he had heard from her. Knowing James, I thought it would be unlikely if he rang me, whatever the news.

In the midst of halcyon weather, I struggled with a spate of problems. Miss Briggs fell ill with some sort of stomach trouble, and so was absent from school. My anguished pleas to the education office were met with some sympathy but little practical help. Supply teachers, it seemed, were like gold dust in our area.

I put down the telephone and racked my brain. In the old days, Miss Clare used to step into the breach. Sometimes Amy, a first-class teacher, had come to our aid. Old helpers like Mrs Bonner and Mrs Finch-Edwards had now moved away, and the outlook appeared bleak.

I struggled all through the first day of Miss Briggs' absence with the dividing door open, and by making sorties between the two rooms, a certain amount of work was kept going, but this state of things was far from satisfactory.

In the evening I rang Miss Briggs' landlady in Caxley to enquire how my assistant was progressing. I must confess that I hoped she was soon going to be fit to return, as much for my own sake as hers.

'Still in bed,' was the depressing response to my enquiry. 'To my mind, it's just nerves, Miss Read. Getting upset about the coming wedding. Girls do get these funny ideas, as no doubt you know.'

I had to admit that pre-marital qualms had never been experienced by me.

'Oh, it's quite common,' she assured me. 'You wonder if you're doing the right thing, you know. And then all the arrangements are a dreadful worry. Should you ask everybody, or nobody? I well remember how suicidal I got before my own wedding. I took such a dislike to my wedding dress, I threatened to go in my mackintosh. My mother couldn't do anything with me!'

She sounded rather proud of the fact, I thought, and privately congratulated myself on having escaped such traumas. There are many occasions when I thank my stars that I am single. This was one of them.

Getting back to the point, I asked if Miss Briggs seemed likely to be back within a few days.

'Oh, I doubt it,' she replied cheerfully. 'The doctor came this morning and I've just fetched the tablets he prescribed, and she says they make her feel awful, so what with the germs she's got and the cure the doctor's given her, I should say she'll be laid low for at least a week!'

A real Job's comforter here, obviously.

'Well, give her my love and I hope she will soon feel better,' I replied civilly.

And I went to prepare my modest supper for a little comfort.

I awoke about four o'clock the next morning with a stupendous idea. Why not ask Isobel Annett if she could come as a supply teacher in the infants' room in Miss Briggs' place? As Miss Gray, many years before, she had been one of my most successful assistants, until whipped from under my very nose by Mr Annett, the headmaster of our next village school, to become his wife.

It has been a happy marriage, for which I am doubly grateful, for his first wife was tragically killed, and when our paths first crossed he was a most unhappy and irritable fellow. Isobel has been the means of turning him into a cheerful family man. They are both musical and energetic, and much in demand at local concerts and musical festivals. Would she consider dropping her hobbies and household duties to hold sway in the infants' room she knew so well? I intended to ask her.

She sounded somewhat taken aback on the telephone.

'But it's years since I stood in front of a class,' she began. I burst in to tell her that, like riding a bicycle, one never quite lost the knack of teaching.

'And I half-promised to play for community singing at the concert for the blind in Caxley next Tuesday.'

I said that surely someone else could do that?

'How long would you need me?' she asked. This sounded much more hopeful, and I said that with any luck a week, or perhaps ten days, would see us through.

I could almost hear her brain working at the other end of the line, and began to plead my extreme necessity.

'I simply can't manage without help, and honestly I have tried. The office is a dead loss, and Miss Clare is past it, of course. As for Amy, she seems to have disappeared –'

'*Disappeared*! How do you mean?'

I hastily back-tracked.

'Well, she's away at the moment, so that's another person unavailable.' Better not to let rumours fly unnecessarily, I told myself. The village would have Amy eloping before one could turn round.

'So you see,' I added pathetically, 'I am in a terrible quandary, and would be so very grateful, Isobel, if you could manage to help us.'

'I'll have a word with George, and ring you back,' she

promised. 'One thing, if the weather's like this I could cycle.'

'And if it's wet I can fetch you,' I said enthusiastically. 'Don't let the travelling worry you. I'll see to that, and if you want to get away early to get a meal ready I can easily manage both classes for the last period in the afternoon.'

'Well, I won't be long making up my mind. Will you be in all the evening?'

'Yes, yes,' I cried.

And with my hand ready to snatch up the telephone, I thought, and with high hopes.

For the next hour or so I hovered about the house within earshot of the telephone bell. I wanted to get in touch with James to hear if he had any news of Amy, but I knew that Isobel would undoubtedly try to ring me at the very same moment, and so I resisted temptation.

My mind turned to another of my present problems. Mrs Pringle's limp seemed to have worsened in the last day or two, and her manner was distinctly frosty. It stemmed, I guessed, from my shortness of temper after enduring her ghastly descriptions of Basil Pringle's and Mrs Coggs' afflictions. However, I had no intention of apologising, and we had had far worse tiffs before this one. No doubt she would come round in time, but that morning's conversation had certainly been heavily ominous.

'How's Minnie getting on?' I had enquired. 'Not giving you any trouble?'

'No more than others I could name,' said the lady blackly.

'Good!' I replied, with false cheerfulness. 'So things are going smoothly?'

'I wouldn't say that.' (I bet you wouldn't, I thought.) 'With all there is to do in this place, I've more than enough on my plate. And all taken for granted! Not a word of praise from one week's end to the other.'

'Oh, come now, Mrs Pringle! You know your work's appreciated, but you can't expect praise all the time. Why, I don't ask you to admire our work when it's done, do I? I mean, that nature table is exceptionally splendid at the moment, but I don't expect you or anyone else to gush over it.'

'I don't feel like gushing, as you call it, when I've got to bend down to sweep up the mess it makes. It's more work for me, and just when I could well do without it, with my leg.'

Mr Willet had arrived at this moment, and the conversation ended with Mrs Pringle limping heavily into the lobby. Obviously, something more than her usual grievances was worrying her, but Mrs Pringle's martyred moods appear so frequently that it is impossible to waste much time on them.

But still, I told myself, the poor old dear was getting on, and perhaps I should make the effort and be gentler with her in the future.

And with this rare charitable thought, I went to cut up raw liver for Tibby's supper.

As was only to be expected, the telephone rang whilst I was in the midst of this gory operation with hands that rivalled Lady Macbeth's.

It was Isobel, and yes, she could come tomorrow, and it would be absolutely splendid to be back, but what about The Office?

I said I would see to that. I told her that she was an angel, I should sleep easily in my bed that night, and it would be marvellous to see her again in her own infants' room.

And now for James, I thought, when I had replaced the receiver.

The bell rang for such a long time that I decided that Amy's house must be empty, and was about to ring off when James answered.

He sounded breathless.

'Oh, it's you!' he panted. 'Sorry I was so long answering. The bacon was spluttering, and I think I've burnt the frying pan. Heck of a lot of smoke in the kitchen. What temperature do you use when you're frying?'

I said I had no idea. I turned the heat down if the pan smoked, and up if it didn't. It seemed to work.

'Any news of Amy?' I asked. 'I've been worrying about her.'

'Not half as much as I have! The police know she's missing, and I've had to give a minute description of her. As though I know how tall she is, or how much she weighs! As for what she was wearing "on the day of her disappearance", as they keep saying, I simply don't know.'

I expressed my sympathy.

'I suppose you haven't any idea where she could be?' He sounded suspicious. 'I mean, you two are pretty thick, She might have dropped a hint, or even told you outright, and then sworn you to secrecy.'

'I don't know any more than you do,' I said indignantly. 'You ought to know I wouldn't be such a rat as to let you worry like this!'

'Oh, sorry, sorry!' he cried hastily. 'It's just such a problem! How on earth do you begin to look for a wife who has vanished?'

'Well, I imagine you do exactly what you have done – told the police, rung up friends, had a word with the neighbours. I suppose you could put an advertisement in the Personal Column,' I ended doubtfully.

'You don't happen to know,' said James, sounding carefully casual, 'of any men friends she has been seeing lately? I know I have to be away a lot, and I believe Horace Umbleditch has been calling.'

'*Horace Umbleditch?*' My voice emerged as a startled yelp. Horace Umbleditch is a blameless bachelor who teaches at a local prep school. The very idea of his pursuing any married lady – or a single one, for that matter – was quite unthinkable.

I rose to Horace's defence.

'I'm horrified to hear that you are even suspecting dear old Horace of such behaviour! And of course Amy would never countenance such conduct anyway. I advise you to keep a check on your jealousy, James, for that's what this is.'

I could have gone on much longer, so incensed was I, but James burst in.

'Oh, don't be such an old schoolmarm! Here I am beside myself with worry, the house is a shambles, and I can hardly see across the kitchen for smoke! Do you reckon the frying pan's too hot for sausages?'

'How should I know?' I replied crossly, and slammed down the receiver.

Thank God I didn't have a husband!

Mr Annett dropped his wife at Fairacre School at half past eight the next morning.

'No, I won't come in,' he said in reply to my invitation. 'Must get back to my own chores.'

'I promise to look after her well,' I said, waving him off.

Isobel looked remarkably cheerful for one thrown into an arduous job with such suddenness.

We went together into the school. Mrs Pringle was brandishing a duster.

'Here's an old friend come to help us out,' I cried.

'Good morning,' grunted Mrs Pringle.

'I'm quite looking forward to a few days in my old classroom,' said Isobel pleasantly, ignoring my cleaner's hostility.

'Daresay it'll be left a good bit tidier than usual,' conceded Mrs Pringle. 'But no one can hold a candle to Miss Clare. The place was always left like a new pin. She thought of others. Not like some.'

'I don't think any of us can come up to Miss Clare's standards,' agreed Isobel, and went on her way with a smile.

'What's the matter with her?' she whispered when we were in the infants' room. 'She's worse than ever!'

'I think I've upset her. It'll blow over. You know our Mrs P.'

Isobel began to unpack her basket. It contained a pink and white checked gingham overall, I saw with approval, as well as other things.

'I daresay infant fingers are as messy as ever,' she commented. 'And I'm bound to be clumsy with poster paint and clay and all the other paraphernalia. I only hope I don't fall foul of Mrs Pringle with my activities.'

'And what are those?'

'Templates of cats in different positions. I found them on holiday and couldn't resist them. I'm going to read them *Tom*

Kitten some time, and thought they could draw round these and then paint them. Perhaps make a frieze if Miss Briggs wouldn't mind. What do you think?'

'They'll love it, and I'm sure our Miss Briggs will approve. In any case, she can always take them down later if she wants to. Honestly, Isobel, you certainly haven't lost your touch, and I can't begin to tell you how marvellous it is to have you here again.'

Ernest bustled in importantly to tell me that one of them new little 'uns what lived up street next to Eileen Burton's gran was took bad his mum said, and wouldn't be acoming.

I thanked him, decided that any grammatical correction of this statement must wait till later, and invited him to ring the bell.

'Well,' I said turning to my assistant, 'the day's begun.'

A blessed period of peace now enveloped Fairacre School. Isobel slipped back into her former quiet and efficient ways, the infants seemed to relish her efforts and I was delighted to have a tranquil infants' room after Miss Briggs' somewhat hectoring manner which tended to make her charges noisy.

Mrs Pringle continued to wear a martyred look, and the leg, always of an inflammable nature in times of stress, appeared to be in a steady state of combustion judging by the lady's limp.

I was not surprised, therefore, when she informed me that she would have to 'give that place of yours a miss this week.'

'A rest will do you good,' I said. 'I hope it will be better next week.'

'I may not come next week either,' said Mrs Pringle, her mouth turning down grimly. I began to feel some alarm, not on my account, but the school's.

'Do you want a few days off all your duties?' I enquired. 'Have you seen the doctor? I'm sure we could manage somehow if you have to be laid up.'

Mrs Pringle gave a snort of disgust.

'I saw that young whipper-snapper that Doctor Martin's got to help him. A fat lot that boy knows! Gave me a prescription for some ointment, and told me to keep it up, and wear an elastic stocking.'

'Sounds sensible to me,' I was rash enough to comment.

'Except that's what I've been trying to do for the last twenty years!' snapped the lady. 'What chance have I got to put my leg up?'

'Well, I've just been telling you – have a few days off – a week, say – and see how you get on.'

'And what good will a week do? There's times when I reckon I'll just have to give in my notice.'

There was a menacing note in Mrs Pringle's voice which has become familiar over the years. I used to try and placate the old virago. Now I am hardened. One can cry 'Wolf!' once too often.

'Only you can decide that,' I told her. 'Meanwhile, I quite understand that you won't be coming to my house until you feel up to the work. But if you do decide to give up the school cleaning, do try and give me plenty of notice so that we can advertise the job.'

'And that,' said Mrs Pringle venomously, 'is all the thanks one gets for Faithful Service!'

Her limp was more severe than ever as she retreated.

Mrs Pringle's threat of leaving, although depressingly familiar, gave me some secret disquiet that evening.

Infuriating though she is, at least she does her work conscientiously, and is proud of the way she keeps the school. I have had periods without her assistance, and I know how quickly our ancient building and its furnishings lose their surface sheen when the lady is absent.

Getting someone in her place was not going to be easy. I

feared that her crazy niece Minnie Pringle might apply for the post. Worse still, she might be the only applicant! Anyone, I decided, would be better than Minnie about the place. I had suffered much from her administrations in the past, and would be alert if she made any approaches. Apart from her complete incompetence, the tangle of Minnie's love life in which one soon became reluctantly involved, was too horrific to contemplate.

It was while these thoughts were tumbling about in my head that I first noticed a pain in my right eye. There was also a blur when I read, or watched the television screen.

Rushing to the mirror, I surveyed my eye. It looked absolutely normal. I covered it and read and watched with my left eye. That was fine, but the right one was definitely defective.

Like any other robust person, the slightest deviation from perfect health throws me into a panic. First thing in the morning, I told myself, I must ring the optician for an appointment. With any luck, my left eye would still work, otherwise it might be as well to memorise the position of the holes in the dialling plate of the telephone. Would it take me long to learn Braille, I wondered? And how quickly would one get used to a guide dog?

Pondering gloomily on these things, I turned out my medicine chest and found an ancient eye shade, which reeked, for some reason, of camphor. This fragrant article I adjusted over a pad of lint over my afflicted eye, and then wondered how quickly the left one would give out with double work to do.

'At this rate,' I told Tibby, 'I shall be out of a job, like Mrs Pringle. We'll be hard put to it to find a crust for me and a quarter of liver for you.'

Why, I thought, I can't even play a mouth organ in the gutter! When it comes to it I'm completely useless, I decided hopelessly.

Perhaps the optician could think of something – not in the

way of future employment, of course – to give me a little hope. Everyone said how marvellous Moorfields Eye Hospital was, come to think of it, and as long as one did not have to have the retina stuck on again with those awful laser beams, which presumably did a sort of stapling job like clipping papers together, one could cope with ordinary treatment, although that, perhaps mercifully, was at present unknown.

John Milton had managed quite well, I told myself, though his daughter had a tough time copying down his poems as he dictated them, as far as I remembered from accounts of the poet's home life read years ago in the pages of Arthur Mee's *My Magazine*. And I had met several active and cheerful blind people who seemed to enjoy life. Should I ever be as brave?

I made my way to bed enveloped in a cloud of apprehension and camphor, and counted the stairs earnestly on my way up.

It is as well to be prepared.

10   Mrs Pringle Deserts Us

I WOKE to bright sunshine and the blessed relief of finding that both eyes were in first-rate working order.

Nevertheless, I told myself, it would be as well to make
an appointment with the optician. Why bother him, asked my
craven half? He has probably more than enough to do with
genuine sufferers, and could well do without panic-stricken
hypochondriacs.

My craven half usually wins on these occasions, but I
decided to be firm this time. So far, I had not needed spectacles,
even for fine work, but no doubt I was now at the stage of life
which demanded some help. At playtime I bravely made my
appointment, and promised to be at the optician's the next
Saturday morning.

Now and again, during the day, I toyed with the thought of
the best design to suit me. I rather fancied half-glasses. They
looked decidedly efficient, and a little intimidating, which is
always useful for a school teacher.

On the other hand, the more modern owlish variety were
definitely fashionable. Several ladies in the village favour
upswept shapes, and Mrs Finch-Edwards, a somewhat flam-
boyant lady who acted as a supply teacher here, actually had a
pair shaped rather like butterflies, with a flashing jewel in the
upper wing tip. Frankly, I could not imagine myself in such
dashing numbers.

When Mrs Pringle appeared, as haughty as ever, I decided
not to let her manner put me off. Fairacre folk who are

proposing a trip to Caxley usually offer a lift now that we have no buses to take us to the market town.

'I'm off to the optician on Saturday morning, Mrs Pringle,' I said. 'May I give you a lift?'

'No, thank you,' said she, pulling in her three chins, and looking grumpier than ever. 'Got to have glasses at last, have you? I've never felt right about them since my Uncle George fell off his bike on Coronation Day, and the splinters of glass was rammed something cruel into his eyes. He was never the same!'

She swept off into the lobby without the hint of a limp.

To my delight, Amy rang me at half past five that evening.

She sounded calm and cheerful, and in answer to my query about where she had been, said airily: 'Oh, here and there, you know. I'm ringing now from Vanessa's.'

Vanessa, her niece, lives in a castle in Scotland, and my frugal soul was shocked at the thought of such an expensive telephone call.

'But you should have waited until after six,' I protested. 'It's so much cheaper then.'

'Well, never mind that, you old miser! I'll manage, no doubt. The thing is I'm coming home, probably tomorrow, and am arranging a little party for June the first. It's a Saturday, as you probably know. About eight or ten of us. Can you come?'

'I'd love to.'

'Good, then I'll try and get Horace Umbleditch, and the young Mawnes. Horace will balance you nicely, and I'm very fond of him.'

Remembering my last conversation with her husband James, I wondered whether I should warn her not to get too fond of the unsuspecting Horace because of James's jealousy, but even a friendship as long and sturdy as Amy's and mine would probably not stand up to such bluntness.

112

'Have you rung James?' I said.

'Oh lord, yes! What an old fuss-pot he is, to be sure! Now, I'm relying on you then for June the first. About seven, shall we say? I'm going to ring the others now, and get things organised from here while I have the leisure. Vanessa's feeding the baby, but sends her love.'

The line went dead, and I put down the receiver, mightily relieved to know that Amy was alive and well, and obviously in excellent spirits.

But just what had she been up to?

The school house had not received any of Mrs Pringle's attentions now for two weeks, and frankly it began to look like it.

Dusting and vacuum cleaning I did fairly regularly, but the kitchen floor really needed a good scrubbing, and the cooker was approaching the stage where it should be dismantled, immersed in soda water, and generally forced to endure the stringent measures which Mrs Pringle regularly undertook.

There was no doubt about it, if the lady was determined to leave me then I must try and get a substitute.

Matters came to a head one morning when we both arrived at the school door to find that a tap had been left on, and the wash basin having been plugged with some unknown substance, the floor was awash.

Mrs Pringle drew in her breath sharply. Her face grew redder than ever, and I began to wonder how one coped with a sudden attack of apoplexy.

'That's the last straw!' she gasped. 'That's it then! You can take my notice now. I've had enough.'

'Mrs Pringle,' I begged, 'please don't desert me now! Think things over, do!'

But she turned away, dewlap quivering with rage, and her black oilcloth bag swinging dangerously on her arm.

She stumped off towards the school gate, and one or two early arrivals hastened to get out of her way, like refugees hurrying to the side of the road when a tank comes along.

I rolled up my sleeves, turned off the tap, unplugged the basin, (bubble gum yet again, I noted), and set to with the floor cloth.

Well, at least we knew where we were. I proposed to call to see the lady that evening to get her resignation in writing, or a firm promise to return to her duties with as much willingness as her nature could muster.

After that, I must work fast to find a cleaner for my house, and if need be one for Fairacre school.

I was still wringing out the floor cloth when Isobel arrived, and I told her the tale.

'You would really be far better off without her. She's been a blight on your life ever since you came here.'

'Oh, I don't know,' I protested. 'I'm quite fond of the old harridan in a perverse sort of way, and she needs the money, I know. I can't just kick her out without giving her a chance to retract.'

'Well, see how you get on this evening,' advised Isobel. 'And if she persists in going, I should count your blessings. As a matter of fact, I think I could find a young woman for you. She lives between Fairacre and Beech Green, and wants a job, I know.'

'That sounds hopeful. One thing I'm determined not to do, and that is to employ that nutty Minnie Pringle.'

And on this note we parted to go to our respective registers and the day's business.

The weather was so balmy and seductive that it was impossible to worry about Mrs Pringle, Amy, or anything else.

May was at its loveliest. It was true that the best of the daffodils awaited deheading, and the crocuses were drooping tattered heads, but the lilac was in bud, and the peonies and irises were flaunting their showy beauty.

My peonies are of the dark red common kind which flourish here and delight me with their blowsy top-heavy blossoms. Several times I have tried to grow the white and pale pink varieties, both single and double, but despite my cosseting they have faded away. The old-fashioned crimson ones flower bravely year after year, and I bless them for their hardiness.

The mats of aubretia and golden alyssum were still a cheerful sight, and the cotoneaster by the wall was spangled with pink and white flowers. The bees droned in it all day, and the birds sang with springtime fervour.

The earth was warm and friable, just right for scattering poppy and marigold and larkspur seeds to take their chance of providing summer colour in the gaps in the border. The air from the downs was soft and soporific, so different from the usual fresh breezes that buffet us, in all seasons, in this area.

I had my tea in the garden, relishing all these delights, and watching Tibby rolling on the gravel nearby. If only one could have more of this blessed solitude, I pondered, just enjoying the simple joys about one, when 'every prospect pleases', how good and loving and noble one would be!

But the hymn continues:

'And only man is vile', I recalled, which reminded me that I must tear myself away from my miniature Eden, and go to visit Mrs Pringle, my personal serpent, and get the interview over.

The lady opened the door a matter of two inches, and from what I could see of her stern visage, I fully expected her to slam the door in my face.

However, she pulled it open and invited me to step inside. I felt like Daniel entering the lions' den, but tried to appear calm.

'Best sit down, now you've got here,' said Mrs Pringle grudgingly, and we both sat one each side of her empty fireplace. Every metal surface gleamed, every tile shone, not a crumb or cotton end showed on the carpet, and the windows were crystal clear. I was glad Mrs Pringle could not see my own home at the moment.

As if she could read my thoughts, she said: 'I'm not up to coming back to your place, you know. There's work and work, and some's *back-breaking* work, like your kitchen floor. So it's out of the question.'

'I quite understand that,' I said, 'but my chief concern is the school cleaning. I know we have had our little upsets in the past, but I wouldn't like you to give up entirely, and I came to see whether you would change your mind.'

The lady's expression changed. One could not, in all truthfulness, describe it as *softening*, but the down-turned mouth was perhaps a little less severe, and the eyes a trifle less flinty. My hopes grew.

'I'm not one to change my mind, as you well know, Miss Read, and I feel I owe it to myself to have a break. I'm up and down the street to that place, day in and day out, and my leg is not what it should be. Doctor said as it needed rest, and I ought to do as he says, though I doubt whether he knows much about it, nor cares, for that matter.'

She surveyed me belligerently, evidently waiting for my comment, but I stayed silent. Mrs Pringle is a wily fish, and has to be played with care.

'Well, let's put it like this,' she continued. 'I'll have a week off and see how things go. Then I will let you know, one way or the other.'

'Right,' I said, rising. 'You rest your leg, and think things over, and have another word with the doctor. But I really must know after a week. Meanwhile, we'll do our best to manage while you're laid up.'

She showed me to the door limping heavily, and wincing every now and again.

There were some splendid madonna lilies in bud in the shelter of the cottage wall, and a line of early pinks smelling divine along the path. There was not a weed in sight.

I complimented her upon the show of flowers.

'Not got without hard work,' was the reply. 'But nothing is in this wicked world!'

A serpent all right, I thought, smiling over the gate at my old enemy.

I drove alone into Caxley on Saturday morning, dodging a number of fledglings who sat bemusedly in the middle of the road and nearly gave me heart failure.

The hedges were beginning to turn green, and some copper

beech trees on the outskirts of Caxley were hazily pink with tiny leaves. What a morning! What a blessed time of year! Even the thought of my coming ordeal could not quench my spirits on such a glorious day of early summer.

The optician was a spruce young fellow smelling deliciously of eau-de-Cologne after-shave. He shone a bright light into my eyes, making strange little grunts as he did so. I earnestly hoped that they were grunts of approval and not horror at his findings. Perhaps I should be rushed to Caxley Cottage Hospital immediately, I thought, panic returning, or there would be an urgent call to Moorfields to stand by.

After this ordeal, I submitted to the usual tests with each eye, trying to read as far down as I could so that my new spectacles, if needed eventually, would last as long as possible.

I can't say I cared for the lenses being dropped one after the other before my eyes while I attempted to say if the red light was brighter than the green. After a bit, one really cannot be sure, just as the last pair of shoes after a fitting always feels worse than the one before, until a superbly comfortable pair is greeted with cries of relief, bought and borne home, only to find that it is miles too big.

'Yes,' said my nice-smelling optician. 'You definitely need reading glasses. I will write a prescription, and then my assistant will show you the different frames available. Actually, I should advise you to have half-glasses. At the moment your long sight is perfect.'

I was ushered into another room and there spent a most agreeable twenty minutes selecting suitable frames, ending up with some rather sedate gold-rimmed affairs which gave me a granny-like appearance which I rather liked.

'Perhaps I ought to have chosen something more dashing,' I said doubtfully to the young man who had taken such pains. 'Those scarlet ones look gorgeous, and those thick black ones might make me look studious.'

'Oh, I'm sure you don't want to look *studious*,' he said rather primly, as though such a condition was rather shameful. 'And the scarlet ones are really for the young. I think you will find the half-glasses very flattering to your own, er, quieter expression.'

All the way home, I wondered if a 'quieter expression' meant plain dowdiness, and had a horrid feeling that it did.

It was an enormous thrill to see Amy's car waiting by my door when I came out of school a day or two later.

My old friend was sitting on the garden seat, her face tilted towards the sun, and her eyes closed. She looked blissfully happy and ten years' younger than when I saw her last.

'Amy!' I cried. 'What a marvellous surprise! Come and tell me all about your disappearance. You had us all rattled, I can tell you, and James rang me in the most awful lather.'

'I'm delighted to hear it,' said Amy, giving me a kiss. 'It was one of the objects of the exercise, but not the *chief* one, let me say.'

'And what was the chief one?'

Amy bent down to pull a long piece of grass and began to nibble it before replying.

'I suppose you could say it was to catch up with myself. You see, for years now, like most married women, I've always had James in mind. Would he like this frock I've just bought? Would he like a holiday in Italy, or would he prefer to go to Frinton as usual? Even down to: "I'd better not put bananas in this fruit salad because James doesn't care for them." Of course, women with children must find it even worse, I do realise that, and must be torn in several directions at once when trying to come to a decision, but it suddenly struck me that I hardly ever did *exactly* as I wanted, *when* I wanted, and it seemed a good idea to try it.'

'And did it work?'

'Perfectly. I decided just to go off without a word to anyone. The whole point was to be alone without agitated friends and relations harassing me. I remember you saying once that the days one enjoys most are those one spends alone. I know it doesn't hold good for everyone. Some people are lonely anyway, but for you, among folk all day, I can quite see the need for a breathing space.'

'But, Amy,' I protested, 'you live alone a great deal. Why the sudden flight?'

'Believe it or not, I am hardly ever alone, and it's largely my fault. Dear old Mrs Hopkins comes in three times a week to char. Bert does the garden on Tuesdays and Thursdays. I play bridge twice a week, and go to innumerable committees and good works, more fool me, I suppose. Do you think I was wrong to go?'

She sounded anxious, and quite unlike her usual confident self.

'No, I don't,' I assured her. 'I know exactly how you were feeling, and I think you were right to recognise that you must take the plunge to keep your own personality. But, tell me, where did you go?'

Amy gave a chuckle.

'Well, I drove to a health farm a few miles south of Cambridge, and stayed there for a few days being massaged and creamed and bathed – and starved, incidentally – and generally being cossetted. It was marvellously therapeutic, and I lost five pounds too, which was a bonus. And they had the best hairdresser I've ever come across. I must say, I prefer a man to do my hair, do you?'

'I think you're right. They don't seem to slice your ears off with long sharp talons as the girls do, and they don't rub your hair into tangles so viciously.'

'After that I went on to dear old Cambridge for a couple of nights, and simply drifted about the Backs, and up and down

Trumpington Street, and round the Fitzwilliam and the Botanical Gardens. It was so peaceful, and Cambridge was looking lovely, and really warm for a change. It did me a power of good.'

'I wish I'd been with you.'

'So did I, now and again, but that would have defeated my aim. I must say I began to feel more balanced with every day that passed.'

'Then what?'

'I rang Vanessa and asked if I could come up for a few days, and she was wildly welcoming. So I took two days ambling northward through some of the most spectacular country, and spent the rest of my time with Vanessa and the children.'

She threw away the chewed grass and sighed happily. 'Of course I was *slightly* guilty about James worrying, but after all he keeps me guessing often enough, and I think it's given him food for thought. I was sorry he'd bothered the police though. The poor things have quite enough to do trying to catch house-breakers and muggers and murderers, without badgering them with a perfectly happy truant wife. But what about you? Did you worry?'

'A bit,' I admitted, 'but I had the comfortable feeling you were in full control of the situation, and you see I was right. Like a cup of tea?'

'Lead me to it,' said Amy.

While the kettle boiled, she told me more about the proposed party.

'Well, Horace is free, and so are Irene and David Mawne, and I came across that nice Gerard Baker again. He called at Vanessa's on his way to some Highland village with a name like a sneeze. He's coming too. So sad his wife Hattie died. Do you remember he wrote about a poet called Aloysius Something who used to live in Fairacre?'

'Indeed I do. He called with Vanessa one morning when he

was finding out about our Loyshus, and I directed him to Mr Willet.'

'Well, he's got mixed up with a television programme about Aloysius and I think they may do some filming in the village soon.'

'What excitement! I must ask him all about it when we meet at your house.'

After tea, we walked in the garden and I picked Amy a real country bunch of mixed flowers, irises, columbine, sweet rocket, some late narcissi, and a few early roses.

She sniffed them appreciatively as she made her way to the car.

'I must get back to poor old James,' she said smiling. 'He's all of a fidget now, in case I take off again.'

'So you've still got a conscience,' I quipped.

'It's well under control,' she assured me, and drove off with a flippant tootle on the horn.

11 Amy's Party

I WAS sad to see the last of May despite the problems it had brought me. Would June ever be as glorious, as fragrant, as tender with new blossoms everywhere? Fairacre delights me in all seasons, but May is the crown of the year for me, and when exceptionally early warmth is added to its blessings, then everything is perfect in this upland village.

However, the weather forecaster, on the last evening of May, promised us a continuation of the balmy conditions, and the weather map was nicely sprinkled with high pressure areas, and isobars widely apart foretelling very light winds.

And it looked as though he would be right.

I woke on the Saturday morning to a cloudless sky, and spent a few luxurious minutes relishing the fact that I need not get up at my usual early hour. A robin was singing in the plum tree, and there were occasional chirrupings from foraging blackbirds. But the rapturous dawn chorus of some weeks earlier was fading now that the young birds were hatching and fledglings needed feeding. A sudden furious chattering and scolding fetched me from my bed and, as I had guessed, Tibby was looking up at an irate blackbird a few feet above him in the lilac bush.

As I soaked in my bath a few minutes later, I thought how lucky I was to have a bathroom to myself, and hot water at the turn of a tap.

It was not always so. I recalled the effort of dragging the zinc bath from its nail on the side of the woodshed, the boiling of rainwater in the old copper and the sloshing of buckets into the bath. It had been hard work, but the water, brownish and silky, had left one's skin as smooth as satin, and the soap had lathered in half the time it took with the water from the mains.

Nevertheless, I told myself as I stepped out, I would not want to return to the primitive sanitary conditions of my early years at Fairacre, and I praised the Lord for mercies received.

That evening I was due at Amy's party and I donned my new pale green silk frock with some trepidation. Amy has an eagle eye for the cut and colour of garments, and although I flattered myself that the colour suited me, I was not too sure about the sleeves. They seemed rather tight at the top to me. No doubt Amy would tell me if anything were drastically wrong when we were alone together.

The sun was still quite high as I drove to Bent, slanting rays through the young foliage and dappling the road surface with sunlight and shade.

Within a mile of Amy's house, I recognised the car in front of me as David and Irene Mawnes', and saw that Horace Umbleditch, Irene's brother, was also with them. They did not see me.

I slowed down to let them get ahead. It was quite a change to realise that I was not first as usual. Amy tells me that it looks as though I don't get enough to eat and have rushed ahead to get my trotters in the trough first. I thought these porcine allusions were very rude, and I told her so.

'Well, I apologise,' she had replied, 'but it doesn't alter the fact that as soon as you enter the hall you raise your head and sniff the air ravenously like a Bisto Kid!'

'I wonder I get invited at all,' I answered. 'Anyway, it's because there are usually such luscious smells drifting about that I automatically respond.'

This time, I told myself, watching the Mawnes' car draw

ahead, I must remember my manners and try not to sniff.

James let me in. He looked as debonair as ever, but I thought he seemed a little more subdued than usual. However, he kissed me on both cheeks gallantly and led me towards the party.

I was pleased to find several people already gathered together in Amy's splendid drawing room. The French windows were open, and some of the guests, glasses in hand, were watching a little bevy of chaffinches splashing in the bird bath. Roses seemed to be everywhere, inside and out, and their perfume was marvellous.

Most of the people were old friends, but I was glad to meet Amy's new young vicar and his wife. They had only recently moved to Bent from a parish in north London, and were enthusiastic about country life.

There was also an elderly cousin of Amy's, recently widowed, who was staying for a week. Luckily I remembered that she was a fairly well-known writer of detective novels and we had plenty to talk about when we found ourselves on the same sofa.

'Do you know Basil Bradley?' I asked her. 'He writes historical novels, and lives near here.'

'We share the same publisher. Now, he really is an enormous success! I believe they print ten thousand copies at first go.'

She spoke with awe.

'I once tried to analyse his great hold on the public, but I came to the conclusion that it could not be true literary worth. That may sound catty, but I don't mean to be. His style is rather florid, I think.'

'I think he gives his readers exactly what they want,' I replied. 'They only have to look at the book jacket, and see one of his heroines, all ringlets and a high-waisted muslin gown, to know that she is going to have wild romances every ten pages, and lots of wicked villains hoping to entice her, and probably a cruel guardian into the bargain, and a few ghosts in the background, and it's all going to be the mixture as before, and very nice too.'

'I don't grudge him his popularity, for a moment,' said she bravely, 'but it would be nice to know its secret. Have you met him?'

'Frequently. He's a perfect dear, and we all love him. He opens bazaars, and empties jars of coins in pubs at Christmas, and generally pulls his weight most satisfactorily. What's more, he's as modest as they come.'

'Really? Well, it's nice to know that he is as popular in private as in public.' She sounded rather wistful, and I wondered if she had hoped for some terrible secret vices to be disclosed, but I was unable to gratify her. Basil Bradley is exactly as I described him, and although the men locally tend to make disparaging remarks about his pink shirts and bow ties, and his rather too-gorgeous silk suits in pastel shades, we women uphold him loyally, always ending with:

'And he's so very kind to his mother!' On the whole, this tends to be the last word on our dear Basil Bradley, and what's wrong with that?

At this moment, Gerard Baker was ushered in by James, and after introductions around the room he arrived at the sofa. Mrs Hare, Amy's cousin, had been collected by the vicar and his wife to go and inspect the garden, and so he sat by me, and I enquired about Aloysius, our local Victorian poet.

'It's really rather exciting,' said Gerard. 'We shall be coming out to Fairacre pretty soon to film Tyler's Row where he lived.'

'Do the Hales know?'

'Oh, I expect so,' he said, somewhat vaguely. 'The producer is a very conscientious young fellow.'

'Will they keep pretty closely to your script?'

'I'm not doing that!' He sounded taken aback. 'There are three, maybe four, chaps doing the writing. You need a large team for a half-hour on the telly, you know.'

It sounded extravagant to me, especially as I had read Gerard's excellent and masterly account of Aloysius's life and work. I should have thought anyone could have knocked a script into shape with some of Aloysius's regrettably flowery poems interspersed to make up the time.

'I suppose it makes work,' was the best I could do by way of comment.

We strolled out into the garden with the others. The sun was going down fast behind a clump of beeches in the distance.

Against a south-facing wall there were already some scarlet flowers on the japonica, glowing even more brilliantly in the rays of the setting sun.

Horace Umbleditch appeared at our side.

'My sister Irene makes the most marvellous japonica jelly,' he said to Gerard. 'We have it with cold meat. Delicious!'

'Japonica Jelly!' exclaimed Gerard. 'Now that sounds exactly suitable for the name of a film star, don't you think?'

'Or the title of one of Aloysius's poems perhaps?'

'Far too obvious,' observed Gerard. 'Aloysius liked such titles as "The Winnowed Seed" and "The Bashful Maiden". But look, Amy is calling us to heel.'

The vicar was on Amy's right and I was next to him. On my right was Horace whom I always enjoy meeting. He teaches at a local prep school, and his first words at the dinner table were surprising.

'I thought you were an excellent speaker at that children's do a month or so ago.'

'Good heavens! Were you there? I didn't see you. Come to think of it, I really saw *nobody*, I was so terrified. Just a pinkish splodge of mixed faces. A horrifying sight.'

'Well, we enjoyed it. I brought along our new school secretary, Eve Masters. You must meet her sometime.'

I said that I should like that and wondered privately why Horace should choose such a dreary outing for the poor woman.

As if he knew my thoughts Horace said:

'Her uncle is a big noise in the Save The Children business. It was her idea to go to the Caxley evening. To be honest, I wanted to go to the Marx Brothers' revival.'

'I wish I'd seen you. Did you linger after the show and have some refreshments?'

'We had to get away fairly early as one of the chaps on the staff was standing in for me until ten o'clock, and I didn't want to be too late back. But we heard Miss Crabbe.'

'Oh good!' I said politely.

'What a misguided old fathead she is!' observed Horace, turning over the delicious chicken in a creamy sauce which was our main course. 'She'd have been burnt as a witch two hundred years ago!'

I found myself feeling fonder of Horace than ever. What a wonderfully perceptive fellow he was, to be sure!

'Well, she was warmly applauded,' I replied, trying to be fair.

'That was only general rejoicing at the cessation of the lady's voice,' Horace assured me, and turned to talk to Amy's cousin beside him.

'I have met Gerald Partridge of Fairacre this week,' said the vicar. 'What a charming fellow! Tell me, does he let the children address him by his Christian name?'

'Good heavens, no!' I exclaimed. 'I shouldn't allow it for one thing, and I don't think it is respectful, do you?'

'*Respectful*,' repeated the young man doubtfully. 'I was not so much thinking of *respect* as of *friendliness*. I wondered if the children of Bent would like to call me "Cyril".'

128

'Well, that's your affair,' I answered, trying not to sound too shocked. 'I only know I should never dream of letting them use my Christian name. They don't seem to suffer any terrible traumas by having to address me as "Miss Read". What did you do about the problem in your last parish?'

'I'm afraid the children there were rather impudent, and some of them took advantage of my goodwill.'

I suddenly felt sorry for him.

'Well, if you'll take an old schoolmarm's advice, I'd say, remember that children on the whole *are* impudent, and *will* take advantage of gentleness. Time enough to indulge them when you know you can control them, but they soon get the upper hand if you are not firm from the beginning.'

'You are probably right,' he said, looking downcast.

'This is fresh fruit salad,' announced Amy, lifting the lid top from a beautiful scooped-out canteloupe melon. 'Or James will give you chocolate mousse, if you prefer it.'

The vicar cheered up at once, I was relieved to see. Food is a great comfort in times of stress.

As we were going to our cars at the end of the evening, James caught me alone as I was about to drive off.

'I'm sorry I was so brusque with you on the telephone the other evening. I was worried to death, as I'm sure you knew.'

'Of course, James. I was feeling just the same. I think Amy's little break has done her good, don't you?'

'Funny affair, really. After all, she has everything she can want here. It seemed so odd to push off into the blue like that. I can only think it was a slight mental breakdown.'

I felt a twinge of irritation. Was he really so obtuse or was he trying to square his conscience?

'She told me,' I said, 'that she simply wanted to be herself – to be her own person – with no ties of any sort. I can understand it.'

James studied his fingers on the edge of the car window. He looked thoughtful. James is no fool and I was wondering how he would react.

'I do love her, you know,' he said at last, very seriously.

'I don't doubt it for a minute,' I told him truthfully. 'And she's equally devoted to you. But no matter how happily people are married, they are still *individuals*, and have to have time now and again to realise it.'

'Yes. It's a point to bear in mind.'

'Dear old Donne,' I went on, watching Amy waving to a departing car, 'stressed that no man was an island, and so on. But I think each man *is* an island, and no one knows his neighbour completely. That's what's so shattering when someone we think we know well does something horrifying like stealing or committing suicide.'

James laughed suddenly. 'Do you want me to have night terrors? No more sermons now, or I'll burst into tears!'

He gave me a kiss through the window, and ruffled my hair as though he were my big brother.

'Goodbye, James, and thank you,' I cried, moving off.

'Thank you for casting pearls,' he replied cheekily.

Trust James to have the last word.

It was quite apparent that Mrs Pringle was not going to come again to clean my house, and so I felt free to accept Isobel's kind offer to approach the lady who lived between Fairacre and Beech Green.

'Just see if she's willing,' I said, 'and I'll pop along after school one day, or at any time that suits her, to arrange things.'

Isobel was as good as her word, and two days later I found myself sitting in little Mrs John's kitchen watching her spoon custard into her youngest's mouth.

She was small and neat, with quick movements and bright dark eyes. She reminded me of a wren or a robin.

'You wouldn't mind if I brought Teresa with me, I suppose?' she asked tentatively.

I assured her that Teresa would be very welcome. If she liked, I added, she could play with some toys with the babies' class.

This seemed to clinch the matter and it was arranged that the two of them would come on Wednesday afternoons, and a satisfactory wage was negotiated. Then a thought struck me.

'You will have to push Teresa in the pram, won't you? It's a good mile and a half. Can you manage it? Suppose it rains?'

Mrs John laughed.

'I sometimes push her to Caxley,' she replied. 'Not often, I grant you, but I enjoy walking, and when I was a child in Wales we walked everywhere.'

'If the weather is really bad,' I insisted, 'you mustn't venture out. I shall understand.'

'I'll be there,' she promised, and I felt pretty sure she would be.

By the end of the week the school was looking grubby

despite all our endeavours at self-help. Curmudgeon though she was, and a sore trial at all times, Mrs Pringle was a first-class cleaner, and the school missed the touch of her heavy hand.

On the following Saturday she arrived at my house, and I invited her in.

'No, I'm not stopping,' she replied.

'At least sit with me in the garden,' I said, making for the rustic seat. 'It will rest your leg before you go back.'

She lowered herself slowly and sighed as she came to rest.

'Well, doctor says my leg's no better, and forbids me to work,' she told me, with evident relish. I was not surprised.

'That settles it then,' I said. 'I'll advertise at once for someone to take over. Does this mean you will be retiring for good?'

She drew in her breath sharply.

'Who said "*for good*"?' she demanded. 'I'm not giving in my notice and stopping "*for good*" for anyone! It's just while my leg's flared up. I told the doctor that.'

'In that case,' I said, 'we shall have to advertise for temporary help.'

'No need to waste money on advertising,' said the lady. 'My Minnie'd give a hand while I'm laid up. That house of yours could do with a bottoming by now, as well as the school, I don't doubt.'

I explained, with secret pleasure, I must admit, that Mrs John had been engaged for my work.

Mrs Pringle bridled. 'And who might she be? You'd better warn her about the weight of that spare bed of yours, and the way the bath tap comes apart if you aren't careful. Poor soul, whoever she is, she'll find plenty to do.'

I explained who she was, and mentioned young Teresa.

Mrs Pringle shook her head gloomily.

'Ten to one she'll put her fingers in the electric sockets,' she warned me, 'and play with the switches. And you'll find fingermarks all over the place, no matter how careful this lady is. We knows children, Miss Read. You'll rue the day, I've no doubt.'

She rose to her feet.

'Well, I must struggle back, leg or no leg. Shall I tell Minnie to come up?'

Panic enveloped me. I thought of the state of the school wash basins, and the floor of the infants' room. I also thought of the time it would take for the advertisement to be answered, and wondered if hopeless Minnie might just possibly be of use for the next few days.

I took the plunge.

'Yes, ask Minnie to come and have a look at the work. Make it clear to her that it will only be for a day or two until we get someone to take your place.'

'She'll have to bring her youngest with her,' said Mrs Pringle. 'But if you're having that Teresa I suppose you won't mind a toddler under your feet.'

'Take care of your leg,' I said in farewell.

'I'm the only one that does,' she replied bleakly.

I returned to the garden seat and pondered on the future. The thought of Minnie, toddler or no toddler in tow, was daunting, but surely she could not do much damage to the basins with a tin of Vim and a dishcloth. It might be wise to supervise the scrubbing of the infants' room floor, I told myself. Minnie was quite capable of shaking Harpic into the hot water instead of soap powder, as she could not read, and any white powder would seem suitable to her.

And I'd better make sure all the cupboards were locked, I decided. On one never-to-be-forgotten occasion she had decided to wash the shelves of the stationery cupboard, and had put back all the exercise books, coloured tissue paper, gummed squares and cartridge paper on the wet shelves, with disastrous results. As for the sacrosanct register which all teachers are supposed to guard with their lives, snatching it from any fire which may be engulfing the school, I thought it would be prudent to take it across the playground every night to my own house, while Minnie was at her mayhem.

Tibby appeared from a clump of clove pinks, a mouse dangling from his mouth.

Seeing me, he gave a triumphant mew. The mouse, having been dropped, beat a rapid retreat, pursued in vain by Tibby.

Two minutes later, he returned lamenting loudly.

'Cheer up, Tib,' I said, 'we all have our troubles.'

12   Minnie Pringle Lends a Hand

MISS Briggs was now back in the infants' room and the dividing partition shuddered every now and again from the impact of her stentorian tones. I thought wistfully of the peace we had enjoyed during Isobel's brief reign, but tried not to dwell on the change.

The girl looked rather pale and thinner than usual.

'It was a tummy bug,' she told me, 'and the first lot of pills disagreed with me, which made matters worse. The only bright thing is that I'm an inch smaller round the waist, and my wedding dress will have to be taken in.'

I complimented her on her svelte appearance.

'You should be getting your invitation this week,' she continued. 'I do hope you can come. Do you know Leamington?'

'No, but I shall look forward to the wedding very much.'

'Good. I expect Mum can put you up, although I know we've some aunts and uncles, and my father's mother coming up from Cornwall, and some cousins from Holland that have been invited, but I'm sure we can find room. We've three bedrooms.'

I said hastily that I would not dream of troubling her mother when so many of the family would need accommodation, and I would look out for a modest hotel for my overnight stay.

'Do you know, I'm quite looking forward to it,' she said, sounding surprised. I remembered her landlady's surmise that girls about to marry frequently suffered from prenuptial nerves. Obviously our Miss Briggs was made of sterner stuff, and good luck to her.

Mr Willet summed it up when he met her on her first morning back at school.

'Looks a lot better with half a stone off, don't she? I mean, she's still a fair old lump of a girl, but got a livelier look about her. That young Wayne's done her a power of good. Nothing like marriage, Miss Read, for setting you up. You wants to try it some time.'

'Chance would be a fine thing,' I told him, opening the register.

The prolonged heat, which I relished, began to take its toll of the garden and of the children's energy.

The crimson petals pattered down from the peonies on to the dry soil. The downs shimmered in a blue haze, and I had to draw the curtains in my house against the heat of the midday sun.

The rainwater butts were empty, and a loudspeaker van from Caxley toured the villages exhorting us to save water and forbade us to use sprinklers and hoses in the parched gardens.

'I turns a deaf ear to that blighted van,' Mr Willet told me. 'It's only old Ted Bates anyway, throwing his weight about, and him no better than he should be with that fancy woman of his over Bent way. I've got some seedlings just up nice, and they gets a drop of water when needed, Ted or no Ted.'

Here was another instance of sturdy country independence born of personal knowledge. What cared Mr Willet for a flashy van and the might of the local water board? Such power was soon cut down to size by knowing old Ted who was running the thing. I found it all very heartening.

The children were listless. Perhaps they are so accustomed to the exhilarating freshness of our downland breezes that a warm and langorous environment, which suits me very well, saps their energy immediately.

Our lofty windows were propped open to their fullest

extent, and the door to the lobby, as well as the outside one to the playground, were permanently ajar. Two large flower pots made sure that they stayed open and Tibby took to sitting on the outside one, washing his face and occasionally looking into the lobby and classroom, much to the children's delight.

But despite my efforts to mitigate their sufferings the children remained lethargic. I took them outside for lessons under the trees at the edge of the playground, but there was so much noise we did not get on very well.

People from the towns have the fond idea that we in the country could hear a pin drop, and that silence enfolds us. Here, in June, Mr Roberts was busy hay-making. The baler thumped its way round and round the fields adjoining the school. The vicar's lawn mower, a few yards away over the vicarage wall, seemed to be doing overtime. Various dogs in the village enjoyed a healthy barking, and Mr Roberts' cows added their lowing every now and again.

We also get a number of aircraft from a nearby aerodrome,

and are in the flight path from an international airport. Some distance away, but quite audible when the wind is in the south-west, there is a motorway, and the hum of the traffic can become a roar in high summer. Fairacre itself is little changed, but sometimes I wonder if it is not a place besieged by outside pressure.

There was little activity at playtimes. Even the coke pile was neglected as children were too idle to climb it. Mostly they sat in the shade of the trees, rolling marbles or chewing grass in a desultory fashion, whilst only the really industrious essayed such feats as making daisy-chains or knocking the heads from plantains.

Nevertheless, it was rewarding to see how tanned and well they all appeared in their skimpy tee-shirts and cotton shorts or skirts. Even Joseph Coggs who rarely seems to enjoy a change of clothes, was clad in some good summer garments which I suspect had been bought at the W.I. jumble stall so bravely supervised by Miriam Quinn. With any luck, I told myself, this blissful spell of sunshine should set us up for the coming winter.

Mrs John began her ministrations much to my relief, and although I did not see much of her as I was in school, I did nip across at playtime to make sure she had a cup of tea.

Teresa seemed to be a model child and played or slept in her pram in a shady part of the garden. I returned to my duties congratulating myself on my new helper.

It was a different kettle of fish, of course, with Minnie Pringle barging about in school. She was only engaged to work after school had ended. The thought of facing Minnie Pringle at the beginning as well as the end of a school day was more than I could endure, and I said that we could easily manage first thing.

I stayed with Minnie on her first visit, hovering protec-

Minnie Pringle Lends a Hand

tively, not on my helper's account, but to look after the school property. Fortunately, the toddler had been left with a neighbour, so I only had Minnie to direct. I let her start on the wash basins, putting out the Vim tin, drawing her attention to its size and colour, and even – such is the ardour of the true schoolmarm – pointing out that the three letters on the side spelt VIM. Minnie nodded her tousled red locks energetically, grinning madly the while, and I wondered how soon she would forget my first lesson.

I managed to dissuade her from giving the lower panes of the lobby windows a brisk drubbing with the Vim-coated dishcloth, but she attacked a mirror with such vigour while my back was turned, that I feared the resultant scratches were there for good.

She swept the floors rather well, I thought, and I initiated her into the art of filling a pail half-full rather than brimming over, and showed her where the kneeler and scrubbing brush were kept, and the carton of soap powder. The latter perplexed her.

'You just put in enough powder to make a lather,' I told her, demonstrating with the plastic beaker kept inside. 'One measure is enough for half this size bucket.'

I swished about energetically until we had a useful mixture.

'There isn't time to do much this evening, Minnie,' I told her, 'but if you could start at the other side of the infants' room, it would help. Do a little each evening, I suggest.'

'It's dirtier by the door,' she pointed out. 'I'd best begin there.'

'Start over by the windows,' I directed, 'and work gradually this way.'

'Why?'

'Well, you won't be walking on the bit you've scrubbed, and you'll be kneeling on a dry part of the floor.'

She gazed at me in mystified silence, before bursting into a cackle of laughter.

139

'What a head-piece you've got on you, miss! No wonder you can learn them kids right.'

She spent the last quarter of an hour of her time working hard on the further strip of the floor. I dusted both rooms, partly to help and partly to keep my eye on our property.

'Time's up,' I said at last. 'It all looks splendid, Minnie.'

I was about to tell her that when the short hand was at five and the long one at six it meant that her duties were at an end, but somehow the thought of giving a lesson to Minnie on telling the time, after a full day's teaching, became insupportable. After all, she had already been initiated into the whereabouts of her cleaning materials, and the desirability of washing the floor without treading on the clean part.

I felt it was enough for one day. If not for Minnie, certainly for me.

On Sunday morning I breakfasted in the garden. The sun was pleasantly warm. Later, it would be too hot to enjoy its direct rays, but at nine o'clock all was perfect.

The grass was still dewy, and the Albertine rose growing over the garden shed was breaking into flower. What a marvellous old rose it is! I love the dark tight buds, the glossy foliage, and the pale pink open flowers. But best of all is its sharp-sweet scent. What matter if it only flowers once in the season, and drops its petals with profligacy? It is a true herald of summer, and I think I am fonder of it than any other rose in my cottage garden.

Later I went to church. The altar had roses on it, and some madonna lilies had been arranged on a pedestal by the lectern. Their heady scent perfumed the ancient building. Outside, the sun blazed and the distant thumping of the baler could be heard. All the farmers in the neighbourhood were literally making hay while the sun shone.

Inside, the church was cool and shadowy. I closed my eyes

the better to attend to Gerald Partridge's sermon, and hoped he would not think that I had dropped off.

It was a good theme, a celebration of summer and all its blessings. He spoke of the beauty of natural things, noticed so much more sharply when one could loiter out of doors. He touched on the renewal of friendships which winter weather had discouraged, and I thought how true this was. I recalled the joys of our nature walks and my own garden, and the trips to see Miss Clare and Amy and other good friends.

He went on to point out that beauty begets beauty, quoting an incident in the woods near Beech Green where he came across members of the Caxley art group busy transferring the woodland scene before them on to their canvases. He added another instance, dear to his heart, of the happy sound of the bees collecting nectar to transform into honey. The vicar has only recently taken to bee keeping, and his charges are very dear to him.

It was a good sermon, I thought, as we scrambled to our feet at the end of it. It encouraged us to look about us, to be grateful for all we could see, and for the bounty of the earth, and to ponder on many hidden meanings in an apparently simple message as we truly celebrated summer.

I remembered to ask Miss Briggs for her wedding present list, and pored over it anxiously one evening. The children and I would get together when Miss Briggs was absent to decide on the school's offering. Judging from the list of things needed it would probably turn out to be: 'Soup Ladle, not plastic' or one of 'Trays, various sizes'.

I was pleased to see that she also wanted 'Vases, various sizes', and I decided to plump for something which I liked as my personal present to her. It is always a pleasure to buy china and good to have an excuse to indulge one's desires.

One hot afternoon, I prevailed upon Miss Briggs to take her

charges into the shade of the trees for story time. This gave me the chance to consult my fellow conspirators about the present.

Patrick was all for giving her a pair of guinea pigs, as his pets had recently had a fine litter. It seemed to me that Patrick's guinea pigs produced litters far too often, and supply outstripped demand heavily in Fairacre.

Eileen Burton suggested a silk eiderdown and bedspread, preferably pink 'because it's always pretty', and Ernest thought a wheelbarrow would be useful.

When I could get a word in edgeways, I pointed out that all Miss Briggs' needs were listed, and I put forward the ideas possible on our modest budget. No one was to contribute more than twenty-five pence, and ten would probably be the average.

After much heart-searching, I was delegated to buy a tray.

'As big as the money goes to,' Patrick said firmly, and I meekly agreed to do my best.

Ernest, who had been allotted the job of Miss-Briggs-observer, and had been keeping an eye on the infants' movements from the lobby door, now called out:

'She's acoming, miss! She's acoming!'

At this, the children hastily took out their readers at my suggestion, and were engrossed in their pages, with unnatural fervour.

But when Miss Briggs came in to speak to me as she went to her own room, the nudges and knowing winks would have alerted anyone more observant than my assistant to the fact that Something Was Up.

Fairacre children are not very accomplished dissemblers.

As I was taking some letters to the post a day or two later, I met Peter Hale who lives at Tyler's Row. He bought the property a

few years ago, and he and his wife have turned the row of four
dilapidated cottages into one fine house.

He taught for many years at Caxley Grammar School, but
has now retired and takes an active part in village affairs. I
asked him if there were any developments in the proposed
television programme about Aloysius, an earlier dweller at
Tyler's Row.

'Well, two chaps were supposed to be coming down one day
last week to see if the interior of the end part where Aloysius
used to live was worth filming. It's so altered that I think it's a
waste of time myself.'

'What did they say?'

'They never arrived. Diana and I stayed in, putting off an old
school friend of hers who was coming to tea, incidentally, but
not a word and no TV chaps.'

'Too bad. Do you think there's enough material for a
programme?'

'All I can discover is a pathetic collection of dreadful dog-
gerel in the public library, and Mr Willet's recollection of our
poet's personal dirt. I can't see it making a national appeal
somehow, but no doubt a skilful producer could turn it into
something on the lines of "The neglected poet in a hostile
world".'

'Well, I hope you don't have to hang about for the telly
people anyway.'

'I don't intend to. They can fit in with my plans next time.
That is, if there is a next time!'

Spoken like a true schoolmaster, I thought, as I went on my
way. That was the tone of voice which had sent many to
detention in times past. The telly men had met their match
there.

I heard a little more about the proposed programme when
Gerard Baker rang up. He seemed somewhat agitated, and
wanted to know if the television team could film the school.

'You see, Aloysius attended it as a boy,' he explained.

'I suppose it would be all right,' I said doubtfully. 'What do they want exactly?'

'You may well ask! I'm beginning to wish I had no hand in it at all, there's so much to-ing and fro-ing. If I were you, I would refuse to let them inside.'

'Why? They don't take all that long, do they?'

He gave what novelists call a hollow laugh.

'They took two hours flat arranging some of Aloysius's manuscripts and a candle on a suitably scruffy table. You see, they have to play about with the lighting and sound, and heaven knows what. I should advise you to limit them to taking outside shots only. If that!'

'Well, thanks for the warning.'

'I said I'd sound you out, as I knew you. Don't let yourself in for too much. I know you are not too patient at the best of times, and this could drive you barmy.'

'Thanks,' I said. I was not exactly thrilled to hear that I was obviously an impatient harridan. Still, it was good of Gerard to give me advice.

'Tell them they can have a brief spell taking one or two shots outside the school,' I said. 'But inside is out.'

'I know what you mean,' said Gerard, and rang off.

'The wonders of modern science,' I told Tibby, 'can prove very exhausting.'

13 Mr Willet to the Rescue

I MUST say I was rather pleased with my new spectacles.
I expected a few whispers among my class when I
donned them first for marking the register, but an awed
silence engulfed the schoolroom as I was made the object of
concentrated scrutiny.

It was not until the morning was halfway through, and the
sun was beginning to get to its full power on yet another
cloudless day, that the first comments came.

'Do them glasses hurt you?' Patrick asked.

'Why, no!' I responded. 'I've got them to *stop* my eyes
hurting.'

Somewhat emboldened, other children now joined in.

'But why ain't 'em big enough to go over your eyes?'

'Is it cheaper, miss, to have them funny little 'uns?'

'I feels frightened when you've got them on.'

I did my best to explain the difference between long and
short sight, and the difficulty in focusing as one grew older,
which drew a spate of comment about the spectacles used by
their elderly relatives. Ernest, who is sometimes a lot brighter
than he appears, began to ask quite difficult questions about
lenses which were beyond my power to answer, and when he
actually used the words 'concave' and 'convex', to my aston-
ishment, I had to admit my ignorance, and direct his attention
to the mobile library van whose kind librarian might be able to
find a book to answer Ernest's questions.

By the time we had exhausted the topic of my new half-
glasses, and I had firmly refused to let anyone *touch* them, let

alone *look* through them, as Eileen suggested, it was almost playtime. It was so blissfully sunny outside, and the birds were chirping so merrily, that it seemed like cruelty to children to keep them indoors.

We all had an early playtime.

Amy was rather less respectful about my newly-acquired aids when she called one evening.

'They tend to *age* you, my dear,' she announced, after studying me keenly for a full minute. 'Why did you pick that particular design? Terribly academic they look, I must say!'

'Well, what's wrong with that? I am academic after all.'

'Yes, dear, in a rather juvenile sort of way, I suppose you are. But those glasses make you look like someone engaged on the third volume of somebody's biography. Tacitus, say, or Cicero.'

'That's all to the good. It's nice to look learned.'

'Yes, I suppose it's quite pleasant to look *learned*, but one doesn't want to appear *eccentric*.'

I began to get alarmed.

'You are not trying to tell me, Amy, that these spectacles make me look like a nut-case?'

'Well, not exactly like a *nut-case*,' said Amy, but with a certain doubt in her tone which increased my dismay. 'No, I wouldn't say that – quite! It's just that somehow they make you look odd. If you know what I mean,' she added.

'I can't see this conversation getting us anywhere but into deep waters,' I said. 'Tell me why you've really come.'

'Gerard Baker is getting ready to help with this television nonsense, and I offered him a bed if need be while the flap's on. I just wondered if you would like to see him while he's here?'

'That's nice of you, Amy. I always enjoy seeing Gerard.'

'Oh good!' exclaimed Amy, with unnecessary elation.

'Not in the way you mean,' I said firmly. 'Just that he's good company, and I'll be interested to hear how the programme's going. I gather from Peter Hale that they want to do a few shots in his house, Tyler's Row.'

'Well, I hope he'll be firm about it. A friend of mine spent five hours solid being badgered from pillar to post for exactly five minutes on the box itself. She said her carpets have never been the same since, and she had to have a weekend in an exceptionally quiet hotel in Sidmouth to recover from the ordeal.'

We wandered into the garden. The sun was still quite high in the sky despite the fact that it was early evening.

'Come round to the front door,' I urged, 'and have a look at the swallow babies. I think there are five, but Mr Willet swears there are only four.'

The parent birds were still swooping across the neighbouring fields catching insects for their young. Tiny blue-black heads projected over the rim of the nest, and a mad twittering broke out whenever one of the parents returned with a beak full of provender.

Amy surveyed my front doorstep which was heavily covered in bird droppings.

'Can't you fix something to catch all this?' she asked, looking rather disgusted.

'Mr Willet has tried, but they don't like it,' I replied.

'What with that tyrant Tibby and this family of intruders,' said Amy, 'I can see you are hopelessly out-classed. What you need is a man about the place to look after things. Now Gerard, I know for a fact, is very practical underneath that rather dilettante exterior. When can you come to meet him?'

'Oh, Amy!' I wailed. 'Won't you *ever* realise that I like being single?'

She began to laugh, as we left the shameful doorstep and went to smell the early roses instead.

'I think I know how you feel,' she said at last. 'My few days of solitary life were wonderfully refreshing, I found. And wasn't it Katherine Mansfield who said that one of the pleasures of living alone meant that if you found a hair in your honey at least you knew it was your own?'

To my dismay there had been no answer to the advertisement for a school cleaner. I guessed that Mrs Pringle would be delighted to hear such news, and I had no intention of telling her, although I had no doubt that she would soon be in possession of the knowledge, by means of village bush telegraph.

Although I was careful to say nothing to Mr Willet, he guessed, I think, that there was no particular stampede for the job. I must say, that when one read in the newspapers about the thousands of unemployed people crying out for work, it seemed strange that no one wanted to come to Fairacre school as cleaner.

'You keepin' that dratted Minnie on then?' asked Mr Willet one afternoon. We were in the playground, and the children were fast disappearing round the bend in the lane. The sound of clashing pail and broom came from the recently-vacated classroom.

'Just until we can get a permanent person,' I said guardedly.

'You want to watch her,' warned Mr Willet. 'She was letting that little 'un of hers suck the floor cloth yesterday. Saw it myself.'

'No!' I said horrified. 'Surely not! He might get some awful disease!'

Mr Willet waved his hand airily.

'It wasn't the kid I was worrying about. But it can't do the floor cloth no good to have it chewed up like that. They costs a fortune these days, Alice says. She cuts up my old pants into nice squares for jobs like that, and that saves a pretty penny I can tell you.'

148

'I suppose,' I said doubtfully, 'that Mrs Pringle is really under doctor's orders still? I mean, we know she has her drawbacks –'

'You can say that again,' interjected Mr Willet.

'But she is a marvellous cleaner, and I don't think Minnie is capable of carrying on much longer.'

'You could go and see the old tartar again, I suppose,' said Mr Willet, smacking his thigh and killing a fly which the swallow babies would have relished. 'But I reckon she just wants to see how long you can stick it out with Minnie. Enjoying it, I don't doubt. There's a spiteful side to Mrs P., as well you knows.'

I did indeed, but I dare not say so to Mr Willet.

I sipped my tea in the garden, pondering on this problem. It would be a waste of time to go and see my old cleaner again. She had told me, squarely enough, that she intended to return, but in her own good time. There was no point in begging the lady to return. I must simply set about finding a stand-in for her, and get rid of the deplorable Minnie before she wrecked the school premises.

At this moment there was a sudden shindy from the school. I put my cup on the garden seat, and hurried across the playground. What horrors would appear, I wondered, as I ran? Broken windows, smashed wash basins, shattered desks, all swam before my eyes. Minnie was capable of anything.

I noticed a battered van standing in the lane by the school gate, but did not recognise it in the heat of the moment.

I burst into the building to be confronted with a ferocious-looking man, Minnie screaming behind my desk, and the floor-cloth-chewing infant yelling its head off.

'What's all this?' I shouted above the uproar.

Minnie pointed an accusing finger at the intruder.

'It's Ern,' she shrieked. 'He's upset.'

This, I thought, was stating the obvious. The fellow was

149

grinding his teeth, and breathing heavily. His face was flushed and his fists clenched. I had never met Minnie's husband, but it hardly seemed the time to say: 'How do you do?'

'I must ask you to leave,' I began, with as much authority as I could muster. What if he started on me? I began to wish I had taken karate lessons at Caxley Technical College.

'This is school property, and Minnie is at her duties,' I went on.

He turned on me menacingly. 'You shut your mouth! She's been at her duties all right, and with that flamin' Bert of hers. She's coming home with me. I'll sort her out without your help.'

Surprisingly, I was not frightened. I suppose it was because I was so furious with this intrusion.

'Minnie will stay here until half past five,' I told him, standing my ground. 'I advise you to go home, or I shall send for the police at once. I won't have brawling in my school.'

He let out a string of interesting expletives, many of them new to me, but to my relief he made for the door.

'I'll be waiting for you,' he said ominously to the cowering Minnie, and then strode off.

The toddler was still emitting head-splitting yells, and I made for the sweet tin before coping with Minnie. A large pear drop successfully gagged the child, although it seemed a dangerous object to put into any child's mouth in the circumstances. However, better asphyxiation than pandemonium, I thought, setting an upturned bucket to rights.

'Now Minnie,' I said, 'sit down and tell me all about it.'

It appeared, from the disjointed account that the tearful Minnie embarked upon, that Bert, her old admirer, had been visiting her in Ern's absence.

'I don't get no fun,' wailed Minnie, wiping her moist nose on the back of her hand. I went again to the cupboard and supplied a handful of tissues.

Minnie looked at them wonderingly.

'Wipe your nose with them,' I directed. She obeyed in a sketchy fashion before continuing with her narration.

'Ern don't never take me out, nor give me enough to buy the kids food and that. He'd have the bit I earns here if he could find it.'

Here she gave a damp giggle, tugged at her neckline and bent down to display a couple of pound notes pinned inside a grubby vest with an enormous safety pin. It looked mightily uncomfortable, I thought, but at least it showed that Minnie had a certain resourceful cunning.

'Auntie told me to do it,' she went on, scratching her mop of red hair. I might have known it. Trust Mrs Pringle to be one jump ahead in any conflict, as I knew from experience.

'But, Minnie, you can't go on like this. He is your husband, after all, and he's bound to be – er – upset if you carry on with other men.'

She looked at me in amazement.

'It ain't other men, only Bert. And he don't come often. I mean, only when Ern's out.'

I gave up, and turned my attention to matters other than Minnie's marital affairs. 'The point is that I can't have this sort of thing going on in the school. What if the children had been here? Ern's language alone was –'

'He didn't say nothin' real bad. Not today, he didn't. He can say a lot worse'n that,' she added boastfully.

'Well, all I can say, Minnie, is finish your work here, and then come over to the school house before you go, and we must get something settled.'

I looked down the lane as I went home, and sure enough, Ern's van was still lurking a little farther down. To ring the police or not, I wondered?

Minnie arrived, toddler in tow, twenty minutes later, and I sat her down at the kitchen table with a restorative cup of tea. While she drank it, I washed the child's face and hands with a J-cloth which went straight into the dustbin. He was not a bad looking little boy under the grime.

' 'E's still there,' said Minnie.

'I know. I'll run you home.'

' 'E'll come after me.'

'Well, it is his home too.'

Minnie began to cry again.

'You must behave yourself, Minnie, and see it from Ern's point of view.'

We set off for Springbourne as soon as Minnie had composed herself. The van had vanished, and was not parked anywhere near Minnie's council house. The coast appeared clear.

'You'd better nip in quickly,' I said, opening the door. 'And

Minnie, start looking out for another job. I think we'd better get someone else to do the school next week.'

I wondered if the tears might flow again, but she gave me a mad grin instead.

'Bert knows a lady in Caxley who'd have me,' she said. 'Cleaning out a pub.'

I watched her enter her house, turned the car round and went thankfully home. I felt as though I had been engaged in a tough wrestling match which, come to think of it, I had.

May always seems to me to be the loveliest month of the year, but a sunny June runs it very close.

Fairacre, in high summer, takes a lot of beating. The early mornings were fresh and dewy, and I sometimes took the children for a walk as soon as the register was closed at nine-thirty.

According to the timetable we should be at our arithmetic lesson, but that could be done later when the sun was too hot to be out of doors, I told myself.

The hedgerows were at their most lush, the young leaves thick and green, with sprays of cascading wild roses, pink and fragile as shells.

The lambs were getting larger daily, but were still young enough to cavort about, butting each other and their patient mothers, and chasing up and down the fields, shaking their woolly heads, and bleating loudly.

There were birds everywhere. Bemused fledglings sat in the playground, lapwings fluttered in scores over Mr Roberts' fields, and rooks and pigeons were equally numerous as they foraged for their young. The bearded barley crop in the field near the school was beginning to bleach in the heat, and the heavy ears were bending over. There were dozens of varieties of silky grasses on the verges of Fairacre's lanes, and the nature table was adorned with them.

The swallow babies were now almost as big as their parents and made short flights from the telephone wire to the television aerial on the school house. Their bubbling chatter began at four o'clock in the morning, as I knew only too well.

The many tits seemed to have vanished, and were probably in the oak and hazel wood at the northern end of Fairacre feeding their broods on the dangling maggots which fed on the young oak leaves. No doubt they would be back, clamouring for peanut kernels, within a few weeks.

The robins too were scarce in this hot weather, although the children were delighted to see one particularly tame one perched on the upturned flower pot which held open the door. His folded wings were tipped up behind him, and he looked exactly like a man with his coat tails lifted, warming his back by the fire.

These summer nights were as lovely as the day. The moon rose each night, enormous and golden, and at its height it was almost bright enough to read a book.

There were strange movements in the garden, as hedgehogs snuffled and scuffled about. A stoat yapped, and an owl gave its eerie quavering cry. The shadows of the trees lay still and black across the silvered lawn, and moonlight glimmered on the school windows and the church roof. There was a lot to be said for being sleepless on such nights of beauty too rarely seen, and I relished them accordingly.

It was at times like these that I could forget the petty problems of the daily round. It was good to have the pinpricks of Mrs Pringle and Minnie put into perspective by the unchanging values of nature.

The Caxley Chronicle, our local paper, carried a report about a man who appeared in court on charges of indecent exposure. It sounded like Amy's 'Awful Man', and he had certainly visited

quite a number of villages in the neighbourhood, although he
had been arrested in Caxley itself, in one of the parks.

The Caxley magistrates were remanding him for three
weeks for psychiatric reports, I read. One day, no doubt, he
would end up in a hospital for the mentally disturbed, poor
fellow.

I felt guilty about forgetting to prepare myself with vegetable dye as instructed by Amy. However, I could now relax
presumably, and perhaps Amy would not cross-question me
further.

I folded the paper and went across to the school. This
morning there was a different feel about the early hours. The
sun was up, but seen through a light haze, and there was an
uncanny stillness about. Already it was oppressively hot, and
the open windows admitted no refreshing flow of air.

'Well, that's the end of summer,' said Mr Willet flatly, when
he arrived. 'Thunder before night, you mark my words. Good
thing really.'

'Why? We can't have too much sunshine, surely?'

'Seen them water-butts? Empty as egg shells. I see yours is
splitting already. I give mine a splash of water now and again
when old Ted Bates isn't on the prowl. Them slats shrink,
see, in the heat.'

'Do you mean to say, I shall lose all the rainwater, as soon as
it starts to pour?'

'Quite likely, I should say,' replied Mr Willet cheerfully.
'But on the other hand you might be lucky, and the cracks
close up when the wet gets to 'em. They say the devil looks
after his own.'

'Thanks,' I said tartly.

Mr Willet chuckled.

'Only my joke, Miss Read. You're a bit fazed with this
cleaner business, I don't doubt. But thank heavens that Minnie
Pringle finishes today. She's enough to set your teeth on edge,

and no better than she should be with them two fellows she leads on. You was right to sack her.'

I was too taken aback to comment on this, and while I was thinking, yet again, of how little I knew of bush telegraph, he made for the door.

'You might try Bella George,' he said, pausing with a gnarled finger on the latch. 'Her old man's changed shifts this week, and she's a rare hand with a floor cloth. That is, if that dratted Pringle kid has left us any.'

He gave me a wink and vanished.

Bella George! Why not try her?

Dear Mr Willet, I thought lovingly. Ever the teacher's friend!

14 Rain and Romance

AS always, Mr Willet was right about the weather.

By mid-morning the sky was overcast and the sultry heat was oppressive. There was a curious coppery colour on a bank of clouds to the west, and no bird sang. No breath of air stirred the leaves of flowers or trees. It was as if the earth waited for what might befall.

The first distant rumblings of thunder came as the children played after school dinner. Then it came nearer, and vicious lightning cracked the skies. I called the children in, just as the first spots of rain began to fall.

Within ten minutes there was a deluge. Raindrops spun like silver coins in the playground, and the chalky dust at the edge of the field was first pock-marked and then turned to silt within seconds.

Water gushed from the gutters and cascaded from the roofs. Little rivers pelted along the sides of the lane, and the church was hidden behind a curtain of silver drops.

The noise was tremendous and awe-inspiring. Thunder crashed and lightning flashed, and I could hear some wailing from the infants next door. My own class was scared, but silent, under the onslaught. I pitied anyone caught in the storm. One would be drenched to the skin in a matter of minutes.

It was very dark in the schoolroom and I switched on the electric light. There was an almighty crackle and all the lights went out, amidst groans of dismay from the children.

'Heads down,' I said, 'and have a nap.' Some hopes, I thought, in this pandemonium, but it was impossible to work anyway. They rested their heads on their desks, and I could only hope that next door's wailing was not catching.

As suddenly as it began the rain ceased. The thunder rumbled more distantly, the lightning became less vicious. I let the children stay as they were, and wondered if they had appreciated, as keenly as I had, the patter of the raindrops on summer leaves, and the steady plop-plop from a nearby gutter. The scent of wet earth was refreshing. It made one realise how desperately thirsty the plants and small animals must have been in the long drought.

Listening to the music of 'leaves drinking rain', as W. H. Davies put it, I remembered reading that the Chinese, in ancient times, planted large-leaved trees like the banana for the express purpose of hearing the pattering of rain upon them. The Chinese have always been wise enough to recognise that the minutiae of natural things can enrich life. We could learn a lot from them.

The rain continued steadily, and by the time school was over it was plain that Miss Briggs and I would have to do some ferrying home. Most of the children were clad in shorts and tee shirts, or thin cotton frocks, the light clothing they had worn for the last brilliant weeks.

A few mothers arrived, umbrellas up and children's mackintoshes over their arms. Their offspring were soon on their way.

Mr Roberts' Land Rover squelched to a halt by the gate, and he shouted an invitation to any children going near the Post Office. Half a dozen excitedly swarmed into his shelter.

Miss Briggs took two children squashed together beside her, and I was left with the Coggs' family.

Minnie Pringle arrived as they climbed into my car. She was pushing the battered pram. Its inmate looked dry enough, but

Minnie was running with water, and her red hair was in wet wisps on her forehead. Her grin though, was as fanatical as ever.

This was, with any luck, the last stint of work she would do at the school, and although I felt relief at the thought, my heart smote me.

'Minnie,' I shouted from the car, 'why don't you put your wet things in my kitchen and make yourself a cup of tea before you start?'

'Oh, lovely! Ta ever so!' enthused Minnie, turning the pram and making for the school house.

It was only when I was halfway to the Coggs' house that I began to wonder how much havoc Minnie could cause in making tea in my kitchen.

Mrs Coggs' back door opened directly into the kitchen, and I hustled the three children inside. At their mother's pressing invitation I went in too.

I have visited the house on several occasions, and always left it with relief, and yet a feeling of hopelessness. It must be the slummiest place in Fairacre, and the smell of unwashed clothes and dirty dishes can be appalling.

I cannot pretend that it was a vision of order and delight on the present occasion, but there was certainly an improvement. For one thing, there was no overpowering stench. There were only a couple of used saucepans on the draining board, and they had been filled with water and were soaking.

Most of the shabby chairs had newspapers or drying clothes spread on them, but the table was clear and even had a cloth on it. Mrs Coggs herself seemed considerably cleaner and happier. No doubt the last few weeks of sunshine had added a tan to her usually pale face, and improved her appearance, but to my mind she looked stronger altogether. Arthur's absence in prison had certainly improved his wife's health, and I suspected that kind Alice Willet's and Bella George's assistance had helped the family enormously.

At the thought of Bella George, I recalled Mr Willet's advice. Now that I was so close, I would call at once, I decided.

I said my farewells to the Coggs, and hurried to see Bella.

I found the lady in her kitchen busy rolling out pastry. She looked as cheerful as ever and invited me to sit down, as she washed her floury hands.

'No, I'll call another time,' I said. 'You are too busy now.'

But I was overborne.

'Pastry does better for standing a while,' said Bella. 'Can I help?'

'I do hope so,' I said sincerely, and told her of my difficulties.

She looked thoughtful, and my hopes rose.

'Well, I don't see why not,' she said at last. 'Jack's on this new shift for six weeks, which means he leaves here at two in the afternoon and sometimes doesn't get home at night. There's a couple of runs a week to East Anglia and he stays overnight there. I could do what Minnie's doing now easily, but I wouldn't want to face the early morning cleaning.'

I hastily explained that that could be left until the permanent cleaner was appointed.

I told her about wages and invited her to call in the next day or so to have a look at the work involved. If she kept Fairacre School even half as clean as her own immaculate establishment we should be jolly lucky, I thought.

'Any chance of Mrs Pringle coming back?' she asked, as we stood looking at the rain.

'Not yet, I think. She knows the job is hers if she wants it, but I think we shall have to rely on kind folk like you in the meantime.'

'She did say to me,' said Bella diffidently, 'as though she wasn't going back to the job at all.'

'Oh, did she?'

In that case, I thought, I should have to think again about a permanency. Maybe it was just the lady's way of rubbing salt into my wounds. Time alone would tell.

I ran through the rain to my car, and left Bella to cope with her pie-making.

As the car swished through the puddles, I felt a surge of relief at the thought of Bella taking over from dear demented Minnie.

I must break the news to her now, I decided, and then have a much-needed cup of tea. That is, if Minnie had left me a tea pot intact.

I put my foot down, and splashed home.

There was a thick white mist over the countryside the next day, but by noon it had cleared, and the sun shone again.

It was a blissful Saturday, and I was at leisure to enjoy the refreshed garden. The lawn, recently so drab, had turned green overnight. Raindrops still sparkled on the roses, and the soil steamed gently.

My water butts were brimming over, and I should have pleasure in telling Mr Willet that they were as watertight as ever when he came on Monday morning.

Minnie Pringle had accepted her wages and her notice with cheerful inconsequence, and was far more moved by my parting present of a jar of instant coffee. Amazingly, nothing had been damaged during my brief absence, and she had even spread out the teacloth to dry.

I had said goodbye to her with infinite relief, and watched her pushing the broken-down pram through the puddles in the lane, until the bend of the road hid her from sight, and I had returned indoors.

Over my supper of scrambled eggs I had pored over the

television programmes for the evening. I was offered a nice
half-hour or so of open heart surgery, in glorious technicol-
our, no doubt, an interview with survivors from a pit disaster,
a discussion by drug addicts about their problems, or another
on the subject of abortions.

'Well, Tibby,' I had said, putting aside the paper, 'I think
we'll play that old record of Jack Buchanan's, and get on with
the P. G. Wodehouse book from the library.'

All in all, we had a splendid evening.

Miriam Quinn called one evening after school to borrow a
book of knitting patterns which I had offered to lend her.

It was an ancient book of children's garments, and its
value to me was that each and every pattern was absolutely
simple and turned out exactly the right size – a rare virtue in
patterns.

'I thought I'd start now and knit Lovell's three a good
thick woolly apiece for next Christmas. You can do with
all the woollies available in that Norfolk vicarage,' said
Miriam.

She often spoke of Lovell, her brother, who had a living not
far from Norwich. The two were very devoted, and she was an
attentive and loving aunt to his three children.

While I was pointing out one or two of the patterns which I
had often used and found most effective, Amy's car drew up,
and she and Gerard Baker came in.

Miriam had met Amy before, and I was about to introduce
Gerard when I became conscious that they were eyeing each
other with somewhat perplexed interest.

'I think we know each other,' said Gerard. 'Surely I know
your brother Lovell?'

'Cambridge?' hazarded Miriam.

'Yes indeed, but I have come across him several times since
then. A cousin of mine lives in his parish.'

I felt it called for a celebratory drink and went to fetch the sherry while they investigated farther.

They were hard at it, recalling old memories, when I returned to the sitting room.

'I saw you first at a May Ball,' said Gerard. 'You wore a cream-coloured frock and had a camellia in your hair.'

'Good heavens!' cried Miriam. 'What an incredible memory you must have! I must confess I don't remember that occasion half as well as you do.'

'You were rather engrossed,' commented Gerard, 'with a young fellow called Martin Farrar, if I remember rightly.'

To my surprise, Miriam turned pink. I had never before seen her confused.

'Miriam is busy planning her Christmas presents already,' I said hastily, and passed the knitting book to Amy.

Outside, a blackbird scolded from a lilac bush. Tibby, no doubt, was being provocative. A light warm breeze ruffled the curtains, the air fragrant with all the scents of summer.

'Do children still wear knitted leggings?' asked Amy, studying a photograph in my ancient book. 'Or "winter bodices", as it says here?'

'Well, not in this weather,' said Gerard. 'Have you ever known a summer like it? Why, it must be warm even in Norfolk! If it stays like this we should get the outside shots of Aloysius's cottage done in two days. We start on Thursday, incidentally.'

'Come and have supper with us on Wednesday,' said Amy, 'and I hope you will come too,' she added, turning to Miriam.

'I should love to. Thank you very much.'

'Let's take our drinks into the garden,' I suggested. 'It's too good an evening to stay indoors.'

Amy drew me aside as Gerard and Miriam went to inspect my rose bed.

'Gerard seems remarkably animated and attentive,' she said,

somewhat severely. 'I had planned to let him partner you on Wednesday, but I must see if Horace is free.'

'Oh, Amy,' I cried impatiently, 'what does it matter? It's good to see them getting on so well, and being an extra woman won't worry me, I assure you.'

'I like the table *symmetrical*,' said Amy, 'but there it is. At least, James will be with us. He tries to be home these days, particularly when I'm entertaining.'

'Good,' I said. 'I could stay away, you know,' I offered nobly, 'if you really will worry about the table plan.'

'Rubbish!' said Amy. 'Of course you must come. No doubt Gerard will be himself again by then.'

There seemed little to comment upon after this remark, and after a few turns about the garden, Amy and Gerard made their farewells.

'Well,' exclaimed Miriam, when they had gone, 'what an extraordinary encounter! You know, I do remember him now. He was terribly kind to me on that occasion. I was horribly shy, and he took the trouble to look after me beautifully in the early part of the evening. Later, Martin turned up, and I fear I paid all my attention to him for the rest of the ball. Unforgivable really.'

She looked unhappily contrite.

'All young people are a bit heartless,' I comforted her. 'Here, don't forget the knitting book. You quite inspire me to start knitting for Christmas myself.'

I awoke suddenly that night to a windowful of stars. Their brilliance was unbelievable, as bright as in a clear October sky.

There was no moon to be seen, but for the first time in my life I saw the room lit with a soft light from the stars, and recalled the old skipping rhyme which the children still use:

Moonlight, starlight,
Boney won't come out tonight.

I wonder if they know who Boney was, I thought. Tomorrow
I must remember to tell them.

I climbed out of bed to survey the shadowy garden. Everything was hushed, not even a hedgehog stirred, and every leaf
was motionless. I stood enchanted for several minutes, thanking the stars above me for the delight of living in Fairacre, until
my feet grew chilly, I reminded myself that I must get up in
time for school, and so returned to bed, and an untroubled
sleep.

As is so often the case, I arrived first at Amy's, but did my
best not to sniff the air like the Bisto Kid Amy said I
resembled.

'I'm so glad I've got you to myself for a minute or two,' she
greeted me. 'The most incredible news! I rang Horace after

166

visiting you, and do you know what?'

'He's ill?'

'No, no! He sounded horribly robust.'

'Got a post abroad?'

'No again! Just let me tell you instead of making these wild guesses. I really am terribly upset, and on your account, I may say.'

I stayed obediently silent.

'D'you remember that secretary person, Eve Masters? He took her to that Save The Children do, I remember you telling me?'

'Of course I do.'

'Well, they are *engaged*!'

Amy suddenly became solicitous.

'Would you like to sit down? It must be a shock.'

'Not to me it isn't, Amy. But I expect it is to you. What about your table arrangements?'

'Don't give it another thought. And really you are so brave. I'm devastated. I mean, I always hoped that you and he –'

'I didn't,' I said, 'and frankly I'm delighted to hear the news. I take it they are already booked for this evening?'

'Her parents are coming down to meet him properly, and they've booked a table at The Green Man in Caxley. I only hope they don't choose duck. My helping was unalloyed rubber last time James took me there.'

She gave me a quick kiss.

'Sure you are all right? You look wonderfully calm. I would have been piping my eye in the circumstances.'

'You are not as flinty-hearted as I am, Amy,' I told her, as her other guests came to the door. 'Inveterate match-makers are bound to get their fingers burnt,' I added primly as she went to open the door, and then had a fit of laughter as the appalling pun hit me.

'My mother,' said Amy, 'would have said you've been sleeping in the knife drawer! Too sharp by half!'

Still chuckling, she opened the door to admit the rest of her party.

15   Summer's Bounty

THE golden weather continued. For week after week the sun had gilded all with glory, and it came as quite a shock to realise that July was upon us, and still the sun shone. Soon it would be end of term, with all that that involved for a schoolmistress, and soon our Miss Briggs would be married to Wayne, and I must look out my maps to find the best route for my ageing car to take to Leamington Spa for the happy occasion.

Already some of the cornfields looked ready for cutting, and scabious and knapweed were taking the place of the Queen Anne's lace, or cow parsley, which had frothed along the road verges. The heavy storm recently seemed to have accelerated the progress of natural growth, and I grieved to see a few early asters and dahlias in bud in some of the cottage gardens. I had no desire to end this blissful summer with an early autumn.

The children had never looked so bonny, tanned as they were with constant sunshine. This should set them up properly for next winter, I told myself. Colds and coughs should be cut to a minimum with all this intake of Vitamin D, or whatever it was, with which sunlight was stuffed. I too felt on top of the world, and relished wearing light clothing and shoes for such a length of time. Usually, one's cotton frocks see the light for a few days and are then returned to the cupboard, while warmer garments are thankfully donned again. This summer all was changed, and I almost believed Mr Willet when he told me that the summers of his boyhood were ever thus.

The first brood of swallows were already accomplished fliers, and now the parents were busy building a second nest. For some reason, the first one in the front porch was deemed unsuitable, and there was much chattering and twittering as they inspected other sites.

To my dismay, they chose to build their second nest on a horizontal bundle of draining rods, which were lodged on brackets near the roof in the back porch.

'Knock it down,' advised Mr Willet. 'You get your drains blocked, and you'll be scuppered. Shall I bash it down for you?'

'No, please! Not after all their hard work. We can't do that.'

'I could,' said Mr Willet sturdily. 'You're too soft by half. I suppose if you gets trouble with your dratted drains, I'll be the fool that pushes my rods up here on my bike to see to 'em.'

'It may not happen.'

'It'd better not! Well, if that's how you want it, let's leave the little perishers. And if I gets a hernia I hopes as how you'll visit me in hospital.'

But he smiled as he said it.

Within a day or two of Amy's party a van and a car duly arrived outside Tyler's Row.

Four men, and a great quantity of paraphernalia were unloaded, including miles and miles of cable, and a number of interesting lights on stands.

The inhabitants of Fairacre tended to pause by the gateway of the Hales' place, as they went ostensibly about their business of shopping, posting letters, or simply taking their daily constitutionals.

Speculation ran rife about the true nature of their activities.

'Mr Hale ain't having 'em anywhere indoors,' said Mr Willet. 'And I don't blame him. They look a proper lot of down and outs. Not a tie between 'em!'

'They do say they might need extras. Wouldn't it be lovely to be on the telly?' said his wife.

'Mr Hale wouldn't let them cut off a branch of his apple tree what was in the way of the cameras. He can be awkward, you know. Him being a schoolmaster, I suppose. Does seem to spoil your nature,' went on Mr Willet.

'Thanks,' I said.

Mr Willet appeared unmoved by my sarcasm.

'That chap Baker what takes an interest in Loyshus, he's about.'

'I know,' I said.

'Is he hanging his hat up to Miss Quinn, would you know?'

'Not that I know of,' I said frostily, inwardly marvelling, yet again, at the village's uncanny interest in other people's private lives.

'Well, I only asks because he's been at Holly Lodge once or twice. Lost his wife in an air crash, I'm told.'

'He and Miss Quinn knew each other years ago,' I admitted. 'He was at college with her brother.'

I always work on the principle that it is as well to let others know a limited amount. It keeps their minds occupied with the little that one is prepared to be known publicly. With any luck – a forlorn hope usually – the nub of the matter will remain hidden.

I pondered on this little snippet of information as I sat in the garden that evening. Mr Lamb, of the Post Office, had brought me a basket large enough to have been a baker's, and filled to the brim with gooseberries.

I set about topping and tailing them with my best nail scissors. They seemed to be the only sharp pair in the house.

It was very pleasant sitting there, with Tibby rolling about at my feet. A starling had taken up a most peculiar position at the far end of the lawn, either sunning itself, with wings outstretched, or engaged in that odd activity called 'anting'. I was too ignorant to know exactly.

There was a distant crackling from the vicar's bonfire next door, where he was busy burning hedge cuttings. Occasionally, a wisp of blue smoke drifted across my garden towards Mr Roberts' corn. I knew the vicar himself would be in charge of this operation. He has a horror of setting fire to things, and with everything tinder-dry it would have been easy to set alight not only the corn, but the brittle hedges and trees, and even a neighbour's thatch. We have seen these tragedies in Fairacre when other people, not as careful as Mr Partridge and Mr Roberts, have burnt their stubble when the wind has been high.

How on earth, I wondered, was I going to store all these gooseberries? I supposed that I could make some jam and jelly. Gooseberry jelly is delicious with cold meats of every sort. But there is a limit to the amount of such preserves that a lone spinster can get through.

I decided to bottle some and to freeze some, but there would still be a vast quantity left. Mrs Coggs sprang to mind. She should be presented with jam and some of the bottles. Home-made gooseberry jam should go down well with all those hungry mouths to feed, and if the fruit were bottled in a good syrup then Mrs Coggs' desserts would need the minimum of cooking attention. The only difficulty would be smuggling it to Mrs Coggs without Mr Lamb knowing.

Thus settled, I turned my mind again to Mr Willet's speculation. Would Miriam ever consider giving up her happy solitude at Holly Lodge? Certainly, she seemed very animated in Gerard's company, and Amy herself had remarked on her vivacity and Gerard's attentiveness. Mind you, I reminded myself, Amy was no fair judge of the situation, biased as she was towards my own single state which she was constantly hoping to rectify. The behaviour of poor Horace Umbleditch, who had rushed into an engagement with the school secretary, had much offended Amy, who had ear-marked him for me.

As I had pointed out gently, Horace was now approaching forty, and presumably knew what he was doing. Personally, I wished him well, and the little I had seen of Eve Masters pleased me. They should make a success of marriage.

Somehow I could not imagine Miriam taking Gerard seriously. She seemed dedicated to her career, worked harder than anyone else I knew, and relished her little abode behind the holly hedge. Irene and David Mawne were ideal landlords, ready to help if need be, but respecting Miriam's strong desire for privacy.

No, on the whole, I decided, as I snipped the last top and tail and shook the fruit level in the basket, Miriam would remain as she was. She liked her own company as dearly as I did.

I staggered into the house and put the basket on the cool bricks of the larder floor. Tomorrow would be time enough to tackle them.

There was a knock at the back door. There, on the doorstep, stood Mrs Pringle. She was carrying a basket in each hand.

They contained gooseberries.

'Come in, come in,' I invited, trying to look enthusiastic about the gifts she was bearing.

The lady smiled graciously and stepped in, putting the baskets on the kitchen table. I must be careful, I thought, not to open the larder door in her presence.

'I knows you likes a few gooseberries,' said Mrs Pringle. 'And it seems to have been a bumper crop this year.'

'It does indeed,' I agreed. 'Now come and sit down, to rest your leg, and tell me how things are going.'

Mrs Pringle seemed in a remarkably amiable mood, and I wondered if, by any chance, she had made up her mind to return.

Much as I wanted it, I refused to ask her outright. Let her make the running, I thought.

We spoke of things in general, skirting the main topic which was in our minds. That dear old standby, the weather, occupied our polite exchanges for a few minutes, while I was conscious of Mrs Pringle's beady gaze upon the furniture which was normally in her care, and which, I guessed, she hoped to see in an advanced state of dilapidation.

'And how are things at your end of the village?' I enquired.

'Well, now, I expect you know as much as I do, but let's see. Mr Mawne seems to be more settled now his wife's back. To my mind, he's a man who needs a woman to keep him company, but then what man don't?'

I took this to be a rhetorical question, and refrained from comment.

'Same as that Wayne,' went on Mrs Pringle, leaping from her end of the village to mine. 'He's proper soppy about his Miss Briggs. It's *love*, you see. Makes the world go round, as they say.'

A look of maudlin sympathy appeared on Mrs Pringle's face. I was too taken aback by this rare display of tenderness to respond.

'I take it you'll be going to the wedding?'

'Yes, I am,' I managed to reply.

'I loves a wedding myself. No matter if it's doomed from the start, I still enjoy it, though I don't hold with these pregnant girls wearing white. Minnie did, you know. I told her it was a scandal, but she would have it so.'

'How is Mrs Coggs?' I asked, anxious to steer the subject to safer ground.

'Doing nicely without Arthur. Though she's been to see him, of course.'

This was news to me.

'Yes, Mr Partridge has been up there twice, and taken her

with him. She don't say much about how Arthur is, but after all, she must feel sorry for him, and she must love him to stick by him all these years.'

Privately, I thought that poor Mrs Coggs had little alternative but to stay with her unsatisfactory husband with the tribe of children she had depending on her, but such astringent comment would have passed over Mrs Pringle's head in her present romantic mood.

And how typical of our good-hearted vicar to visit one of his most notorious back-sliders in prison! He put us to shame with his practical Christianity.

'I see that nice Mr Baker is helping the telly men,' went on Mrs Pringle. Ah, I thought! Are we now approaching the heart of the matter? Will Miriam Quinn's name crop up?

It did.

'I do hear as how he used to know Miss Quinn years ago.'

'That's right,' I agreed.

'Well, they seem to enjoy each other's company. My cousin in Caxley saw them in The Green Man one evening.'

'Really?' I said coldly.

'My cousin is barmaid there, and having a terrible time trying to slim. She's a convulsive eater, the doctor says, and with all them peanuts and crisps laying about it's a rare temptation.'

Was Mrs Pringle skating away from thin ice, I wondered? She was getting no more information from me, I vowed secretly.

'Well, there it is,' said the lady, rising majestically. 'It's the same for high and low, isn't it? Mrs Coggs, Mr Mawne, Miss Briggs and Miss Quinn, all Touched by Love, as you might say.'

I followed her into the kitchen. There was no trace of a limp, I noticed.

'Let me empty your baskets,' I said, lifting out the bowl from the sink to take her largesse.

I accompanied her across the playground to the school gate. She glanced across at the school porch.

'I take it Bella is still doing her best?'

'Yes indeed. She's doing a splendid job.'

A slightly malevolent expression crept over my old adversary's face. It gave me a feeling of relief. This was the Mrs Pringle I knew!

I walked a few yards down the lane with her. The sun still shone, and there was dust at the side of the road. Pink and white striped bindweed crept along the dusty verge, as pretty as marshmallows.

'Well, thank you again,' I said warmly. 'I shall enjoy those lovely gooseberries.'

Should I ask her outright if she proposed to return? It was on the tip of my tongue to do so, but something held me back.

Pride perhaps? Or the remembrance of that wise old adage: 'Least said, soonest mended'?

We said goodbye, and each went on her way.

While I was marking the register the next morning, there came a knock at the door, and a young man put his head round.

'I wondered if we could take a shot or two of the outside of your building?'

He had a winning manner and seemed clean enough, although Mr Willet was quite right about his lack of a tie.

Memories of the tale of the person whose carpets had suffered from five hours of programme-making assailed me.

'When do you want to come?'

'Say three o'clock?'

'That would be convenient.'

He came farther into the room. The children stood up politely, and I nodded to them.

'Good morning, sir,' they chorused.

'Oh, ah! Good morning to you too.'

He seemed somewhat startled by this everyday civility. Perhaps he was not used to being called 'Sir'. Probably just Nigel or Basil, I imagined.

'This might make rather an interesting sequence,' he said, gazing round appreciatively. 'I believe Aloysius sat at one of these desks.'

'Hardly,' I said. 'They were new in the fifties.'

'I suppose we could make a mock-up of an earlier desk,' he went on dreamily.

'I'm afraid it would be most inconvenient for you to film in here,' I said firmly. 'And anyway, I'm sure my governors would not want the children's work to be interrupted.'

'I could have a word with them,' he offered.

'I wouldn't dream of troubling you. By all means film

outside, but this interior is so much altered since Aloysius's time –'

I broke off.

'By the way,' I added. 'What was Aloysius's surname? I've never heard him called anything but Loyshus in Fairacre.'

He began to laugh. He was quite a nice young man, I thought, even if he did not wear a tie.

'Stone! Loyshus Stone! How's that?'

'First-class,' I said, as he waved goodbye.

The children, of course, were wildly excited at the thought of 'being on the telly', although I did my best to explain that their presence would be unwelcome.

'Your clothes would be all wrong, for one thing,' I pointed out.

'We could dress up.'

'We've got them things –'

' "Those things".'

'That's right. Them things as we had for that show we done when us was a hundred.'

I gave up trying to correct this last sentence, forbade further discussion, and threatened them with no-story-this-afternoon if they continued to waste time.

The day wore on. The sun blazed away, and obviously the school would look splendid in this wonderful light when the cameras began to turn.

Three o'clock came and went. Apart from some chirruping from a few sparrows, and a ring dove rippling throatily from the school roof, all was quiet as the grave.

Nothing happened throughout the reading of *Treasure Island*, although I sensed that the children were alert for the sound of approaching vehicles.

At a quarter to four we said grace, wished each other 'Good afternoon', and I accompanied my flock to the school gate.

'And don't loiter,' I adjured them. 'Go straight home. I expect the filming will happen tomorrow.'

They went off reluctantly. They were bitterly disappointed, poor things.

At a quarter past six, four young men arrived, including Nigel – or possibly, Basil – and they began to wander about the playground, discussing the best vantage points.

I carried out a pot of tea, four mugs, milk, sugar and biscuits and left them to it.

I must say they were extremely grateful for their sustenance, and all the biscuits had been eaten when I went to fetch the tray an hour later.

I spent the evening making jam and bottling the first lot of gooseberries. Whilst waiting for the bottles to get done, I began to tackle Mrs Pringle's offering with my hard-pressed nail scissors.

It was while I was so engaged that Amy arrived.

'Heavens, I'm so glad to see you!' I cried. 'I'm awash with gooseberries.'

I ushered her into the kitchen. Eight pots of ruby red jam gleamed from the draining board. A rich fruity smell emanated from the oven.

'Lucky you!' said Amy. 'It smells marvellous in here.'

She gazed with wonder at the bowl awaiting my nail scissors' attention.

'Do you want some?' I asked. 'Please say you do. I'm getting to loathe the sight of a goosegog.'

'Can you really spare a few? I adore them. I like all the nice cheap fruits like rhubarb and gooseberries that other people look down on. I think they are blissful.'

I began to tip a few pounds of Mrs Pringle's gooseberries into a bag, expressing my pleasure and relief at the same time.

'Seen anything of Gerard?' asked Amy when at last we were resting in the sitting room.

'No. Well, I can't say I expected to. He's probably busy.'

'He's not too busy to visit Fairacre daily,' said Amy, somewhat severely. 'It's my belief he calls to see Miriam each evening. He only seems to use our house to sleep in.'

'He probably doesn't want to take up your time,' I said.

Amy blew three perfect smoke rings, one of her many accomplishments.

'That's as maybe,' she said eventually. 'Personally, I think that Miriam is a charming girl, and far too good for Gerard. You would have been much more suitable.'

'How do I take that?'

'You know what I mean. You have quite a lot in common with dear Gerard. Now Miriam would find a lot of things about him which she would want altered. I know James had some tiresome ways when I first knew him.'

'And is he now a reformed character?'

'I hope not. Despite the few tiresome ways just mentioned, I liked him as he was. And still do.'

'That's good. I think James is a dear. I should have snapped him up myself, if you hadn't got in first.'

Amy looked gratified.

'Yes, I'm glad I did get in first, taking it all in all. You know, it amazes me how many women think that if they marry a man they will be able to mould him to their own requirements.'

'Do they think that?'

'Indeed they do! The times I've heard a girl say: "He'll be different when he's married"! It's not only colossal cheek, I think, but such a ghastly waste of time. After all, if you don't like a man as he is, then why marry him?'

A sizzling sound from the kitchen ended our conversation. I was about to tell Amy of Mrs Pringle's sudden absorption in love, but bottled gooseberries came first.

I saw her to the car, and helped to prop the bag of gooseberries safely.

'A thousand thanks for them, my sweet,' she said, as she let in the clutch.

I returned to my fragrant kitchen. There were still gooseberries waiting in a bowl to be topped and tailed. Six bottles were now standing beside the jam jars.

The telephone rang. Mrs Mawne was at the other end. Could I do with some gooseberries? They had a bumper crop this year.

I expressed my gratitude, but explained that I really had rather more than I could cope with at the moment.

In more ways than one, I thought, when I replaced the receiver, what with end of term, Miss Briggs' wedding, Mrs Pringle's continued absence from duty, television crews and tales of Gerard into the bargain.

Too tired to cook a proper supper, I spread a hunk of bread with still-warm gooseberry jam, and washed it down with a glass of milk.

I must say, it was jolly good.

16   Sunshine and Sports

DURING the last week of term I drove to Beech Green
to have tea with Miss Clare.

Despite the brilliant light and scorching heat outside, the interior of the little cottage, which would one day be
my own – to my everlasting amazement – was dim and cool.
Thatch is a wonderful insulator, and despite its drawbacks of
attracting birds to nest in it and needing a good deal of skilled
maintenance, it is good to see this natural roofing blending so
beautifully into the countryside.

Her garden was as trim as ever. The borders on each side
of the brick path were bright with pansies, pinks and early
asters.

The vegetable plot was a miracle of tidiness. Miss Clare was
now past gardening herself, but a young neighbour with a
growing family was glad to have the garden, and kept Miss
Clare supplied in return for her generosity. Thus everyone was
pleased.

'He's almost as good as Mr Willet,' I said, surveying the
rows of shallots ready for lifting, the swelling bronze onions,
the peas thick on the sticks. The tops of the pea sticks, I
noticed, were all cut neatly to the same level. It all looked most
efficient.

'He was always a tidy boy,' said Dolly Clare indulgently,
when I commented on his handiwork. 'He was at Fairacre just
before your time. Very neat with his hands, and could use a
ruler even as an infant.'

I rubbed a leaf of sun-warmed mint between my fingers, and inhaled the sharp scent.

'The only trouble is we are short of parsley,' went on Dolly. 'But you know what they say. It goes seven times to the devil before it germinates. I'm afraid ours never came back at all this year.'

I promised to bring her a root of mine, and we went indoors to put on the kettle.

The round table in the window had already been set. The best china, sprigged with violets, the silver teaspoons, thin with age, and bread and butter cut wafer-thin awaited us, with a splendid sponge cake of Miss Clare's own making.

One always sat up to table at Dolly's house. Only the odd cup of coffee was partaken of in an armchair, and even when she was alone the mistress of the house set the solitary place and dined, as if she had friends present, with simple dignity.

I spread some of our vicar's honey on my bread and butter,

and thought how marvellous it was that Dolly Clare, despite her age and physical frailty, had never lowered her standards. My own casual meal arrangements seemed positively slatternly in comparison.

I said as much to Dolly. She looked somewhat surprised.

'I suppose early training has something to do with it,' she said. 'My mother was a stickler for having things just so. And then, when you are as old as I am, you wonder if you might be taken suddenly, and it would be so dreadful if you were found in squalor, wouldn't it?'

'I hadn't thought of that.'

'You see, I now look upon each day as a bonus. When I wake in the morning I think how lucky I am to have yet another day to spend.'

'Even if your arthritis is painful?'

'Even then.' Dolly laughed. 'After all, some part of one's body must play up when one is over eighty. I'm luckier than some, and I still love living.'

When we had washed up, we took a turn along the field track which borders Hundred Acre Field behind Dolly's house.

The blackberry flowers were thick in the hedges, and great creamy plates of elderflowers still nodded on the northern side of the hedge.

'I tie a head in a muslin bag,' said Dolly, 'and steep it in my gooseberry jelly. It gives the most marvellous tang to it.'

I told her about my gooseberries, and my own less elegant means of coping with them.

'And look at my hands,' I said, holding out my stained fingers.

Dolly held out her own fragile hands, and I was surprised to see that they were even more stained than my own.

'Broad beans, and then blackcurrants,' she said, surveying them calmly. 'I know one should wear gloves, but the feel of fresh young things is so pleasant that I would sooner have stained fingers. It's a small price to pay for pleasure.'

I drove home feeling all the better for an hour or two of Dolly's company. In a feverish world she is like a cool drink.

The birds were still foraging although dusk was beginning to fall, and I narrowly missed a cock pheasant, gleaming bronze in the westering sunlight, as he strolled haughtily across the lane.

The sheep had been sheared recently and they looked almost like white goats moving leisurely across the meadows. All creatures, it seemed, were flourishing in this glorious summer, and I felt lucky to count myself among them.

It had not dawned on me, until I had the wretched things, how remarkably elusive a pair of spectacles can be. If I am at school the children help me to locate them with an eager chorus of:

'On the piano, miss!'

'On the window sill, miss!'

'You're still wearing 'em, miss!' This last, of course, accompanied by much hilarity.

But in the house, it is not so easy. If I am downstairs I have left the things upstairs, and vice versa. I reckon that I take far more exercise these days simply tracking down my glasses.

Gradually, I am learning to look first by the telephone, where I need them for studying the small print of the book, then by my fireside book shelf, and thirdly by any newspaper lying about.

What happens when advancing age compels me to have two pairs, one for reading and one for long distance, is too horrific to contemplate, and bifocals, so Mrs Pringle told me once, send one headlong down any flight of stairs.

I think I shall have to get a fetching chain affair to lash them to my person, like the spectacled half of Hinge and Bracket.

The television crew remained in the village for three days, and were soon accepted as a welcome addition to Fairacre's amenities.

Peter Hale, who had evidently been very much on his guard when first approached, now seemed quite sorry that the excitement was over, and that the van and car had gone for good.

I met him on one of my evening strolls.

'D'you know, I was at school with the father of one of those chaps? The oldest one incidentally. Makes you realise your age.'

'I'm constantly meeting old pupils in Caxley,' I told him, 'and I am not only incapable of remembering their names, but also if they left three or thirteen years ago.'

'Well, that's some comfort. It was quite interesting to watch them at work. One wonders, of course, if it really takes half a day to take a few shots, and I'm jolly glad they decided against coming indoors.'

I told him that I too had banned interior filming.

'They are making a set, I gather, of a Victorian schoolroom, all hanging oil lamps and slates, and the cane well in evidence.'

'When is it going to be shown?'

'Sometime next month. They said they would let me know. I'll give you a ring as soon as I know anything.'

'Many thanks. I'm looking forward to seeing Aloysius Lloyd.'

'Was that his surname? First I knew of it! By the way, are you all right for gooseberries?'

I assured him that I was, and added: 'It seems to have been a bumper crop this year.'

After all, if I had not said it, then he would have done.

The highlight of the summer term at Fairacre School is our Sports Day. Mr Roberts, the farmer, lets us have one of his meadows for the occasion, and obligingly turns out sheep or cattle, a day or two beforehand, so that Mr Willet can rope off the course from the spectators.

It is also Mr Willet's unenviable task to clear the course of the more obvious of the cow pats, and to flatten any molehills. In this job he has the enthusiastic support of three or four of the bigger boys. I have no difficulty in maintaining order in the classroom as Sports Day approaches. The hope of being chosen as one of Mr Willet's course-clearing team makes for a very well-behaved class.

Normally, we study the barometer and listen anxiously to the weather men as Sports Day approaches. The final word, of course, is Mr Willet's, who knows all the local signs of a change. But this year, with weeks of 'Set Fair' and even 'Very Dry' on our barometers we hardly bothered to consult even Mr Willet.

'Might get a bit of wet in a day or two,' he volunteered on the morning of the day, 'but it should hold up for this afternoon.'

'It all looks splendid,' I told him, surveying the course before school began. The grass was still dewy, the sky cloudless. The meadow had been cut for hay a few weeks earlier, and presented a trim face to the world.

'Had a mort of trouble knocking in them posts though,' observed Mr Willet. 'Never known the ground so hard. Better tell the kids to pick their feet up or we'll have some good ol' banged knees.'

Excitement ran high during the morning, and it seemed prudent to let off some of their suppressed steam with number games, and oral work rather than risk bodged pages of written exercises. As always, on these occasions, the girls were much calmer than the boys. The latter seem to have a much stronger competitive spirit which shows itself in tiresome boasting about their physical prowess.

'Look at my muscles then!' bragged Eric, flexing his arm to his neighbour.

'No bigger'n a sparrow's kneecap,' responded Ernest.

During playtime there was a good deal of sprinting from one end of the playground to the other, and some perilous jumping over skipping ropes obligingly held by the girls. I turned a blind eye to these activities, only warning the infants of tender years, to keep out of the way.

Miss Briggs had thrown herself whole-heartedly into preparations for the day, and had organised most of the timetable, including a mothers' race and a hideously difficult obstacle race for any fathers who were courageous enough to attempt it. As well as a pegged-down tarpaulin, kindly loaned by Mr Roberts, under which one had to wriggle, there were the usual hoops to negotiate, ropes to leap, and a stretch of grass to be covered by means of stepping on flower pots manhandled in a bent-double position. The children were tackling the course themselves, but at half the size and twice as agile they certainly had the edge on their fathers.

Several parents had been coerced into being judges, and keeping the scores of each child. I had been responsible for buying innumerable bars of chocolate, and making badges from cardboard embellished with gold stars. It made a change from making gooseberry jam on recent evenings.

The dinner lady brought us sliced cold ham, jacket potatoes and some salad, for our first course, and a sloshy dish, which she told us was trifle, for dessert. Her offerings were greeted with general approval.

'That's just right for today,' Patrick said graciously. 'Us don't want no stodge and that. Slows you down, stodge does.'

One or two hardy boys professed to despise food altogether

just before racing, but I noticed that they ate as heartily as the rest when it was time to serve out.

At two o'clock we were all out in the sunshine. Chairs had been arranged for the elderly on one side of the course, but most of the mothers, and a sprinkling of fathers who were not at work, sprawled on the grass looking after the many toddlers.

Miss Briggs and I had decided that the first few races should be the straightforward hundred yards (we don't bother with metres at Fairacre) for boys and girls, divided into three age groups. Then came the girls' skipping races, and after that the infants had their turns.

Apart from one of the infants running the wrong way, and Patrick taking a tumble over a tough tussock of grass, and wrenching his ankle, all went beautifully.

Linda Moffat's mother, in charge of the score sheet, was kept busy with a stream of breathless children arriving at her table clutching red, blue or yellow cards for first, second and third places. I had the fairly easy job of being judge for first place in each race, and two brave mothers coped with being judges of second and third positions.

The obstacle race proved to be the most exciting, and the frenzied shouts of the children spurring on the contestants were deafening. Even the cows in the next field came to look over the hedge at the goings-on in their former grazing ground.

Mr Lamb's collie dog had escaped from the Post Office garden and romped energetically among spectators and competitors, licking the children's faces as they emerged from under the tarpaulin, and greeting all with great enthusiasm. It would not have done at the Olympic Games but at Fairacre it adds to the enjoyment.

In the midst of this hubbub, I was surprised to see Mrs Pringle sailing majestically across the grass, wearing her best navy-blue straw hat decorated with a white duck's wing. Obviously, this was an occasion, and I felt very flattered that she had honoured us with the hat, as well as her presence.

She took a seat on the end chair, and raised a hand in greeting to one or two neighbours. Hard on her heels came Mrs Coggs, the ancient pram making heavy weather of the uneven meadowland.

I was particularly glad that she had arrived in time to see Joseph's age group tackling the obstacle race. He gave her a dazzling smile as he lined up, and whether it was his mother's presence, or simply his own skinny agility, which turned the scale in his favour, no one could say, but he won by several yards and the spectators applauded his success.

The mothers' race was a decorous affair, a straight sprint down the hundred yards. The younger ones took off their shoes, but older ones, like Mrs Moffat, who abandoned her duties to me for this race, rattled along creditably in high heels, and she it was who came in second, yielding first place to Patrick's mother.

I went over to talk to Mrs Pringle when Mrs Moffat returned, flushed and triumphant, to her table.

'I'm glad you could come,' I said, taking the next chair.

'Well, it was a nice afternoon,' said she grudgingly. 'And I guessed I could sit down after my walk.'

'You should have entered the last race,' I told her mischievously.

'The mothers' race? I was a mother too long ago for that lark,' she replied, and who was I to gainsay it?

And now the highlight of the afternoon occurred when seven brave fathers toed the line. Privately, I backed a newcomer to the village, one George Fuller, father of a blonde daughter in Miss Briggs' care. He was slim and lively, and looked a certain winner.

Ernest's father, all of fifteen stone, I reckoned to be out of the race before the whistle blew, and the other five were fairly run-of-the-mill in weight and athleticism.

Mr Fuller justified my hopes by reaching the hoops first and sliding through them at speed. He also leapt the ropes with the aplomb of a hurdler, and was first to emerge from the confines of the tarpaulin. He was greeted rapturously by Mr Lamb's dog, and the cheers of the spectators.

Now came the flower pot problem, and to my dismay it was quite apparent that balancing with one foot on a flower pot whilst transferring the other by hand a yard or so ahead, was a skill which this young father had never attempted. If he fell off, and he did, he was in honour bound to start the flower pot bit again.

It was here that Ernest's father came into his own. His

struggles under the tarpaulin had been heroic, and the spectators were convulsed with laughter, even Mrs Pringle managing a smirk. Only one father was behind him. The rest had progressed to Mr Fuller's stage of the proceedings.

But despite his girth, Ernest's father had the uncanny sense of balance which so often makes large people excellent dancers. He fairly nipped along with his two flower pots, overtaking all the others, and almost colliding with the hapless Mr Fuller who was returning, yet again, to base.

He won by yards, and Ernest rushed to greet him by throwing his arms round his father's impressive waist, and jumping all over the poor man's feet.

He received the loudest clap of all when he came to receive his chocolate bar.

'He deserved that,' said Mrs Pringle.

And we all agreed.

By the time we had returned the chairs to the school, cleared away the remains of the biscuits and lemonade kindly provided by the Parent-Teacher Association, and carried the ropes, hoops, balls and so on to their rightful places, we were all pretty tired. The bigger boys folded Mr Roberts' tarpaulin with much shouting and falling over, but at length it was done, and dragged into the shelter of the school lobby.

'What about them posts?' enquired one.

'Leave them for Mr Willet,' I replied. 'He will see to them tomorrow.'

The parents drifted away, children darting around them, still glorying in their recent triumphs.

Miss Briggs refused a cup of tea in the schoolhouse, saying that she was meeting Wayne to choose the bedroom carpet.

And so I had my own cup with only Tibby for company, and very peaceful it was after the clamour of the afternoon.

Later that night, I was awoken by the pattering of rain. Mr Willet had been right as usual, and we had got through Sports Day by the skin of our teeth.

17 Off to the Wedding

IT was still raining when I dressed the next morning. It was not the violent torrential downpour which the earlier thunderstorm had brought, but a gentle steady pattering on dry earth and thirsty plants.

The air was mild. It was the sort of day the Irish call 'soft', and it described it well. The downs were veiled in mist, and no doubt the valley of the river Cax, not far from Fairacre, would be just as misty.

It seemed strange to see the children arriving in mackintoshes or carrying umbrellas. For weeks the lobby pegs had held only a cardigan or two, or a floppy sun hat. Now raindrops spattered the floor from the dripping mackintoshes and, true to form, the skylight, so recently renovated, let through an occasional spot of rain near my desk top.

This change in the weather seemed to affect the children in a rather peculiar way. I should have thought that cooler conditions would have enlivened them after the oppressive heat, but the reverse happened. Possibly they were physically tired after yesterday's efforts on the sports' field. There was a good deal of yawning, and a number of children complained of feeling cold. Those that had woolly jackets in the lobby were sent to get them, and to warm and wake the rest we did a few brisk exercises. I cannot pretend that these efforts wrought much change, but at least they were galvanised into taking out their arithmetic books and attempting some work in a desultory fashion.

At playtime I compared notes with Miss Briggs as we sipped

our coffee. Her class too was remarkably soporific and three of the infants had actually fallen asleep.

'I think this place is damp,' opined Miss Briggs.

'It's been that way for over a hundred years,' I told her, 'and unless the stoves are alight, or there is a nice long spell of heat, such as we've been enjoying, the school never really dries out.'

'Time we had a new one,' said Miss Briggs. 'Wayne says this one ought to be pulled down. I'm sure he could build a much better one – and with a proper damp course too.'

'I'm sure he could,' I agreed. 'But with the nation's economy as it is, I can't see our local authority giving him the chance.'

As well as finding the cash, there is another difficulty which is ever present in my mind at Fairacre School. Our numbers have been perilously low for years, and I cannot help thinking that, before long, our little school will go the way of so many more in the country.

It has always been a worry to me. I hate to see these rural schools closing, and yet what is the practical decision?

Parents do not want to see their five-year-olds carted off by bus for a long day some distance from home. Those who attended the school in their own youth are often fiercely loyal, and want it to stay open.

On the other hand, when numbers get into the twenties, or even lower, are the children getting the competition and stimulus they need? The battle continues.

For my own part, the obvious difficulty, in my first few years at the school, was the fact that my school house would be taken from me when the whole property was put on the market. I had no doubt that I should be leniently dealt with, and probably would be offered first refusal, but it was a problem nevertheless. Now, thanks to Dolly Clare's over-whelming generosity, I need not fear the future, but not many school teachers, in the same position, have such comfort.

'Ah well!' said Miss Briggs collecting our coffee cups. 'Only one more week, and it's end of term.'

It was a cheerful thought.

One evening, during the last week of term, Bella George came over to my house after finishing her stint in the school.

The air was still cool. The really hot sunshine seemed to have deserted us, but I hoped that it was only for a few days. We sat indoors, and Tibby, unusually demonstrative, climbed on her lap and settled down, purring loudly.

'You're honoured,' I told her.

'Well, I'm not all that fond of cats actually, and I think they know, so they come and try their luck. Contrary animals, aren't they?'

I agreed.

'The thing is,' went on Bella, stroking the cat, 'Jack's shift's changing again next month, and I can't see how I can keep on with the cleaning indefinitely.'

'We've been lucky to have you for so long,' I replied. 'You've been a tower of strength. How long can you stay?'

'Oh, I'll certainly put the place tidy at the end of term, and if need be, I could come in the day before term starts in September, just to see things are all ship-shape, but I can't do more than that. I'm sorry. I've really enjoyed the work.'

'You've saved our bacon, Bella,' I told her. 'We were really in a desperate plight. I can see I shall have to get in touch with Mrs Pringle and let her know how things stand.'

Bella looked embarrassed.

'I don't know if I should say anything, but she still says she's not going to come back at all. Do you think she's just stringing you along?'

'I wouldn't put it past her. The last she told me was that she intended to come back eventually. When, I don't know, which is why I shall have to advertise the post in order to have someone here regularly for next term.'

'Shall I let her know you are going to do that?'

I thought for a minute. Mrs Pringle had certainly got us over a barrel, and knew it too. On the other hand, I genuinely hoped that she might return. Better the knave you know, than the devil you don't.

'Leave it for the moment,' I said at last. 'I shan't be drafting an advertisement until after we've broken up, and she may have come forward by then. What a problem it is!'

I accompanied Bella to the gate and watched her wobble away down the lane on her bicycle. She had served us nobly in our time of stress. I only hoped that Mrs Pringle would see fit to take up her duties again with the same dedication.

On the last day of term we had a little ceremony to present Miss Briggs with her wedding gifts and to wish her well.

The vicar represented the governors of the school and made a graceful speech, brief and to the point, and the children tried not to fidget as they impatiently awaited the unwrapping of presents.

Miss Briggs, flushed with excitement at being at the centre of the scene, looked almost pretty. She made a grateful speech to the vicar, and then set about undoing the largest parcel which was from the children.

I had shown them the tray secretly beforehand, and received their commendations. It was an oval one, with splendid gilt handles, and a garland of wild flowers painted on it. The children approved my choice, and now we awaited Miss Briggs' reaction.

It was altogether satisfactory. Her delight seemed genuine, and she thanked the children warmly. They sat, beaming and smug, exchanging congratulatory glances. Weren't they clever, they seemed to say?

The governors had given her a pretty little travelling clock which folded into a scarlet case, and I had put my gift of a Coalport flower vase with the other presents to swell the pile.

The girl seemed absolutely delighted with everything, and when the youngest infant staggered from the lobby with a bouquet almost as big as himself, she was speechless with pleasure.

After more congratulations from everyone, the vicar said grace, exhorted the children to behave well during the holidays, to help their mothers, and to remember to come back on the third of September.

He then shook hands with Miss Briggs and with me, and departed. Within five minutes the school room was empty, except for Miss Briggs and myself.

The girl was busy rewrapping her presents, and when she looked up I was surprised to see that she was very near to tears.

'It all went beautifully,' I said. 'You gave the children no end of pleasure with such a nice little speech of thanks.'

'Not as much pleasure as they've given me,' she responded shakily. 'And you too. It's a wonderful school. I've been so lucky.'

She blew her nose energetically, and I bent down tactfully to lock up the cupboards.

'See you at the wedding,' she said, collecting her parcels. 'I'll give you a ring before then.'

She still looked Mr Willet's 'fair old lump of a girl', I thought, watching her make her way to the car, laden with her bounty, but a very nice one at that.

There was a full week before I needed to set off for the wedding, and I employed it by doing some shopping, which included a magnificent hat to wear with my wedding ensemble, and various other less glamorous items such as grease-proof paper, jampot covers, a new milk saucepan and a new doormat.

The swallows had not improved the latter, and as it had given me many years of service I thought it would be prudent to throw it out at last.

I also brought back from Caxley some patterns of curtaining, wondering if I might get round to choosing something suitable to replace the present shabby curtains in the sitting room.

When I worked out how many yards I should need and how much they would cost me, even without paying for the making up, pelmets, fringe, lining, tape and so on, my heart began to sink. Perhaps it would be wiser to wait until I had returned from my holiday?

A cousin of mine, recently widowed, had begged me to accompany her for a week in Guernsey in August, and to this I had agreed. We rarely met, as she had married a farmer in Cumbria and been much engaged in bringing up a family of boys, but she sounded so pathetic on the telephone, when she broached the possibility of going with her to Guernsey, that I was glad to be of some use at this sad time.

It was while I was busy leafing through the pattern book and wondering whether it would be worth cashing some national savings' certificates to buy the material and to look upon the transaction as a wise investment, or whether I should shelve the whole idea for a time, that Miriam Quinn appeared.

'Lovely to see you!' I enthused. 'It seems ages since we met at Amy's party. What have you been doing?'

Of course, I rather hoped that she would say: 'Seeing Gerard' but she did not. Miriam is not one for girlish confidences, for which I respect her. Nevertheless, she looked more animated than usual, and I wondered if I should learn more. Or were the village rumours unfounded? They so often are.

'Holding the fort at the Caxley office, I'm sorry to say. Barney had a business tour in the Middle East, all very high-powered and lucrative, and he left me in charge for three weeks. I've hardly had time to breathe.'

I knew that Miriam was private secretary to Sir Barnabas Hatch, the financier, and that he recognised the value of this imperturbable and competent young woman. I only hoped that she was suitably rewarded, and I suspect that she was. If anyone should appreciate a sound investment it was Sir Barnabas, and he certainly had a treasure in Miriam.

I showed her the patterns and explained my problem. Should I or shouldn't I?

'Let's look at the present ones,' said she practically, and we went to study the sitting room curtains.

'I should let them do another year,' said Miriam. 'There's nothing wrong with them. Or do you loathe them?'

'Far from it. And I'm only too glad to take your advice. My mother used to say that Procrastination was my middle name. But in this case the thought of finding two or three hundred pounds is more telling.'

'As much as that?'

'More, probably. I was not going to decide anyway until after my trip to Leamington and then Guernsey.'

I told her about my holiday plans, and she said that she was having a fortnight when Barney returned, and proposed to spend it in Norfolk with her brother Lovell and his family.

'And later,' she added, 'I'm having a week or so, probably in the autumn.'

'That will set you up for the winter,' I said.

'I really called,' said Miriam rising, 'to invite you to a small dinner party I'm giving soon. It's on Thursday week. Can you manage it?'

'Drat it, no! I shall be at Leamington then. I'm so sorry. It would have been lovely.'

'Never mind. There'll be lots of other occasions, and I'll think of you enjoying wedding cake and champagne.'

She waved goodbye from the gate, and I returned wondering, yet again, why it is that one can go for weeks without an invitation to something pleasant, and then when one does arrive it is on the same day as an earlier engagement.

Sometimes life seems as contrary as a cat.

When I set off for my few days in Leamington, the sun was reigning once again, and the weathermen, including Mr Willet, forecast a return to halcyon days.

My spirits were high as I trundled towards Oxford. I had double-checked all switches at home, and left Tibby in Mr Willet's care. He had promised to visit the house night and morning and to see that the cat enjoyed his usual expensive meals.

'Not that it'd hurt him to starve for a few days,' he commented. 'If that cat don't die of fatty heart I shall be surprised. Lives like a lord, don't he?'

In the back of the car was a suitcase with my everyday

clothes and toilet things in it. Another one held my wedding garments. A new cream-coloured silk suit was carefully swathed in as much tissue paper as Amy might have used, and my new cream shoes were my pride and joy, surpassed only, in my affections, by the superb large hat smothered in silk tea roses.

Even Amy had been impressed by this confection.

'Why, you ought to be the bride yourself in that gorgeous rig-out,' was her flattering comment, when I displayed my ensemble to her. This was high praise indeed. I am rarely able to impress Amy, least of all with my clothes, and I made the most of it.

'Though when I'm going to get a chance to wear this lot again, I'm blowed if I know,' I told her.

'They'll never date,' said Amy comfortingly. 'Put them aside for other weddings, or even a garden party. You never know – you may need them for your own wedding, but now that Horace Umbleditch has rushed so madly into that quite misguided engagement, I must admit that the outlook seems somewhat bleak.'

'I'll bear up,' I promised.

'Of course, you might meet someone suitable at the wedding,' continued Amy, brightening at the thought. 'An uncle, say –'

'Or a grandfather,' I put in. 'Or some eighty-year-old friend of the family, creaking along on his last legs.'

'Yes indeed,' agreed Amy, ignoring my sarcasm.

Still, I told myself, as I took the northern bypass skirting Oxford, it was good to have such a lovely collection of matching clothes with me, and I resolved to enjoy the occasion thoroughly.

I approached Woodstock on the dreaded A34 road and passed the gates of Blenheim Palace, recalling the action of the Duchess Consuelo, of American birth, who had had the good sense to put out the uneaten food from the ducal halls in two containers, one savoury, the other sweet, for the poor of the town. For years it had all been thrown in together, I gathered, like so much pig swill.

My way took me east of Stratford-upon-Avon but I noticed a sign to Charlecote Park where it is alleged the young William Shakespeare did some poaching, and then on to Royal Leamington Spa.

It was early afternoon when I arrived at the hotel, not far from All Saints' Church where the ceremony was to take place. It was in a quiet street of elegant Georgian houses, and I was glad to be shown to my room to unpack and refresh myself.

The next day was free. The wedding was to be the following day, and I spent my time exploring the town. It reminded me of Bath with its graceful terraces, and I did a great deal of window shopping in the Parade. I even tried the water in the Royal Pump Room, and decided that I should never become an addict.

The Art Gallery and Museum was a pleasant haven on a hot afternoon, and I admired some modern paintings and some Wedgwood and Worcester pieces of porcelain which I coveted.

Altogether, I decided, I should come again one day. This visit was obviously going to be too short.

Our Miss Briggs was a wonder to behold as she came up the aisle on her father's arm, and I wished Mr Willet could see her now.

The Caxley dressmaker had created a beautiful dress of white silk, with a short train edged with ruched lace. She carried a Victorian posy of white rosebuds and wore a little matching garland on her head. Two young friends acted as bridesmaids, and were dressed in sprigged voile. The whole effect was youthful and unsophisticated.

The Briggs were lucky enough to live in one of the tall Regency houses. We walked straight through to the marquee in the garden where the most sumptuous spread was set out.

Wayne, looking handsomer than ever, gave me such an enthusiastic hug and kiss, that my gorgeous hat was knocked askew, but it was a small price to pay for such a warm greeting. In any case, by the time the celebrations ended, I was past caring whether my hat was on or off, and by the time I was safely back in my hotel bedroom all I could think of was the blessed fact that I could sleep as late as I liked, without interruption from anybody, and that I had another two days to enjoy the delectable Royal Leamington Spa.

18 Away From it All

THE sun was setting when I returned to Fairacre. I stopped at Mr Willet's to pick up the key and to thank him for feeding Tibby.

'That cat of yourn don't grieve, you know, when you ain't at home, so don't go thinking you're missed at all.'

'I suspected as much.'

'Golloped down best part of a half-pint of milk, and polished off two saucerfuls of grub a day. Just like them cats on the telly. Which reminds me, we're on tomorrow.'

'On what?'

'The telly. Us. Fairacre. Tyler's Row. Loyshus. The lot. About a quarter past six.'

'Marvellous!'

He walked to the car with me. As always his garden was a picture.

'Alice will be sorry to have missed you. She's over at Springbourne, with her cousin Aggie, on some chapel lark.'

'I hope I haven't stopped you from going too?'

'No, no. It's one of these temperance meetings. Aggie's a great one for abstaining. Well, so are we, as you know, but old Ag's a bit fiercer, if you follow me, and she got this chap from the other side of Caxley to cycle out to give a talk on the evils of strong liquor.'

'Well, I hope he gets a drink of some sort,' I said, 'if he's cycling all that way on a hot evening.'

'Oh, he'll get a cup of tea and a Marie biscuit, no doubt. Maybe a Rich Tea if they start living it up. I think Aggie was afraid there wouldn't be many attending, seeing as it's August, and most people are busy gardening, or away on holiday. That's why Alice has gone to swell the numbers. Rather her than me.'

Driving home, I pondered on Mrs Willet's outing. It didn't sound like 'a chapel lark' to me.

Tibby ignored my blandishments when we met, and gazed haughtily into the distance.

That would teach me to neglect a cat!

There was a good deal of clearing up to do before taking off for Guernsey with cousin Ruth.

I tackled washing and ironing, a batch of correspondence, and tidied one or two cupboards with some surprising results. The larder yielded a Christmas pudding which must have stood in a dark corner for at least three years, and the landing cupboard had secreted a box of stationery I had been looking for for months.

Also I had to draft the advertisement for Mrs Pringle's replacement, but felt it would be only prudent to check, yet again, that the lady had retired permanently before sending it off.

Meanwhile, I hovered around the television set waiting for the great moment.

It did not come. At least, it did not come on the day appointed. Peter Hale rang me in the afternoon to say that he had been told there was some strike trouble, and that the programme was now scheduled for the following night at the same time.

I switched off and decided to post my letters and beard Mrs Pringle in her lair. But just as I put my letters in the box, the lady hove in sight with one of her own.

'Hello!' I called. 'I was just about to visit you.'

'And what was that about?'

'Frankly, about the advertisement which ought to go in this week if you still feel unable to tackle the work.'

Mrs Pringle bridled, her face becoming suffused with colour.

'Who says I'm unable to tackle the work?'

'Well, are you, or not?' I asked. I felt like echoing Lady Bracknell and saying: 'This shilly-shallying with the question is absurd!'

'I don't say as I'm a hundred per cent fit, and that new doctor don't seem to relish the idea of me working again, but there it is.'

'But what is?' I persisted. 'You know the post is still yours if you want it, but I must know here and now, one way or the other. I expect you know that Bella can't do the job next term, so we must get someone.'

Mrs Pringle looked smug.

'Yes, I did hear as Bella was finding it too much for her. Not surprising, of course. It's too much for anyone, let's face it.'

'Well, what's the answer?'

'I don't think I'm up to it.'

'Right. That settles it.'

'Don't be too hasty though. I'm seeing the doctor tomorrow, and shall we see what he says?'

I hesitated. Clearly, the old scoundrel was enjoying every minute of this encounter, and I determined not to lose my temper. On the other hand, it was imperative to get the advertisement in before I went away.

As usual, we compromised.

'Very well. Come and see me tomorrow evening, and we'll decide then,' I said. 'But I must post the advertisement this week.'

'It'll be after The Programme,' said Mrs Pringle.

'Fair enough,' I said. 'I'll see you about seven o'clock.'

And so we parted.

* * *

Mrs John and Teresa came the next afternoon. The sun still blazed, and I thought that she looked tired after her hot walk.

I refreshed her with lemonade, and suggested that she might like to tackle the brass and copper cleaning in the garden, in the shade of the copper beech, while Teresa played on the lawn.

I did some ironing and watched the two outside. Teresa was an attractive toddler, still a little unsteady on her feet, but accepting the occasional tumble with great good humour. She had a large ball which she rolled about happily, and a teddy bear which needed a good deal of motherly attention. I only wished some of my infant class were as well-behaved.

We had a cup of tea at the end of her session. I explained that I should be travelling to Guernsey on her usual day, and back from Guernsey the following week.

'So there's absolutely no need for you to come,' I said, 'for two weeks. You deserve a holiday. You look rather washed out, if I may say so.'

'I have been off-colour this week,' she confessed. 'I put it down to this heat.'

I gave her her wages, and the two weeks' money when I

should be away. She demurred, but I insisted, and she seemed grateful.

'Shall I run you home?' I offered. 'I could get one of the boys to push the pram along later today.'

But she would have none of it, and I watched her go towards Beech Green, Teresa waving to the last.

The television programme was highly enjoyable, and Fairacre looked splendid on the screen. The man who played Aloysius looked rather too clean and well-fed, I thought, remembering Mr Willet's description of the poet, but all in all, it was well done, and I could see that the inhabitants of Fairacre would be basking in reflected glory for some time.

Half an hour later, Mrs Pringle arrived, her limp strongly in evidence. My heart sank.

When the lady was ensconced on the sofa, had refused refreshment, and contributed her share of comment on the weather, I felt it was time to come to the point.

'So how do you feel?' I began, and immediately was re-minded of television reporters questioning some grief-stricken relatives after various disasters. You know the sort of thing:

'How do you feel now that your daughter's body has been recovered?'

'How do you feel now that you know your leg has been amputated?'

It beats me that none of these pathetic and tragic victims do not turn and rend their interlocutor, or at least snarl:

'How would *you* feel?'

Luckily, Mrs Pringle took my question at its face value. She drew in her four chins and a deep breath.

'I'm sorry to say,' said the lady, 'that the doctor says it still needs care. He said it was up to me to decide about the job, and after a night sleeping on it, I think it would be best to say "No".'

It sounded to me as though the speech had been well rehearsed, but it made no difference to the outcome. If Mrs Pringle did not want to return, then that was it.

I felt a twinge of genuine regret.

'Very well. I quite understand, and of course your health comes first. But I really am sorry. We shall be lucky if we ever get such a marvellous cleaner again. However, I'll post off the letter now.'

Having got the matter over, she took a turn round the garden before setting off to her home.

'There's the end of an era,' I said to myself sadly. 'Come rain or shine, that old terror has kept me company for all my years at Fairacre. How I shall miss her!'

However, there it was. I stamped my letter, and put it ready to post. For good measure, I also wrote out a postcard to the same effect to be put in Fairacre Post Office, by courtesy of Mr Lamb.

Something told me that I was far more likely to get results from this source than the advertisement in *The Caxley Chronicle*.

Two days later, my cousin Ruth and I were in Guernsey.

We put up at a most comfortable hotel in St Peter Port overlooking the harbour. At night we could hear the sea hissing over the shingle.

It was fun to see the steamer coming in daily from Weymouth, and to watch the fishing boats setting out.

The weather was as balmy as it was at home, and I had never seen the sea so blue, not even in Crete where I once spent a holiday with Amy. Ruth's spirits rose daily, and I could see that this break was comforting her after the shock of Bill's death.

It was clear that she needed company desperately at this sad time. She told me how good her sons had been, taking it in turns to call daily, or to telephone her, or to take her out for a drive.

I remembered Joan Benson talking about widowhood, and how some people just cannot bear to be alone, whilst others – herself included – needed some solitude to come to terms with changed circumstances. At any rate, Ruth seemed to be glad of my company, and it was good to feel that I was of some help.

We did all the things that visitors to Guernsey do. We explored Castle Cornet, seen on the horizon from our hotel windows. We visited the claustrophobic abode of the late Victor Hugo, some interesting galleries and innumerable shops where we were easily tempted by some first-rate clothes and jewellery. Of course, we bought a woollen guernsey apiece, a fawn one for Ruth and a nautical dark blue for me. They would keep out the winds of winter beautifully, we told each other, though even to think of such conditions seemed absolutely impossible, as we basked in the heat.

One of the places we enjoyed particularly was the Fort Grey maritime museum where everything was imaginatively displayed, and the woodwork and brass so immaculately kept that I thought of Mrs Pringle with a sudden pang. How she would approve of such cleanliness!

But I thrust the thought aside. This was my holiday, and I was not going to spoil it by dwelling on future problems. Time enough to worry when I returned.

As we drove home from the airport, at the end of our holiday, we were greeted by heavy rain.

The windscreen wipers were working madly to cope with the downpour, and every car that passed flung up a shower of spray. In places the road was flooded, and for the last few miles we were accompanied by fast-flowing streamlets on each side of the highway.

Mr Willet had thoughtfully left the key in the secret hiding place known to all, which is under a large stone near the front door. I guessed this meant that he and his wife were away for the day.

The house looked so fresh and clean that I suspected that Mrs John had called in after all to put things to rights.

Ruth was staying the night before setting off north, and we enjoyed our tea in a leisurely fashion with our feet propped up on stools.

I thought of Miss Clare, and her more formal tea time habits. Perhaps I really was a slattern? Nevertheless, it was good to flop back with a cup of tea on a sidetable, with the biscuit barrel handy, and Ruth seemed to be as content with the arrangements as I was.

'This little holiday has done me a power of good,' she said.

'Me too.'

'I do so hope I haven't been a wet blanket. It's difficult to throw off one's cares completely.'

I assured her that she had been the best of company.

'You know,' she went on, 'I think I shall take up a little voluntary job when I get back. We have a scheme at our local hospital where we take it in turns to man the shop or push a trolley round the wards. I rather think the library people are in it too. They've been asking me for years to help out, but so far I've refused. In any case, with Bill so ill I couldn't really be reliable.'

'It sounds just right. I'm sure it would be a great help to the organisation.'

And to you too, I thought. This could be the best bit of self-therapy needed.

'It's always good to feel one is of some use,' said Ruth.

'I endorse that,' I told her.

'You found the old key then?' said Mr Willet when I saw him next. 'Had a good time? You look quite bonny.'

Away From it All

I told him about the trips we had made, and how lucky we had been with our choice of hotel and the weather.

'But we came back to rain,' I said. 'How's it been here?'

'That's our only splash. Came just in time to fill up the water butts again, and plump up the runner beans.'

'Any news?'

'Well now, let me see. Arthur Coggs is due out in a week or two, more's the pity. Mr Hale fell off the garden steps cutting that great hedge of his, and sprained an ankle. Mr Mawne saw some bird that shouldn't be here by rights and wrote to that bird society in London to tell 'em about it. They wrote back to say he was mistaken. *Mistaken!* Our Mr Mawne! You can guess he's been in no end of a taking, and the fur's flying, believe me.'

'The feathers, you mean.'

'Yes, well, maybe. Now what else? My Alice has made sixty pounds of gooseberry jam and forty of raspberry, my marrows are coming on a treat as I've been watering 'em well behind old Ted Bates' back. And they've got the mumps in Caxley.'

'Well, I hope it doesn't spread here.'

'And of course, there's this business of the cleaner.'

I was instantly alert.

'You had any answers yet?' he asked.

'Not one.'

'Not even from *The Caxley*?'

'No. I hardly expected it. I think Mr Lamb's card has more chance of attracting notice.'

'Yes. It's done that all right,' he answered cryptically.

'What do you mean?'

'You'll know soon enough,' he said, making for the door. 'I'm saying no more.'

And the maddening fellow set off for home at a brisk pace.

*   *   *

For the next hour or two I worried over Mr Willet's enigmatic comment. Had I worded the notice wrongly? Was there going to be a rush of candidates for the appointment? Had Mrs Pringle been putting in her spoke, and warning off would-be applicants with terrible descriptions of the work involved? I would not put it past her.

After a great deal of fruitless anxiety, I decided to pay a visit to Mrs John to see if it was she who had put my house to rights unexpectedly, and to deliver a pot of Guernsey honey and a rather splendid teddy bear, made in the island, and to which I was becoming so much attached that I felt it would be wise to hand it over without delay, to its future owner.

The countryside was looking lovely after the recent rain, and already some of the fields were being ploughed after an early harvest. Farmers did not waste much time these days, I thought, remembering the golden stubble which used to stand in the cropped fields for weeks, it seemed, in the old days.

But already there was a shabbiness about the hedgerows and grass verges which told of approaching autumn. It grieved me to think of the waning of this most glorious of all summers, its joys and its splendours. Well, we had celebrated it, every one of us, and must face the inevitable, I supposed.

Knapweed and late scabious coloured the drying grasses. Already acorns and young conkers were formed, and in the orchards the plums were turning colour, and some early apples, like Beauty of Bath, were being picked.

To some people, autumn is the loveliest of the seasons with John Keats' 'mists and mellow fruitfulness'. But for me, I find it a wistful time. 'The dying fall' presages the chill of winter, and this year, particularly, I hoped that autumn would be late in coming.

Mrs John was delighted with her honey and Teresa with the bear. Yes, she had looked in, she said, almost apologetically, and Mr Willet had unlocked the house for her.

'It all looked immaculate,' I told her. 'But you shouldn't have gone to such trouble.'

'Well, I was going to leave a note, but in the end I decided I'd see you myself.'

'Shall I see you next week? Are you feeling better now?'

'It's about that I wanted to see you.'

She twisted her fingers in some embarrassment.

'You see, the doctor says there's another baby on the way. It's a bit earlier than we'd planned, but we're quite pleased about it. The only thing is I shall have to give up the job, and I did enjoy it so.'

'And I enjoyed having you. You did a first-class job and I shall miss you sorely, but you must do as the doctor says.'

We parted affectionately, and I promised to keep in touch.

Teresa was too engrossed in the teddy bear to wish me farewell.

I left them both with much regret.

So that's that, I thought, as I drove home. Now I must look for another cleaner for my home as well as the school.

I was genuinely sorry to part from Mrs John. She was a fine person, and had looked after me beautifully. While the holidays lasted, and that was not for much longer, I could manage well, but once term started on September the third, I should have to find a help-meet.

Perhaps Mr Willet knew about this too? Next time I met him I must put in some third-degree stuff.

Unfortunately, as I knew from experience, the wily old boy was more than a match for me.

19 Mrs Pringle on the War Path

THE last few days of the summer holiday passed with unwelcome rapidity.

Amy called to see me one evening.

'To catch up with the Fairacre gossip,' she told me. 'I haven't seen you since the television programme. I must say they made the village look absolutely Arcadian.'

'It is,' I assured her.

'Oh, come off it! You know there are as many serpents in your Eden as there are in mine at Bent. How's that terrible Mrs Pringle getting on?'

I told her about that lady's vacillations, and my present predicament.

'A pity about Mrs John,' she said, looking closely at the floor and furniture about her. 'She really has pulled this place together. You will miss her.'

I ignored this aspersion on the normal state of my abode, and agreed that Mrs John would be sorely missed.

'I believe Miriam Quinn is in Norfolk at the moment,' she went on. 'Am I right?'

'You are indeed.'

'Well, I asked because I had an extraordinary postcard this morning from Gerard Baker, written from a place called Great Snoring.'

'I don't believe it.'

'Perfectly true, my dear. But it wasn't the address that perturbed me, but the ebullience of the man's message.'

'Tell me more. I'm agog!'

'I ought to have brought it to show you, but the telephone rang just as I was coming out, and I have left it at home, but it was to the effect that he was the happiest man in the world, and what bliss it was to find Fairacre in Norfolk.'

'Good Lord!'

'Yes, you may well say so,' said Amy severely. 'It looks to me as if you have let yet another nice man slip through your fingers. I was afraid from the moment they clapped eyes on each other, in this very room, that no good would come of it.'

'But good *has* come of it, Amy, if Miriam and Gerard propose to get engaged. But somehow –'

'Somehow what?'

'Well, Miriam seemed so very much the confirmed single woman, happy in her work. I wonder if it's true?'

'I can't think of any other explanation, can you? Two people, both connected with Fairacre, now in Norfolk? No, I think it's a case of love.'

'You sound as maudlin as Mrs Pringle,' I told her. 'She's always telling me that it is Love That Makes The World Go Round. Not that she puts it into practice, as you know. I see mighty little love here from that source.'

'Well, there is it,' said Amy rising. 'Let's take a turn in the garden like Jane Austen's heroines, and you can tell me all about Guernsey and the wedding. Was your gorgeous hat admired?'

'It certainly was.'

'And did it attract a flock of eligible men, all soft and wistful in the presence of nuptials?'

'I'm sorry to say it did not.'

Amy bent to sniff at a Gloire de Dijon rose against the wall.

'Never mind,' she said comfortingly. 'There's a lot to be said for living alone in such a heavenly place.'

'I'm always telling you that,' I said.

It was good to have the last word for a change.

★　★　★

That evening I was surprised to have a telephone call from Elizabeth Mawne.

'You haven't forgotten our garden party tomorrow, have you? In aid of the Royal Society for the Protection of Birds?'

I confessed that I had.

'No matter,' said she kindly. 'I only rang because you promised something for the cake stall, and I noticed it hadn't arrived.'

'I'll set to now and make something,' I promised humbly. 'Anything to help the R.S.P.B.'

'That's nice of you. To tell the truth, Henry almost called off the whole thing, as he's been having the most acrimonious exchanges with one of the officers about a rare bird he saw up on the downs.'

'How exciting! What was it?'

'Don't ask me, dear. I'm absolutely ignorant of bird life. Some sort of *Lesser Thing*. A godwit, possibly. No, I don't think it was that. He'll tell you when we see you. The man he wrote to told him he was mistaken, and of course Henry was furious. However, I've soothed him enough to have the garden party here tomorrow, but for two pins he would have changed the posters to "In aid of the Cats' Protection League".'

'He sounds as though he's taken it hard, poor Henry.'

'Well, when you are an authority on birds it's rather annoying to be told you can't distinguish between a Lesser Whatsit and a Greater Thingummy, isn't it?'

'I agree.'

'Then we'll look forward to seeing you about two-thirty. With a cake, of course.'

'Of course,' I agreed meekly, and went into the kitchen to make a batch of flapjacks to atone for my forgetfulness. Tibby, expecting supper, accompanied me, and graciously accepted a morsel of cold chicken, before I began my labours.

What a summer, I thought, as I made my way through the village the next afternoon!

Normally, I am full of fears for those organising outside junketings, but this year one just could not go wrong.

The cottage gardens were gay with red hot pokers, michaelmas daisies, pansies and delphiniums. Roses still glowed from old brick walls, and hollyhocks reached to thatched roofs.

Little birds fluffed their feathers at the side of the lane, glorying in their baths, and sending up little puffs of light dust. Cats dozed on window sills, relishing the heat, while dogs had sought the shade, and lay there panting.

Mr Roberts' cows, now restored to our erstwhile sports' field, stood beneath a clump of trees swishing their tails against the tormenting flies, and an aeroplane, leaving trails in the high blue sky, added its distant hum to the somnolence of the summer afternoon.

In the Mawnes' garden, however, all was bustle. I presented my flapjacks to the cake stall, and asked if I might reserve an appetising fruit cake that caught my eye.

'Not until Mr Bradley has made his speech,' said Mrs Mawne, arriving at my side. 'We can't possibly start selling until then.' She hurried off.

'Bossy old thing,' commented Mrs Lamb, who was in charge of the stall. 'Don't you worry. I'll see you get it, Miss Read.'

I expressed my thanks, but moved in a somewhat chastened mood to listen to Basil Bradley, who had mounted a rather precarious stool to make his opening speech.

As always, he was looking immaculate, his wavy hair beautifully cut, his pink shirt and pale grey suit a vision of delight. We are very proud of our local author, and he is generous with his time and money. Also, a great point, he is always brief when speaking, and this has endeared him to us all.

This afternoon was no exception, and within five minutes I had revisited the cake stall and collected my fruit cake. Mrs Lamb was doing a roaring trade, and the blue and white striped pudding basin which was acting as her till, was almost stuffed with notes and silver.

I noticed a particularly luscious chocolate cake, decorated with walnuts, lurking in the shade under the table. Seeing my interest, Mrs Lamb said:

'Put aside for Mrs Mawne,' and rolled her eyes to heaven.

Tea was served at the card tables collected earlier from the village hall, and covered with a fine assortment of borrowed tablecloths. Even on Henry Mawne's level lawn they proved uncomfortably wobbly, but it was pleasant to sit among friends admiring the flowery dresses of the women, and the bronzed near-nakedness of the children.

By four o'clock I felt I had done my duty, and set off for home. It seemed hotter than ever. A few small children, clad only in shorts, were accompanying a man, and were walking towards me.

To my surprise, when they were nearer, I saw that it was Arthur Coggs and all his offspring except Joseph.

He looked rather sheepish as he approached, but we stopped and had a civil word. He looked all the better for his time in prison, I thought, fitter and leaner without his beer, but naturally I did not say so.

'And where's Joe?' I asked.

'Home with 'is mum,' said Arthur. 'Reading some book.'

'He's getting on famously at school,' I told him.

'It's all he seems to think about,' responded Arthur. His tone was derogatory. He might have been saying that the child was hopelessly delinquent from the disgust shown in his manner.

'Good!' I said heartily. 'I'll look forward to seeing him, and the others, next week.'

Mr Lamb was weeding the front garden of the Post Office as I passed.

'Got our old friend back,' he said, nodding to Arthur's departing figure. 'Pity he didn't do his full time. Still, there's a chap at Beech Green has offered him a labouring job on that new building site, and Arthur starts on Monday. If he feels like it,' he added.

'Well, I hope the employer knows what he's taking on.'

'You can bet plenty of people have told him.'

'It's good news for Arthur though. He might go straight for a bit.'

'So might a corkscrew,' replied Mr Lamb.

He came close to his gate, and dropped his voice. 'You had a visit yet about that cleaning job?'

'Not a word. Why?'

Mr Lamb looked furtively about him, and came even closer. 'Well, you know that card you left with me?'

'Of course.'

'While you were away, Minnie Pringle came in for her children's allowance, and wanted to know what it was. You know she can't read?'

I said I did indeed.

'Proper scandal, isn't it? Had compulsory education here for a hundred years, and you get duffers like that Minnie still! Anyway, I was reading it out to her, when in comes Ma Pringle.'

Here Mr Lamb's husky whisper changed to a falsetto.

' "And what may you be doing?" she asks Minnie. "Thinking of going to see about this job," said Minnie, all pert. And Ma Pringle turns as red as a turkey-cock and says: "Oh, no you don't my girl!" and stumps off without buying anything.'

'This is the first I've heard of it,' I said. 'Although Bob Willet did say that that card had caused problems.'

'Problems? Murder, near enough, from what the neighbours told me! When Min went back, the old girl set about her something terrible, and threatened to black her eye if she dared to put in for what she called "her job". Minnie went off home to Springbourne, but she stuck out and wouldn't swear not to apply, and her old aunt is still seethingover it.'

'What a kettle of fish,' I remarked. 'All I know is that Mrs Pringle has said she doesn't want the job, and I'm still hoping to hear from someone, though time's running short. In any case, Minnie is not at all suitable.'

'That she's not,' agreed Mr Lamb. 'Does more harm than good, I should guess.'

'Well, thank you for telling me,' I said, picking up my basket. 'At least I'm prepared.'

The news was disturbing, but I did not intend to let it upset me unduly. Mrs Pringle had had her chance. Minnie Pringle would certainly not be taken on permanently, if she were rash enough to apply, and that was that.

The next thing to do, was to get in touch with dear reliable Bella, and to see if her offer of getting the school in good trim, for the beginning of term, still held.

I determined to see her the next day and went home to follow Mr Lamb's example, and to do some weeding as the evening cooled.

I awoke to another dewy morning, and looked forward to yet another golden day.

Full of good resolutions, I planned to give my house a thorough cleaning, secretly rather stung by Amy's remark about it looking in need of Mrs John's ministrations.

In the afternoon, I proposed to visit Bella, and to tell her how grateful I should be if she would put things straight before term started.

Life, of course, was already waiting with a spanner to throw in the works.

When I was at my most dishevelled, and had spent some time on my stomach attending to dust under the beds, the door bell rang.

Annoyed, I ran downstairs. It was nearly half past ten. Whoever it was could have a cup of coffee and then, I hoped, they would leave me to my chores.

Not many people come to the front door. I fully expected to find a gipsy selling pegs, or some earnest soul with a handful of tracts asking if I were saved. Friends and neighbours usually come to the back door and halloo cheerfully to see if I am in.

On wrenching open the door, which tends to stick with infrequent use, I was severely shaken to be confronted by Miss Crabbe and my past assistant Miss Jackson.

'Well,' I said with false enthusiasm. 'This is a lovely surprise!' Sometimes I wonder that I am not struck by a bolt from heaven when I dissemble in this fashion – but there it is. Civilisation rears its head yet again.

'Do come in. I was just going to make coffee.'

The two ladies followed me into the sitting room, where a

full dust-pan lay on the hearthrug, a vase of roses had been upturned by Tibby in his understandable haste to leave home on seeing the visitors, and water dripped steadily, and a few dead leaves had blown in the French windows and added to the general squalor.

'We were just returning from a marvellous course in Dorset, and saw the signpost to Fairacre, and we felt we must pop in,' said Hilary Jackson, teeth and spectacles flashing as brightly as ever.

'I'm so glad,' I said, picking up the dust-pan with one hand, and trying to arrange some stray locks of hair with the other. 'Let me put on the kettle, and then you must tell me all about it.'

I escaped to the kitchen, and did my best to tidy myself. It was a pity that I was wearing a paint-splashed cotton frock, no stockings and sandals with two straps adrift. Minnie Pringle was probably a good deal tidier than I was at the moment, I thought.

I put out cups and saucers, and surveyed the deplorable fragments in the bottom of the biscuit tin. Luckily, I had some oat cakes of Scottish derivation, as hard and gritty as the Grampians, and I added these to my offerings.

The ladies accepted my invitation to call upstairs, and I only hoped that they would not measure their length falling over the vacuum cleaner on the landing. The beds had been stripped, and piles of bedclothes were festooned over the banisters. The whole house must give the impression of total chaos.

However, it could not be helped, and I managed to mop up the water, and straighten a cushion or two, before they returned smelling nicely of my Morny's pink lilac soap.

'We hoped to see you at the course,' said Miss Crabbe, accepting a Scottish rock. 'It was really inspiring, wasn't it, Hilary?'

'Yes, indeed,' said the girl earnestly. She had had the sense, I noticed, to select half a Nice biscuit from the rubble in the tin. 'It dealt with Difficult Children. Half of them, of course, as we know only too well, are the Victims of Unhappy Marriages.'

'But there are so many other factors,' went on Miss Crabbe, who was gamely trying to chip off a fragment from her oat cake with an eye tooth. 'Unsympathetic Teachers, Hereditary Defects and the Pressures of Modern Life.'

'We had some wonderful lecturers,' enthused Hilary. 'So understanding and really jolly. In the evenings we played old-fashioned games like charades and I-Spy.'

Privately, I thanked my stars that I had not been among those present, and changed the subject by offering more coffee and enquiring which route they had taken to Fairacre.

Miss Crabbe was still fighting her oat cake, and was now attempting to snap it into pieces before transferring the morsel to her mouth. I began to feel quite sorry for her.

'Do leave that if it is too hard,' I said.

'Indeed no! It is absolutely delicious, and full of nourishing roughage,' said the lady. 'I am a great believer in Fibre.'

'I have bran with everything,' volunteered Hilary, who had finished her half biscuit. I offered the oat cakes, but she declined.

Coffee over, I took them round the garden. I do not think they really noticed anything, they were so agog with the mental stimulation of the past course.

However, they seemed to be content to sit on the garden seat to continue their discussion, and I excused myself as the telephone rang.

It was Bella George.

'I was coming to see you,' I said. 'Are you still game to tidy up the school before term?'

'Yes indeed, that's why I rang. But I thought I'd better find out if Mrs Pringle was definitely not returning. I shouldn't like to get across that lady.'

I was in firm agreement with Bella's feelings, and said so.

'No,' I told her. 'Mrs Pringle told me herself that she can't manage the job at the moment, so it will be marvellous if you can help out.'

'You haven't heard about *The Upset* then?'

'With Minnie?'

'Yes.'

'Mr Lamb told me that Mrs Pringle had threatened Minnie when she expressed an interest in applying for the post.'

'That was a while ago. She's been up since evidently, and is still talking about putting in for the job.'

'Well, she wouldn't get it,' I said flatly. 'The work's beyond Minnie, so you need not worry on that score.'

'I see. Well, I'll be along tomorrow and put things straight. I do hope someone turns up for the regular work. What about Mrs John?'

I told her about the coming baby.

'Oh dear! So you're without help too?'

'It looks like it. But I'm not too worried.'

'See you tomorrow then,' said Bella, and rang off.

I took the opportunity of clearing away the coffee cups and straightening the sitting room. Upstairs must wait.

Through the window I could see my two visitors engaged in earnest conversation still. The clock now said a quarter to twelve, and I wondered if I should offer them lunch. And if so, what?

Those of us who live alone do not have cold joints, or large stews standing ready in the larder.

On this occasion, I had one chop which I had intended to grill, with some lettuce from the garden as a side salad. All that I could manage, if the worst came to the worst, was an omelette which should suit Miss Crabbe, the non-flesh-eater, with a somewhat more interesting salad with chives, radishes, spring onions and any other snippets from the garden added to the lettuce.

I mentally reviewed the bread situation (poor), the cheese situation (disastrous, mouldy cheddar only), the fruit situation (two black bananas, and some sharp apples). Of course, I thought, I could always open a bottle of gooseberries.

I returned to my guests.

'It will soon be twelve o'clock,' I said brightly. 'Would you like to stay for lunch? Or I could take you to the Beetle and Wedge for a sandwich, if you prefer?'

My enquiries were met with a flurry of agitation.

'Nearly twelve? Good gracious, Hilary, we must set off at once!'

Miss Crabbe had leapt to her feet, and Hilary was scrabbling about for her handbag.

'No, no! Most kind of you to offer us lunch, but we have an evening engagement in Cambridge, and must be on our way.'

I did my best to look regretful.

'We are very much refreshed by your delicious coffee and oat cakes,' said Miss Crabbe, as they entered the car. 'By the way, do call and see us if you are ever in Cambridge.'

I thanked her, and helped to guide the car out of my somewhat awkward drive, before returning to my neglected duties.

The lamb chop was delicious, and all the more enjoyed because it was eaten in blissful solitude.

20 The End of Summer

TRUE to her word, Bella appeared the next day and got down to her scrubbing, dusting and polishing.

At mid-morning I went across with our coffee, and we sat on the desks and I admired the tortoise stoves, already gleaming like jet, and the glittering brass rail round the fireguard.

'It looks marvellous,' I told her.

'I like a bit of a shine-up,' she answered, stirring her coffee dreamily. 'I was talking to Jack last night, and he says he don't mind if I want to help out for another week, say, until you get a new cleaner.'

'That's very noble of him. I appreciate that. As a matter of fact, things are slightly more hopeful. Mr Roberts called in yesterday to say that he has a new stockman starting at Michaelmas, and his wife wants a job. So maybe she will take it on.'

'And Bob Willet said he'd do the stoves when the time came, if need be. That's something I really couldn't take on.'

'I've got all my scouts out,' I said. 'The vicar, the Annetts, Miss Clare, Mrs Mawne and Mrs Partridge. Between us all, someone will turn up. Meanwhile, if you really feel you can come after school for a day or two, I'd be more than grateful.'

As it happened, I saw Mr Willet in the churchyard that afternoon, and went to thank him for his offer of coping with the stoves.

'Lord, that's nothing!' he replied, ceasing his slashing at the long grass, and subsiding on to the flat tomb of Hezekiah Bootle who departed this life in 1832, respected by all.

'I'll see you and the kids keep warm,' he went on. 'I always enjoy a nice bit of stoking. Keeps hot, don't it?' he added, pushing back his cap, and scratching his head.

'A wonderful summer,' I agreed. 'I can't remember a better one.'

We sat side by side in the sunshine. Bees fondled the clover at our feet, and a pair of collared doves pattered about on the gravel path, looking like two curates dressed in clerical grey. High above us, a flock of rooks winged their way westward, their harsh cawing muffled by distance.

It was very peaceful. A country churchyard takes a lot of beating on a sunny afternoon, and I can never understand people's aversion to such places.

We brooded in companionable silence for a time, until Mr Willet sighed, and reached for his bill hook.

'No real news then, I take it, about Bella's job?'

I told him about Mr Roberts' new stockman.

'Oh, I knows that couple! Lived over Springbourne way some years ago. Yes, she'd be a bonny worker if she'd take it on. Fat girl. Name of Martha. Don't get many Marthas these days.'

He creaked to his feet.

'Well, I'd best stir me stumps. Don't you worry about this cleaner business. Someone'll turn up, you'll see.'

I roused myself too, and we parted company.

It was the last day of the holidays and it ended very pleasantly for me with a little party at Holly Lodge, where Henry Mawne's nephew David and his wife Irene, sister of Horace Umbleditch, now lived.

The older Mawnes were there, and also David's boy Simon, as well as the vicar and his wife, and a sprinkling of friends from Caxley.

'It's really to celebrate Horace and Eve's engagement,' Irene told me, as she took my coat. 'But they are not here yet. I can't think what has held them up. I do so hope they haven't forgotten. They are so befuddled with love, I wouldn't put it past them.'

Luckily, at that moment there was a scrunching of tyres, and the couple arrived. I made my way into the sitting room, while Irene welcomed them.

'I've always loved this house,' said the vicar, coming up to me with a tray of glasses. 'And everyone who has lived here has enjoyed it. I know Miriam Quinn finds it a real haven after a day's work in that busy Caxley office. You know her good news, I take it? Unfortunately, she is still away, but I think her engagement to Gerard Baker is now general knowledge.'

I said that I had heard something about it, and thought it was marvellous news. Henry Mawne came up at that moment, and said that he had been keeping a sharp look-out in the *Daily Telegraph* for a notice, but nothing had been seen.

'They are keeping it quiet,' said Mr Partridge, 'but the wedding will take place around Christmas, I gather. Miriam wants to arrange things easily for her employer, I know, although she intends to keep on her job after the honeymoon.'

'I like a winter wedding,' announced Mrs Mawne. 'Plenty of fur and velvet. So pretty always. I suppose they will marry at St Patrick's? I always feel a registry office ceremony is rather like a visit to the bank.'

'Yes, yes. The wedding will be here, I'm happy to say,' said the vicar. 'Her brother Lovell will take part of the service, of course. I look forward to meeting him.'

At that moment, the two chief guests arrived, David hastened to greet them, and then made a short but charming speech, asking us to drink to their happiness.

It was good to see Horace looking so smug and cheerful, and his wife-to-be seemed equally content with her lot.

'This is our last fling before term starts next week,' Horace said, in answer to David's speech. 'And nothing could be nicer than an evening with good friends.'

Speeches over, we began to circulate, and I was pleased to see Simon again. He looked much stronger and happier than when he had been my pupil for a short time, and he gave me a cheerful grin as he proffered a tray of tempting tit-bits.

'When does term start for you?' he asked.

'Tomorrow,' I told him.

'Then Uncle Horace has the edge on you. He doesn't go back until Thursday.'

'Lucky chap,' I said. 'And when do you start?'

'Not till the following Tuesday.'

'Hardly worth going back,' I teased him. 'It will soon be Christmas.'

'Stop chattering, Simon,' called David. 'There isn't a nut to be had over here.'

'Back to my duties!' said my old pupil, and departed.

Elizabeth Mawne hove in sight and I enquired politely about the aged aunt in Ireland who had been the unknowing source of my troubles, and Miriam's, with Henry early in the year.

'Perhaps you know I managed to get her into a nursing home?'

I said I did.

'Well, as you might guess, she's taken a great dislike to it, and is raising Cain according to the matron, and threatening to go home.'

'But can she? I thought –'

'Of course she can't. We sold up everything, and really I'm at my wits' end to know what to do. Henry refuses point-blank to have her with us, and I think he's right. I can see I shall have to have another trip to Ireland to sort things out.'

My heart sank at the thought of Henry left yet again to his own devices. Should I have to be alert for unwelcome visits? Lucky Miriam, I thought! At least, she would now have the protection of a fiancé. It almost made one take to matrimony for sanctuary from lonely grass widowers. However, as Amy had pointed out, with some callousness, Gerard and even Horace were now out of my reach, and I saw no other possibility looming up. On the whole, of course, I was not sorry.

'Old age is a problem,' I said. 'I frequently think about my own, and wonder which will crack first, mind or body.'

'Good heavens!' cried Elizabeth. 'You won't crack at all. Henry's always telling me you are the sanest person he's ever met. You'll go whole and uncorrupted to the grave, believe me.'

I was much taken aback.

'Well, I'm very touched by the compliment,' I quavered, 'and now I must go and see the happy pair.'

Still reeling from Henry's kind opinions, I threaded my way

to speak to Horace and Eve. Perhaps, poor old Henry was not such a bad chap after all, I decided.

Nevertheless, I hoped Elizabeth's absence would be brief.

I walked home through the peaceful village, and encountered Mr Lamb, exercising his dog.

After a boisterous welcome from the latter which left me with laddered tights, and my best fifteen-denier ones at that, Mr Lamb gave me good news.

'I've heard of another likely candidate for the cleaning job,' he told me.

'You are kind. Everyone's been scouting round, and things do look more hopeful. Who's this one?'

'Wife of one of the postmen. They're at Beech Green, and she used to work at that electrical factory this end of Caxley. But it closed down at the end of last month, and she could do with some cash. Nice woman. Plenty of common sense and elbow grease.'

'She sounds marvellous.'

I told him about the possibility of the stockman's wife.

'So now there's real hope of someone soon. I shall miss Mrs Pringle though, awkward though she is. But I can't see her coming again.'

'Would you have her if you could?'

'Yes. She's served the school well for donkey's years, despite being such –'

I searched for a phrase which would be truthful but not libellous.

'Such a wicked old faggot?' suggested Mr Lamb, hauling his exuberant charge away from my ruined tights.

'That's it.'

'Well, now you can have some choice perhaps. I think I know the Springbourne girl, Martha Someone, and I know Reg's missus would work well too. Good luck anyway.'

He set off at a brisk pace, with the dog panting at the delay, and I went home thinking how helpful my neighbours were in times of trouble.

Naturally, the first day of term dawned as sunnily seductive as one might guess, and it was sad to think of us all confined to the schoolroom when summer remained so beguiling outdoors.

The school looked fresh and gleaming from Bella's ministrations and the children equally radiant from their long days in the open air.

Miss Briggs, whom we now had to call Mrs Richards, was in good spirits, and told me all about the work she and Wayne were putting in on their cottage. It was on the outskirts of Beech Green, and they were lucky to have found it.

'That's one good thing about being in the building trade,' she told me. 'You often get to hear of houses going before they get on to the market. The old couple who had it before us were distant cousins of Wayne's dad, so we heard about it from him.'

I enquired about the house. It sounded as if it were not far from Miss Clare's home.

'That's right,' agreed the girl. 'When we're straight you must come and see it. At the moment it's a proper mess, and we haven't got much furniture.'

'That'll come,' I told her. 'Much more fun to get it bit by bit anyway.'

'My mum and dad married after the war,' she said, 'when things were really tight. Dad always says they set up home with two deckchairs and an orange box for a table. I think we've done a bit better than that, but not much!'

She laughed, and went off to cope with the infants. It was good to see her so content.

Joseph Coggs appeared at my desk, pencil in hand.

'Please, miss, the nib of my pencil's bust itself.'

'So's mine,' chorused three more children.

Term had begun.

Amy called that evening, wearing a most elegant turquoise blue suit and matching hat.

'Heavens, you do look smart!' I cried. 'Have you been to a wedding?'

'No. A rather dreary committee meeting, but all the others always appear dressed to the nines, so I thought I'd better do the same.'

'Well, mind where you sit. Tibby left a mouse on the sofa last week, and it was by sheer chance that I noticed it.'

'You certainly live a primitive life out here at Fairacre,' commented Amy, dusting busily at the seat of an armchair. 'How's term going?'

'Much as usual. Luckily our Miss Briggs, I mean Mrs Richards, is in good form, and I really think I may get a cleaner before long. Everyone's rallying round.'

'Splendid! I came to ask you if you would like to come to the opera with me next month. At Oxford.'

'Lovely! To hear what?'

'La Bohème. Suit you?'

'Perfectly. I can always do with a nice juicy bit of Puccini.'

'Right. I'll fix up the seats. James will be coming too, and we'll pick you up.'

'I shall look forward to that.'

'And the week after, James and I are pushing off for a tour of Scotland, and staying with Vanessa for a few days. I must say, he's being very attentive. I think he fears I might go off on my own again.'

'Well, you gave us all a fright, I must say.'

'Rubbish! And don't expect me to feel guilty, because I don't regret it for a moment. It did me a lot of good, and James too, for that matter. By the way, what news of that crafty Gerard? I shall never forgive him for throwing you over.'

'Amy, you know there was absolutely nothing in it, and I'm delighted to tell you that, as far as I know, he and Miriam are engaged.'

'Well! I didn't see it in the *Daily Telegraph*.'

'Quite a lot of things don't get into the *Telegraph*. Their engagement was one of them.'

'Let me know when things are a little more public, and I'll write to them. She's a nice girl. I wonder when the nuptials take place?'

'Quite soon, I gather, from the vicar.'

'I shall have to get a new outfit if I'm invited,' said Amy thoughtfully.

'What's wrong with that present get-up?' I asked, waving at the beautiful suit. 'I hope we do get invited. My hat could do with another airing. But somehow I think that wedding will be a very quiet affair.'

'I should hope so,' said Amy sternly, 'after the way he's treated you.'

'Now Amy –' I began.

'What about a cup of something?' she said swiftly, avoiding a scolding, and we went amicably in search of one.

Next day the storm broke, in more ways than one.

The clouds rolled up during school time, and the air became sultry. Distant rumbling could be heard, but we saw no lightning, and luckily the rain held off.

As before, this sudden withdrawal of sunshine made us all feel chilly, although the thermometer registered a fairly high temperature.

The children went home in dry weather, and Mrs Richards and I returned to our respective homes before the heavens opened, as we fully expected.

At six o'clock, the rumbling came nearer, and there was some lightning. Tibby prudently and stealthily crept under the sofa, and I was about to go upstairs to shut the windows when the bell rang at the back door.

On opening it I was confronted by Mrs Pringle. She was wearing her grimmest expression, and her best navy blue hat complete with the white duck's wing.

'Do come in,' I said, my heart sinking. Now what had upset the old curmudgeon? I knew that look only too well. It boded trouble.

'I've been having a word with Bella George,' was her opening remark, when she had settled her bulk in an armchair.

'Oh yes?'

'And I was that taken aback I come straight up here to have it out.'

'Have what out?'

'You knows as well as I do. About my job.'

Mrs Pringle's face was now scarlet, and she leant forward belligerently. I mustered my defences.

'You told me plainly that you did not want the job, Mrs Pringle. Naturally, I've had to look elsewhere.'

Mrs Pringle's ample bosom was heaving up and down with emotion, and I began to wonder how I should cope if she should have a seizure.

'That Minnie Pringle made me see red with her talk of coming for the cleaning, but I soon sorted her out. The very idea! Why, she's got no more idea of cleaning than that cat!'

She glared at poor Tibby who was trying to make a dignified exit from this upheaval.

'Even if Minnie had applied, she would not have been given the post,' I assured her.

If I had hoped to placate the lady, I was wrong. Mrs Pringle's voice now thundered as loudly as the storm outside.

'But what about Martha Ellis, as is supposed to want it? And Reg Carter's wife? Though what good she'd do looking after a school when she's only fiddle-faddled about in Caxley keeping her hands clean, I don't know.'

'They haven't applied yet –' I began, but was howled down.

'And then Bella had the sauce to tell me that Bob Willet had offered to do the stoves, when we light 'em. I tell you straight, I'm not having him crunching coke all over my floors with them great boots of his.'

'But they are not your floors,' I managed to slip in.

Mrs Pringle took an enormous breath. The duck's wing quivered in time with her four chins, and the flash of her eyes reminded me of the Valkyrie.

'They've been mine for more years than I can remember,' she boomed.

'Are you trying to tell me,' I said, as calmly as I could, 'that you are willing to come back?'

'Of course I am! You don't think I'd let that lot of muddlers mess the place up? Bob Willet doing the stoves! A fine old fist he'd make of it. Wait till I see him next!'

'He was only doing what he could to help,' I pointed out. 'You know quite well you let us all down badly. If it hadn't been for Bella, we should have been really in the cart.'

There was no gleam of remorse in Mrs Pringle's fiery eye. Secretly, I was overjoyed to think of my old adversary returning to the field of battle, but she had led us such a dance I did not feel noble enough to forgive her completely.

'I shall have to think about your offer,' I said formally.

'Think what you like,' said she, 'but I'll be coming to work next Monday, and if Bella or anyone else is mucking about in my school, they'll get thrown out.'

'How do I know,' I countered, 'that you really will turn up? We've had quite enough shilly-shallying, and in any case what does the doctor say?'

'It's up to me, he said. Work if I want to, and now I do. I'll be along first thing Monday.'

She began to struggle from the chair, but I waved her down. This was as near as I should ever get to an apology, I could see. The only thing to do was to accept the situation. In any case, it was what I really wanted.

'Very well. I'll expect you then.'

A crash of thunder nearly split our ear drums, and the rain began to fall in torrents.

'I'll run you home,' I said.

'There's no call to put yourself out,' said the lady, but she sounded mollified.

'We'd better wait a few minutes,' I added, as lightning rent the sky. 'Have a glass of sherry now we've settled things.'

She raised a massive hand in refusal.

'You should know I don't drink.'

'I'm sorry. I forgot. A cup of coffee?'

'No, thank you.'

She sat four-square and studied the room about her with an

eagle eye. An ancient beam runs across my ceiling, and this she scrutinised for some time.

'I suppose no one's touched that rafter?' she said.

'No,' I replied, mystified.

'I thought as much. I give it a good rub down each week with a nice soft cloth wrung out in vinegar and linseed oil. And your copper and brass is a disgrace. I'll come as usual and do you now that Mrs John has given up.'

'Thank you,' I said meekly.

'And anyway, we never got down to any proper spring-cleaning this year, as I recall. I reckon the whole house could do with bottoming.'

As soon as the rain abated a little, we drove down through the wet village street to her house. Little was said on the brief journey, but when the car stopped, she thanked me as she struggled to get out.

'I'll see you on Monday then,' I said.

'Be quite like old times,' replied the lady, nodding the hat graciously, as she opened her gate.

As I drove back I faced the fact that Mrs Pringle had easily won this last skirmish. As usual.

But, on the other hand, I was quite content with the outcome.

To my surprise, I had a letter from Miriam Quinn in the next morning's post. It was written from her brother's vicarage, and ran to three pages.

She was obviously very happy, and had postponed her return to the office, with Barney's blessing, as Gerard was busy with a project in Norfolk and they were both enjoying their holiday together.

'We hope to marry early in the New Year, at St Patrick's of course. It will be a quiet wedding, as befits two sober and elderly people, but we want close friends, such as yourself, to join our families on the day. You shall have a proper invitation when I get back.

'We hope to find a house near Caxley, as we've both made so many friends in the neighbourhood, so look out for one.'

There followed a eulogy of Gerard, which I am sure Amy would not have endorsed, and she ended with loving messages to her Fairacre friends.

'I wonder if my new hat will look suitable for a winter wedding?' I pondered aloud.

Tibby gave a prolonged and painful cry, but I refused to acknowledge it as a derogatory comment.

'So we've got Madam Sunshine coming back!' said Mr Willet. 'You'll never see the last of her now.'

'It was the thought of you coping with the stoves that really settled it,' I told him.

'I'd have done 'em all right,' he said sturdily. 'The fact is the old girl was jealous of anyone getting in here, and when she heard there might be a rush for the job, she knew it was time to stop malarking about and come up here pronto.'

'Well, there it is. Better the rogue you know, than the knave you don't. I'm not sorry she's coming back, to tell the truth.'

'You're too soft by half. She'll be bossing us all about worse than ever after this.'

'We're used to it, aren't we? In any case, I'm not grieving about it with this sunshine all round us.'

'You're right.' He sniffed the air appreciatively. 'That rain done a power of good. Shan't need to look out for Ted Bates now. Won't want my sprinkler for a week or two.'

We parted company. I was off to take assembly, and he to sweep up some of the coke he would not be allowed to scrunch into Mrs Pringle's floors in the future.

* * *

It was good to be back to normal, with Mrs Pringle crashing about in the lobby before and after school, and booming awful threats to children who got in her way.

It was even comforting, in a queer sort of way, to have my house turned inside out on Wednesday afternoons, and to be told of the strange articles she had found in the sides of the armchairs, and the deplorable condition of my kitchen equipment.

'Ah well!' pronounced my old tormenter. 'There's some as have their heads stuffed with book-learning, and don't know one end of a duster from another. But I suppose we was all sent here with a purpose. Mine seems to be looking after Fairacre School, not to mention its teachers.'

The golden days passed, and it began to grow chilly. The hedges were dew-spangled each morning, and the berries were glowing red. Before long the Battle of the Stoves would begin, as it had done for so many years.

'I don't like this nip in the air,' I said to Mr Willet early one morning in the playground. 'I can't bear to think of this blissful summer coming to an end.'

'You take a look at the calendar,' advised my old friend. 'It's September the twenty-ninth, Michaelmas Day. The end of summer that is, and we'll just have to face it.'

'Well, we made the most of summer this year, didn't we? A proper celebration. I'll always remember it.'

'Ah! We celebrated all right! Even though it did start with snow on Lady Day. Remember? We've had something to celebrate too, when you think us had weeks without old Sour-face bossing us about.'

At that moment Mrs Pringle appeared in the lobby doorway.

'I want a word with you, Bob Willet,' she said ominously.

'Here we go!' he said, with a wink.

CHRISTIAN HERALD ASSOCIATION AND ITS MINISTRIES

CHRISTIAN HERALD ASSOCIATION, founded in 1878, publishes The Christian Herald Magazine, one of the leading interdenominational religious monthlies in America. Through its wide circulation, it brings inspiring articles and the latest news of religious developments to many families. From the magazine's pages came the initiative for CHRISTIAN HERALD CHILDREN and THE BOWERY MISSION, two individually supported not-for-profit corporations.

CHRISTIAN HERALD CHILDREN, established in 1894, is the name for a unique and dynamic ministry to disadvantaged children, offering hope and opportunities which would not otherwise be available for reasons of poverty and neglect. The goal is to develop each child's potential and to demonstrate Christian compassion and understanding to children in need.

Mont Lawn is a permanent camp located in Bushkill, Pennsylvania. It is the focal point of a ministry which provides a healthful "vacation with a purpose" to children who without it would be confined to the streets of the city. Up to 1000 children between the age of 7 and 11 come to Mont Lawn each year.

Christian Herald Children maintains year-round contact with children by means of a *City Youth Ministry.* Central to its philosophy is the belief that only through sustained relationships and demonstrated concern can individual lives be truly enriched. Special emphasis is on individual guidance, spiritual and family counseling and tutoring. This follow-up ministry to inner-city children culminates for many in financial assistance toward higher education and career counseling.

THE BOWERY MISSION, located at 227 Bowery, New York City, has since 1879 been reaching out to the lost men on the Bowery, offering them what could be their last chance to rebuild their lives. Every man is fed, clothed and ministered to. Countless numbers have entered the 90-day residential rehabilitation program at the Bowery Mission. A concentrated ministry of counseling, medical care, nutrition therapy, Bible study and Gospel services awakens a man to spiritual renewal within himself.

These ministries are supported solely by the voluntary contributions of individuals and by legacies and bequests. Contributions are tax deductible. Checks should be made out either to CHRISTIAN HERALD CHILDREN or to THE BOWERY MISSION.

**Administrative Office: 40 Overlook Drive, Chappaqua, New York 10514
Telephone: (914) 769-9000**

GC '86